TANGLED SHADOWS

CHRISTINA CROTHERS

For Grandma and Pap
Who lovingly translated the creative spelling in my first trilogy into
English

One

Alexis
Thursday, 2:06 p.m.
Western Shore, MD

"And last but not least," Mia read with gusto to the rest of the car, "don't bring home any unicorns."

"Okay, okay. Give me back my phone." Laughing, Alexis tried to snatch back her cell phone. She looked to Mia's boyfriend for help, but Eric had both hands on the wheel and his eyes on the road. Alexis was tempted to unbuckle her seatbelt and half-climb into the front, where Mia was riding shotgun, but it was an unnecessary risk while the car was going fifty-five on country roads.

"What kind of dog-sitting gig is this, anyway?" Mia gestured with her free hand, causing her assortment of handmade bracelets to dance against her black skin. "I can't believe she texted you all these rules. I get being safe, even if I don't agree, but the rest—ugh. Any other made-up stuff you shouldn't bring home? How about a sea monster?"

Alexis laughed. "You remember Terra. She just says stuff like that."

"It's not fair." Mia made a pretty pouty face at Eric. "I'm the one who loves to climb, but it's my best friend who has all the inside jokes with the camp's ropes-course leader."

Eric's hazel eyes twinkled behind thick-rimmed hipster glasses as he caught Alexis's gaze in the rearview mirror. "Is that so?"

"Mia is the first in line to climb anything, but she yawns whenever there is detail work, like making sure everything is set up precisely." Alexis spread her lightly tanned hands, palms up. "Since I enjoy that part, I got to hear lots of Terra's stories." Including the one with Alexander the Great and the unicorn, which started the running joke with Terra about Alexis and unicorns.

"Hours spent tying knots and checking ropes is too high a price to pay for inside jokes. Look! There's camp." Mia pointed to the right before handing back the phone. Alexis slid it into the front pocket of her green-plaid flannel shirt.

Ahead, a yellow-and-blue sign welcomed them. A little of Alexis's college stress slid off her shoulders. In a break between neighborhoods and small businesses was a patch of familiar forest, now gilded with autumn colors. A long road wound its way to the center of Camp Cattail. It was her favorite spot along the western shore of the Chesapeake Bay, just under three hours from their college in Virginia. There was something special about the woods and marshes here. On a good day, she'd been a vital member of a team that could handle anything. On a bad day, a half-hour escape down a trail with her camera could restore her patience and enthusiasm.

"It won't be the same without the people," Mia said.

"I'm looking forward to the peace and quiet. Plus, the theme for this round of the competition is 'The Natural World.' I've only got four days to submit my photos." Alexis pushed a lock of her shoulder-length brown hair behind her ear, forcing herself not to dwell on how close she was to missing the deadline.

Mia snorted. "Yeah, yeah. You've got plenty of good ones."

"But nothing excellent I haven't already used in the earlier rounds." *And I haven't taken a decent shot in weeks.* There was no point in voicing the last part. Mia would say she was being a perfectionist, and Eric would side with her, but Alexis had been taking her photography seriously since junior year of high school; she knew when her photos were *blah*.

"Semantics. And there's plenty of nature in New York City. I hear there's this really big park," Mia teased.

Regret gnawed at Alexis. She didn't want to think about all the crazy, fun things Mia and Eric would be doing without her, but this competition was too important. She set her shoulders.

"Last chance." Eric's eyes were warm in the rearview mirror, complementing the freckles on his nose. "To ditch this backwater forest and come with us to New York."

Alexis took a breath, considering for one more moment. At first, she'd only seen Eric as a valuable addition to their study group, but quickly realized he and Mia had sparks. A trip for just Mia and Eric was exactly the right next step for their budding relationship. Alexis wasn't needed; Eric could temper Mia's enthusiasm for trouble without stifling her. It was easier to be needed by her friends than to deal with her own goals. Her brow wrinkled into a frown.

She consciously smiled before saying, "Thanks, but I've already promised to look after Prince. I really appreciate you dropping me off on your way, though."

Mia waved an unconcerned hand. "Bring the dog."

Alexis relaxed and laughed at the impossible image. "He'd love being stuck at your cousin's place while we explore the city."

"You mean party!" Mia corrected with a shoulder shimmy, accented by her gold-and-red peasant blouse.

Eric gave a mock wince.

Alexis grinned at him in the rearview mirror. In Mia's vocabulary, *party* and *trouble* were usually synonyms, always interesting, and never comfortable. "I'm good. Honest. I've got several papers to write on top of all the photo taking and editing."

"Just slap the papers together when we get back. Fall break isn't for doing homework."

Eric snorted. His bag had been heavy with textbooks when Alexis helped load the car earlier.

"Good luck finding time to study while you're with this one," Alexis warned Eric before grinning at Mia. "If you had it your way, nothing about college would be about homework."

Mia gave a dramatic sigh. "If only. But this isn't college, it's a break from college. Thus, a break from homework."

Alexis leaned forward to hug her best friend from behind. "I'll miss you too."

Mia wrapped her arms around Alexis's. "I do get it, but New York would be so much more fun with you there."

"You're going to have a great time. I expect details! And don't do anything I wouldn't let you drag me along for."

Mia laughed. "No promises."

It was Alexis's turn to give a dramatic sigh.

"It's nice to get a peek at a place I've heard so much about," Eric said as they passed the cinder-block dining hall.

"It's good to be back," Alexis said. Here her photography would feel right again. It had to.

"I can't believe I'd ever hear you say that!" Mia turned to Eric. "Being a camp counselor was the hardest I've ever worked, for the least amount of money. And for three summers in a row."

"But whose idea do you think it was?" Alexis asked him.

Eric gave Mia a raised eyebrow, his grin barely suppressed.

Mia shrugged an elegant shoulder. "It was one of those ideas Alexis was supposed to talk me out of."

Alexis put the back of her hand to her forehead. "Not only wasn't I able to do that, I got dragged along too. I'm the victim here."

"I feel your pain," Eric said.

"Hey!" Mia swatted at him playfully.

Alexis grinned, but it faded. Camp had been an extraordinary, life-changing experience. Adventures she would have missed if she'd held her ground against Mia. *How much am I going to regret missing this trip to New York?* Alexis did her best to ignore the knot in her stomach and shake off her self-doubt. She was graduating in December. Mia had until the spring to worry about what came next, not that Mia ever worried about practical stuff.

If Alexis could just get one of her photos in the top four, she'd have her dream internship. With a lot of hard work, her dream internship would turn into her dream job as a photojournalist. After that, her five-year plan got a little fuzzy, but that was just for now.

If she didn't place in the top four, she would have to accept the marketing job she'd been offered yesterday. Alexis would be able to pay off her student loans, but she'd have to relegate her photography to the land of hobbies. Not much time for hobbies when she'd be working sixty hours a week. But that wasn't going to happen. She'd made it through eight rounds of the competition. All she needed was one last perfect photo.

She couldn't risk the distractions of New York or life-changing adventures.

"Park up there." Mia pointed to the small lot at the end of the road.

"Thanks again, Eric," Alexis said when the car stopped.

He turned to look at her. "Have a nice, peaceful time."

"Enjoy the chaos," she countered.

He gave her a one arm hug between the seats before tactfully checking his phone, leaving the best friends to say goodbye without him.

Grabbing her camera and overstuffed backpack, Alexis slid out of the car. A breeze saturated with leaf litter and damp earth greeted her. Mia walked her to the door of the log cabin. Trees, cheerful with autumn foliage, stood watch over the gabled roof, making it look like something out of a calendar.

Mia ran a hand along the faded wood railing. "I was thinking . . ."

Alexis pretended to stagger. "Oh, no! What's wrong?"

"Oh, ha ha. But seriously. You're not *not* coming to New York because I invited Eric along, are you? Just because we're dating now . . ." Mia swallowed and looked up from the toe of her knee-high boots. "Well, I hope you don't feel like a third wheel."

"Mia! Quit that. Of course not. I do hope you'll have an awesome time, just the two of you. But, no. I'm staying here for me. Look at this cabin in the middle of nowhere, and a whole camp to myself.

I'm going to take the most-amazing photos ever and finally get ahead on my homework." Alexis gave a contented sigh. "Heaven."

"Sometimes, you make absolutely no sense to me, but I love you anyway."

Alexis hugged Mia. "Love you too."

"Thinking of photos. Selfie," Mia said in a tone that made it clear she was making fun of herself.

Alexis checked her camera, took off the lens cap, and set it on the railing with the timer set. She made a silly face, which Mia matched before demanding a normal photo.

Alexis checked the screen to make sure they'd come out okay. She and Mia looked good standing on the porch in the afternoon light. Mia was a head taller and gorgeous as a princess. Her rich black skin and clothes bold enough to match her personality contrasted sharply against Alexis's boringness. Alexis had brown hair, brown eyes, and white skin that was holding on to most of her summer tan. Her roundish face and sturdy body suited her well as a camp counselor, but didn't look the least bit regal. Her favorite green flannel shirt and old jeans looked muted. But it worked in the photo, contrasting colors and personalities brought together by a deep and joyful affection.

"There—documenting our fall vacation," Alexis said.

"Good."

"See you soon."

"Four whole days! It's an eternity!"

Alexis laughed and hugged her again.

A loud bark interrupted them.

"And there's my prince calling me." Alexis put a hand over her heart.

Mia laughed. "My cue to leave."

And with more goodbyes, well-wishes, and a whirlwind of energy, Mia and Eric were gone. Alexis waved until they were out of sight, fighting the heaviness in her stomach. She shouldn't have felt lonely yet; they'd only been gone a minute. And she certainly couldn't feel abandoned, she told herself firmly; it was her choice to stay. This was what real photographers did.

Shoulders set, she turned her attention to Terra's house. Excited barking emanated from inside, making her smile.

"It's just me, fella," she called before opening the door. A creature the size and color of a black bear greeted her like she was a tree full of honey. Even with her feet planted she staggered back. "I missed you too!"

He licked her face happily, his paws on her shoulders. Terra said he was descended from a long line of warrior dogs that had palled around with the Knights of the Round Table. Alexis figured he was some kind of Newfoundland mix Terra had picked up at the pound.

"Okay, enough. Behave." Immediately Prince dropped to his haunches and looked up at her expectantly. "That's a good boy!" She ruffled his ears. "Let me put my stuff inside, text your mom, and we can go for a walk. I have a photo to find."

He jumped to his feet and wagged his tail enthusiastically. Alexis dropped her backpack just inside the door and sent Terra a quick text to let her know all was well. Grabbing a leash from the hook, she looked back at the inside of the house.

Kitchen, living room, and entryway were only separated by a bar counter and a couch. Above half of it was a loft bedroom. Against the far wall, breaking up the bookcases, were stairs wide enough for Prince to navigate. The decor was rustic and cozy. Flowy cream curtains were pulled to the sides of wide windows, allowing light to spill across the handmade quilt laid over the back of the couch, adding rich oranges and reds to the otherwise pale wood tones that dominated the room.

Breathing came easier, and peace settled over Alexis, despite the excited dog prancing around her.

As anxious to hit the trails as Prince was, she stepped out and held the door for him. "Let's go."

He raced into the sunshine but stopped at the top of the stairs to look back, seeming to ask for permission.

"Go on," she said.

He took off in ecstatic loops around the small yard as if he'd been cooped up for a week instead of half a day.

Alexis laughed at his antics as she tied the leash to her waist. He didn't need it at camp, but she carried it in case of emergencies. Removing the cover from her camera and lifting it to her eye, she snapped several quick shots, trying to capture Prince's enthusiasm.

He pranced back up to her, gazing at her with his big chocolate eyes as if he wanted to know why she was standing there.

"You're right." Alexis had already submitted a photo of him. It was a waste of time to take more.

Her shoulders hunched as she headed for the trail that would take her toward the main camp. It meandered through the forest, bright with sunlight and fall. With a careful eye she watched how shades of color contrasted and complemented each other. Deep gold leaves of beech, red and orange of maples, earthy tones of oaks, and cheerful yellows of tulip trees dominated, interrupted only occasionally by evergreens. The leaves crunched under foot, making it easy to keep an ear on Prince. Alexis could enjoy it later, as soon as she'd sent off her submission for the contest.

She stopped to snap a few photos of the trail, just to warm up. They were technically correct, with decent composition, but even on her camera screen they felt stiff.

Prince sniffed at a small pile of broken, green nut-husks, probably nibbled on by a squirrel, and she drew closer to look. She stemmed her curiosity, though, when she realized they wouldn't photograph well.

Birds flitted among the branches, but she had already submitted bird photos. Five-fingered raccoon or possum tracks were in the mud by the creek, looking like tiny handprints. Terra would know which if she saw the picture, but most people wouldn't be interested.

Alexis stopped at two of her favorite trees. Taking a deep breath and letting it out slowly, she tried to capture how the large beech tree trunks looked like elephant legs. The first angle wasn't right. She walked around to the other side, but nothing gave the photo life. Alexis rubbed the ache forming in her forehead. The light was shifting from crisp to muted. *Why isn't this working?* Here, at camp, she'd always been able to connect emotionally to her photography, not just see it. She needed that now.

Maybe if I get a ladder? Trying to remember where the closest one was, she didn't notice the wind was picking up until the leaves started blowing free from the canopy. She lifted her camera to her eye again. Falling leaves did look rather magical, like snow or rain. She jumped when a branch fell out of a tree with a crash. Prince dragged it proudly to her. A shiver skittered down Alexis's spine as she frowned at the swaying canopy.

The light shifted as dark clouds overtook the sky. *Just great.* The air had gone from crisp to heavy, promising not just rain, but a serious storm.

"It looks like it's getting dangerous out here," she told the dog. "Let's go."

He sniffed the wind suspiciously before bounding off toward home.

Alexis shivered, put the lens cap back on her camera, and let it hang on the band around her neck. Checking her phone, she frowned.

"It's two forty. I still have three and a half days to get my photo," she told Prince in a tone that denied the weight settling in her stomach.

Prince glanced back, as if saying, "Hurry up."

"It's not a bad omen," she told him firmly, lengthening her stride.

A second dead branch broke free of the canopy and hit the forest floor, barely a dozen feet away.

Two

Brian
Thursday, 2:06 p.m.
Chesapeake Bay

"Cannonball!" Brian jumped off the side of the boat. He surfaced with a laugh.

"Seriously?" his sister Vicky shouted at him.

"Sorry," he said, still grinning. "Did I splash you?"

"We were still setting the anchor," Mom said mildly.

Brian dropped the smile and shoved his black hair out of his eyes. "Sorry." It wasn't as if he was going to swim toward the spinning propeller, but this was his parent's boat, not some college party. "Now that the boat's turned off, Em, you coming in?"

"How's the water?" Em asked.

Brian rubbed his tan arms as if fighting shivers. "Freezing!"

His youngest sister didn't disappoint. Shedding her windbreaker and baseball cap, she dove in after him.

She came up beside where he was treading water and splashed him.

"It's not that cold!"

Brian played up the British accent he'd picked up for a few years in elementary school. "If I told you it was warmer than the English coast and colder than the Caribbean, you'd have had to think about whether or not you wanted to get your hair wet. Even though you're already wearing your swimsuit."

Em splashed him again, but didn't contradict his logic. "Vicky, it really is rather nice. Come on in." Her accent, like her wardrobe, adapted to her present environment and was currently as American as the rest of their family.

"Thanks, but it's not what I'd call warm." Vicky pulled her jacket closer. "And I've got my book."

Brian and Em both rolled their eyes. Vicky devoured oversized fantasy novels as if they were candy bars, and she seemed to be able to skip out on fun without a second thought.

"Tag." Brian tapped Em's shoulder and dove underwater. He surfaced, swimming hard.

Em shrieked and chased him. She'd gone through a growth spurt over the summer and made him work to stay ahead.

"Not too far from the boat," Dad called.

Brian dodged, trying to turn around without losing his lead. He dove deep, but Em was ready.

"You're it!" she declared when he surfaced, and she was off.

Laughing, he chased. It was one of those moments too wonderful to waste on thought. Eventually, they got bored of chasing each other around the old fiberglass powerboat and called a truce. Dad tossed in two old, throwable boat cushions for them to float on.

Em hugged the faded-blue square of foam and fabric to her chest. "I'm glad you could make it home."

"Me, too!" Brian ducked under and came up, shoving his hair out of his green eyes again.

"Mom's going to make you cut that before the council meeting Saturday."

Brian groaned and tried to sit on his float, which sank about two feet into the water. "It doesn't even touch my shoulders, and it's not like they need me there. Maybe we can go exploring around DC while they talk serious stuff."

"Really? That would be great! But I want to be back in time for Elliot to give a tour of the vault."

His float popped up with a splash. Brian settled for sliding his arms through the loops. "Haven't you heard his stories a hundred times before and seen all the boring, old artifacts often enough?"

"Boring!" Em said indignantly. "They're amazing."

Brian didn't argue, but personally, he was starting to question if any of it was real or if it was just fairy tales for an eccentric club of antique collectors and an excuse for old friends to get together. Sometimes he thought his dad felt the same way, but they never talked about it. Brian wasn't going to bring up his growing doubts, though, and spoil Em's fun or start a big discussion with his mom and Vicky about the validity of the Guard.

"It's getting chilly, shall we?"

Em agreed by racing to the ladder without counting down.

Brian laughed and followed. He handed up the floats before climbing the ladder. "What's on your hat?" he asked Em as she pulled her dripping blonde ponytail through the back of her baseball cap.

"School mascot."

"I thought the mascot was a bird."

She rolled her eyes. "That was, like, totally three schools ago."

Brian winced. One of the advantages of college was he no longer had to change schools every time Mom got a new assignment. She worked for a multinational company with interests in some pretty cool places, but growing up, Brian had never lived anywhere for more than two years.

"Can I drive?" Em asked.

She might only be twelve years old, but Brian had to admit she could handle the *Kingfisher* almost as well as she thought she could.

"For a bit," Mom said, pulling out a chart to show Em where they were going.

Brian snagged his shirt, jacket, and a towel from the chest before heading to the bow of the boat, where his shoes were. The front was the best place; it bounced the most in the waves. And he could help pull up the anchor from there.

He savored the closeness with the people he loved most. No matter how much fun he had with his friends or how well he got on in class, his core understanding of the world was different. Maybe it was all the moving they'd done together or maybe it was their lineage in the Guard Council, but no one outside of this boat gave him quite this sense of belonging.

Dad and Vicky were in the middle seats, debating Celtic history. It sounded as if they were comparing what they'd learned during their six months living in Scotland and what Vicky was covering in her high-school history class. Brian was just impressed Dad had managed to get Vicky to put down her book for a few minutes.

Looking out over the water, he could see the large tankers in the channel and just make out Thomas Point Lighthouse in the distance. Yellow grasses hugged the shorelines, marking the edges of the wide swath of calm water.

When they got underway, Mom moved up to sit beside him. Her hair was dark like his and Vicky's except for the silver starting to mix in. Her cream skin tended to freckle in the sun the way Em's did. He always knew he was home when he saw her smile, no matter where they were hanging their hats that day.

"So how are classes?" she asked. There hadn't been time to interrogate him earlier; he'd arrived just as they'd been launching the *Kingfisher*.

"They're not bad. Just trying to juggle a lot." Like his busy social life.

"Just as well you didn't try out for the swim team then?"

Brian didn't miss the concern in her tone. His parents hadn't been certain whether or not to encourage him toward more organized sports in his last semester at school.

"I'm so glad I don't have that to deal with!" he said. "You know I'm not competitive enough for it." Everyone having fun was far more important than crushing another team or the drama that came with high stakes. Plus, he was graduating a semester late, so he was off schedule from most of his friends.

"But you're still getting enough exercise?"

"I'm on an intramural basketball team, play pickup games of ultimate frisbee, and go swimming at least twice a week. I'm good." Not to mention all the dancing he did at parties. "I've got a sound mind in a sound body. It's not like we're not keeping up on the phone." They talked most weeks, but he knew she'd like it if he called more often.

"This is better though."

He grinned. "True."

"Are we worried about that?" Vicky called to the rest of the boat, pointing behind them.

Brian could see ripples on the water fifty yards away; it looked like a line where the texture changed from smooth to fuzzy. Above, dark clouds were moving their way.

"I can outrun it," Em said with glee.

Brian winced; that was something he might say, but it didn't sound like such a good idea coming from his little sister.

"The weather forecast said only a small chance of thunderstorms. Probably pass over quickly," Dad said.

"There's a marina in a cove to the left." Mom checked the chart. "I'm sure they'll let us tie up until it blows over."

"Sounds like a plan," Dad said.

"Would you mind navigating, Em? I want to take a shortcut and leave the channel," Mom asked, moving back to the cockpit.

Even from the bow, Brian could see Em knew she was really being asked to give up the wheel, but after another look at the incoming clouds she accepted the chart gracefully.

"Brian, keep an eye out for crab pots," Em called. "We're cutting closer to shore."

"Aye, aye," he said with an exaggerated salute before turning to keep a close watch. She was right, of course. They didn't want to get caught in the lines between the colorful buoys on the surface and the crab pots on the bottom of the bay, but it was still funny to have his little sister tell him what to do.

"On the left." He pointed at the first painted, hard-plastic float, the shape of a rounded cone.

They were easy to spot if one knew to look out for them and wasn't going too fast, so Brian had no trouble pointing the way through until they were back in deeper water. A large powerboat was headed up the channel in their same direction, but didn't seem in any hurry to pass them.

Keeping the red markers on the right, Mom steered them toward the faded marina. Old wood and a tin roof sheltered a fuel station and the boats at the end of the docks closest to them. Beyond that were regular slips, where power boats and sailboats were tied. On land were a few tired-looking buildings with peeling white paint. It didn't look like a place that would mind them seeking shelter from a surprise thunderstorm.

The boat behind them picked up speed. Its wake was a little too high, but Brian couldn't blame the owner for wanting to get out of the storm.

A big wet drop of rain splashed on Brian's forearm. He tucked his neck into his jacket and reached for his shoes. He removed the cuff he'd tucked into one of them and snapped the inch-wide leather band onto his wrist before pulling on his shoes. The surrounding water's surface began to shift with windblown waves and ripples from falling rain just as they made it to the dock.

Brian jumped to the dock to secure the line Vicky tossed him. Dad stepped down to get the one Em passed him. Then they all headed for the sheltered interior of the roofed dock.

"Close one," Dad declared above the sound of the sky opening up on a tin roof.

Grinning, Brian passed around high fives. Vicky humored him before pulling open her book. Thunder boomed in the distance. Mom looked around for someone to check in with. The boat that had followed the channel pulled into the dock behind the *Kingfish-er.*

"Let's give them a hand," Dad said to Brian. But in the ten seconds it took them to get back to the fuel dock, the boat was being tied up with crisp efficiency by a half-dozen men in dark clothes.

Something about them bothered Brian, but he dismissed it. Just because they weren't wearing Hawaiian shirts or carrying fishing gear and beer didn't mean they weren't perfectly normal for this part of the country. Maybe they were SEALs on their day off. Or fire-and-rescue personnel in training.

A blond guy stepped off the boat. He stood out from the group, and not just because he was wearing expensive clothes far lighter than those of his companions. He couldn't have been more than ten years older than Brian but was clearly in charge, and Brian wouldn't have been surprised if the guy turned out to be an up-and-coming politician or someone famous. Even the rain didn't seem to ruffle his composure. The men in dark clothes kept an eye on him, as if checking for instructions. Maybe they were his protection.

"It's drier back here," Dad called, retreating with Brian back to the rest of the family.

The newcomers followed.

"Quite the storm." Mom offered her hand to the blond guy. "I'm Annette, this is my husband Daniel, and these are our kids."

He accepted the handshake with a warm grin. "Nick." He turned to the closest two men, but didn't introduce them. "See if there's anyone around we owe a docking fee to."

All the men looked like they would be people you'd want protecting you in a war zone, but these two were particularly serious looking and the eldest by at least fifteen years. The first looked like a marine extra from a Hollywood blockbuster. He even had a light scar on his square jaw. The second looked like he could number bears and cinder block walls among his cousins. The part of his face that could be seen around his brown beard held no hint of smile lines.

The men gave a nod and walked down the dock toward the rest of the marina. The remaining four guards stood stone-faced. Nick turned his attention to scanning his surroundings, apparently not paying Brian's family much attention.

"We're close to DC," Em murmured to Brian. "Maybe he's someone important."

"I was just thinking the same thing."

"His clothes are expensive."

"As are those guys with him."

Em giggled. "That's not funny."

"True though, bodyguards like that—"

"My stomach hurts," Vicky announced.

The rest of the family turned to her. Brian's own insides clenched. Magic-touched, Mom always said about Vicky's stomach. Dad just said she had good instincts and picked up on signals the rest of them missed. In practice, Vicky's digestive system was an impressive barometer for trouble. Usually, it meant they should move *now*. A convenience store was about to be robbed, political unrest was about to get ugly, or she'd just eaten too much fried food. Glancing at Nick's paramilitary-looking guard, Brian doubted it was the peanut butter and jelly sandwiches they'd had for lunch that was bothering Vicky. They didn't need to get caught in the crossfire between Nick and whomever he was being protected from.

"Probably just a touch of seasickness. You should feel better now that we're on land." Mom sounded convincing enough, to anyone who didn't know her well. She moved over to check Vicky's forehead temperature. As she walked by Brian, she slipped him the boat key. He understood immediately. If Vicky's stomach was right, Em would be too reckless of a driver, Vicky didn't like to drive, and his parents would draw attention to buy them time. He'd have to make sure his sisters made it to safety.

"Em, stop fidgeting," Dad said, looking at his statue-still daughter, in the tone he used when they played improv games. "Why don't you check on the lines holding the *Kingfisher*?"

"Yes, captain," she said, feigning preteen sarcasm, and waltzed off to their boat.

Sometimes her acting skills scared Brian. Still, he'd congratulate her on them when they all got back to the Airbnb if he remembered. Energy was coursing through him, making him want to fidget the way Em supposedly had been.

Lightning flickered. Brian counted the time to the following thunder. Seven Mississippis wasn't too bad.

"Glad we're not out on the water." Nick turned his calculating eyes and smiling face back to Brian's family.

"Me too," Dad said with forced cheerfulness. "Storm came up fast. Guess summer's not quite ready to let go."

Nick's attention slipped away to his returning men. His gaze came back to Brian's dad, and his polished smile returned. "An Indian summer at any rate."

"Boat's fine, Dad," Em said, rolling her eyes as she returned.

"Thank you for making sure," Dad said with exaggerated patience.

Brian would have smiled at the playacting, but his attention was on Nick. Something seemed contradictory about the man. His smile was too pleasant. Perhaps? Hard for Brian to tell. Maybe it was just his reaction to Vicky's nerves.

Nick's scouts returned and joined the blob of people standing in the middle of the dock.

"No sign of anyone else around," the scarred guard said. "Looks as if the workers are gone for the day and the boaters were delayed by the weather."

"Good, let's get this over with." Nick grabbed Em's arm and yanked her to his side of the dock.

Brian moved to snatch her back and found himself looking down the barrel of half a dozen guns. He swallowed hard; his mouth was dry.

"Stand back. This doesn't need to be difficult," Nick said, sounding unnaturally relaxed, as if they were having tea. He was the only one of the strangers not holding a gun, but he didn't need to; the threat was clear.

Em stomped on his foot and tried to twist away.

Nick shook her lightly. "Be still." He sounded almost gentle; it made the hairs on the back of Brian's neck stand on end.

Only then did Em seem to notice the guns; she went so white Brian was afraid she might pass out.

"What's going on?" Dad asked, his voice colder than Brian had ever heard it.

"Just a simple robbery. Bringing these guys might have been overkill, but better safe than sorry." Nick sounded as if he was apologizing for the tea not being quite hot enough. But Brian noticed Nick's free right hand was trembling. *Thank God he isn't holding a gun.*

Nick seemed to notice Brian's gaze, because he put his hand in his pocket. "I'm here to collect Merlin's Knot and the Compass. No one needs to get hurt."

Brian tensed and sensed Vicky, close by, do the same. He wasn't the only one trying to keep recognition off his face. Playing a scenario like this in childhood imaginary games was nothing like reality.

"You're loony. Let me go," Em demanded, fear beneath her bravado.

"Seriously, let the adults talk," Nick said.

If looks could kill, Nick would have been dead on the spot, but he seemed not to notice the expression Em was giving him.

Brian wasn't sure whether to give his sister a metaphorical high five or strangle her. He knew it was just how she reacted when scared, but he wished she would be quiet. Best-case scenario this guy was a collector of old junk. The Knot and Compass were worth a shit-ton of money to the right people, but no one in the Guard had actually been robbed of an Arthurian Artifact in at least a dozen years, and even then, the thief had no idea what he'd taken. The artifact had been recovered less than a month later in a pawnshop. This guy knew better.

Dad cleared his throat. "Definitely overkill then. We're not a Boy Scout troop with a bunch of different knots, but you're welcome to all the ropes and the compass on our boat. Just please, let go of my daughter."

"Ha, ha," Nick said dryly. "Did you really think that would work? I know who you are, Daniel and Annette Weaver. Children: Brian, Victoria, and Emily. Active members of the Guard, an organization originally founded by Merlin over a thousand years ago to keep magic out of the world. You're in town for the Council meeting this weekend. And more importantly, to me at least, you are entrusted with Merlin's Knot and Compass. Now, can we quit playing games and get this over with?"

Each additional fact hit Brian's bloodstream like a block of ice. Fingers numb, he glanced at his dad. *Is he going to try to deny it? Laugh at the idea of Merlin?* Dad didn't, though. His face had gone white, and even if he'd wanted to deny it, no one would have believed him. Just because Dad thought people took the stories a little too seriously didn't change the fact that they did. Having seen Nick and his men's faces couldn't be a good thing either. If they handed over the Knot and Compass, would they even be allowed to live, or was that just a problem in movies?

"Stupid stories and family heirlooms? You'd threaten my children for this?" Mom snapped with no hint that she was lying. "We lost the Compass ages ago, didn't want to admit it to the Guard, so they think we still have it. But here's the Knot." She unclasped the necklace she always wore around her neck. The silver chain reflected a flash of lightning. A flattened tangle of dark, glossy thread, about the size of lime, hung like a pendulum on the chain. "Give Em back and get out of here."

A look passed across Nick's face, like he was lost in the desert and was being offered a drink, but it passed so quickly, it might have been a trick of the lightning. He took the chain with the dangling Knot and handed Em to her mom. "Watch them," he said to his mercenaries, who were trying to hide their confusion.

"Even *if* the stories are true, the only way to gain the power to conquer the world is by untying that tangled knot. That would take you a lifetime, " Mom said. The Guard would track the Knot and find a way to buy it back. It might take years, but that's what they did. "Can we go now?"

Nick leveled a hard look. "No."

"Why not?" Dad asked.

"You're lying about losing the Compass. After four hundred years in your family, I doubt you just misplaced it. Search him," he added to his men.

Brian had to fight not to fidget with the leather cuff on his wrist.

Dad didn't resist the search. All he had on him was a pocket knife, since his wallet, keys, and cellphone were in the box on the boat, to keep them safe and dry. Not that anyone bothered to explain this to Nick.

While they were busy looking, Mom shifted closer to Brian. "You need to run."

Brian snorted at the idea.

"They'll chase you, we'll use that to get away."

That didn't sound like good odds. He gave her a look that conveyed his dislike for the plan. If he'd stopped and thought about it, he probably would have said it wasn't that he was being brave; it just didn't feel real.

"It has to be you. You swore an oath."

Almost five years ago, he wanted to protest. When he was seventeen, and keeping family tradition had felt like an adventure. When he'd still believed in the wild tales without a doubt.

"We'll deal with that later," Nick said, when it became clear the Compass wouldn't be as obvious as the Knot had been. "First things first. Alexander the Great was an interesting guy." He pulled a dagger from his pocket, maybe eight inches long, including the simple hilt. The metal looked old, rather like a museum artifact. But the shine on the blade showed it had been sharpened recently. "When faced with this very same Knot, he didn't waste his time trying to untie it."

The world seemed to slow down for Brian. *If that knife really is the one Alexander the Great used to cut the Gordian Knot, the First Knot … then the stories are real.* And protecting the Compass wasn't just a matter of family tradition. It was the reason the Guard had been founded.

Nick crouched down and placed the necklace on the rough wood of the dock. It looked glossy in the flashes of distant lightning, but not special or powerful. Dagger in his left hand, Nick brought it down hard onto the center of the necklace.

Light screamed out of it in all directions. Watery ripples of color danced and reverberated off the walls and shrieked against the tin ceiling. Clouds of storm-gray steam rose up from the water. Brian nearly lost his footing; Em fell back. The mercenaries fought to stay on the dock.

Everywhere the light hit Brian, it turned emerald green. It laced over his skin like a quicksilver snake, cool but not slimy. He tried to get away, but it spread rapidly over every inch of him before globbing over his heart and seeping into him.

The same thing happened to Nick, but with blue light. Gray steam boiled up around all of them, obscuring Nick from view.

"Run!" Mom's urgent whisper broke him free from the moment. He grabbed Em's hand, pulled her to her feet, and started to run for the boat. Vicky, smart girl that she was, was right behind.

The guards snatched at them. Vicky swung her book like a rock and stopped to fight. One of the men grabbed Em by the waist and pulled her from the dock. Her hand wrenched from Brian's.

"Run!" Mom yelled.

Pulled in two, Brian didn't look back. This wasn't just about his family anymore. He bolted through the rain. Boiling steam made it hard to see three feet in any direction. Gunshots cracked; wood splintered to his right. Reaching the end of the dock, Brian yanked the lines free; Em had loosened them earlier. The key resisted sliding into the lock for an endless second, and then he slammed the *Kingfisher* into gear. She took off like a stung horse, tossing a high wake behind her.

Brian didn't bother to sort his thoughts. He just trusted his instincts. The boat fought the turbulent water. He drove standing up, his legs spread wide for balance, the boat slamming into the surface after riding each swell of water. The waves were higher and more choppy the further he got from the protected marina.

Glancing back through the driving rain, Brian could see Nick's boat coming after him. It was large and powerful; he didn't have a chance of outrunning it under fair conditions. But it needed deeper water than the *Kingfisher*.

Shifting his direction, he headed for the shortcut they'd taken to the marina. The shallower water outside the channel might buy him some time. Lightning raced through the clouds overhead. Thunder boomed a split second later.

The rain was so heavy that he couldn't see the marina. He could barely make out the boat running him down. Lightning reflected off the water. Thunder hurt his ears.

The crab pots!

He was beside one. Couldn't see more. Not in this rain, not with these waves.

The engine screamed, then shuddered. The boat yanked to drift. Brian was thrown forward; pain lanced up his left arm as he slammed into the sharp metal of the steering console. Hitting the emergency stop helped prevent further damage to the boat, but he was without an engine. Warm blood contrasted with cool rain on his arm.

Options! There have to be options! He was stuck on a crab pot. Even if he took the time to untangle it from the prop and used an oar to row the boat, he'd never get far in this gale.

The water looked as inviting as lava, but swimming didn't scare him. What might be hiding in the dark water did. And the lightning made it a supremely stupid idea. Nick's boat was roaring toward him. Land was just visible through the driving rain. Brian kicked off his shoes, tied them to his belt, and then dove in.

It was eerily quiet underwater. Pain burned up his arm, but he could still use it. Staying down, he swam as far as he could. He was being dragged about by the current, but he trusted his body to get him through. Coming up for air was like sticking his head out of a soundproof room and into a rock concert. The pounding storm and waves shoved him about. He took a deep breath and ducked under again. The muted sound of sand sifting and the whine of a boat engine filled his ears. Swimming with long, slow strokes, he tried to conserve his oxygen. The rain that made it so hard for him to see would surely hide him from view.

Surfacing, he looked around. How far had he swum from the boat? Which direction did he need to go? And where was Nick? All he could see was waves and rain.

Fear, choking and mind numbing, grabbed Brian around the chest. A stitch stung his side. *Shit, I'm going to drown.*

He fought to keep his head out of the water; if he drowned, at least the Guard would have time to step in before anyone found the Compass on his body.

A wave slammed into his face.

Kicking hard, he surfaced. Coughs racked his body. More water than air entered his mouth. The stitch in his side screamed. He fought harder. The cloud-tossed sky darkened around the edges.

There was a gap between waves. Something was coming toward him. Not a boat, but too big to be anything that lived in the bay. Too much of it was out of the water to be a dolphin. Brian managed to get a breath free of water. A deer maybe? Vicky insisted they could swim. A sea monster didn't seem out of the question under the circumstances, but a large duck seemed more likely.

It didn't take off. It came straight for him. Brian tried to paddle away while not taking his eyes off it.

Then he recognized it. Though he'd never before seen a unicorn in person, it wasn't hard to identify when it was swimming a few yards away. Just like magic, unicorns hadn't existed in the world twenty minutes ago, but the laws of physics had been altered. Logic had shifted. Unicorns, apparently, were real. Or at least one was. Or maybe shock was causing hallucinations.

The unicorn was the color of a thunderhead, dappled in the low light. Its horn was long and the color of lightning, matching the geometric patterns going down the crest of its neck.

Brian tried to swim away, but the unicorn came up beside him, watching him quietly with large, dark eyes. Treading water, he wondered vaguely if he was about to be eaten, but the unicorn didn't lunge or stab him.

The stitch in Brian's side worsened as he coughed on another mouthful of brackish water. He was swimming away from his family because he was trying to protect a crazy old artifact he'd sworn an oath to guard with his life. The man who'd attacked his family and changed the very fabric of reality was chasing him. So, Brian did the most sensible thing he could think of under the circumstances. He grabbed a handful of silky, gray mane, kicked hard, and pulled himself onto the unicorn's back.

Three

Alexis
Thursday, 3:02 p.m.
Camp Cattail
Western Shore, MD

Alexis watched the storm while nestled on Terra's couch with Prince and her laptop. It would have been a great way to spend an afternoon if she had a photo worth editing. She was wrapped in Terra's homemade quilt with Prince curled up beside her. The window showed hints of spider-webbing lightning between thrashing tree branches and lines of gusting rain. It was better background music than the New Age station she usually listened to.

She scrolled through the pictures she'd taken earlier, but none of them captured her attention. Most felt flat, others were cluttered, and none connected to her deeper emotions. Pretty shots of fall foliage weren't going to make her a professional photographer. She needed something more. Something original without being too out there. If it was a photo of a path, it should make her want to walk down it. If it was of a tree, it should make her want to run her fingers along the bark. Just like photos of plants growing out of a New York sidewalk were overdone, so, too, were pretty shots with no character.

Thinking of Mia, she snapped a quick photo of herself and Prince and another of the storm out the window. She sent them to Mia with a text: *Got here just in time. Perfect day to snuggle with a dog. Cozy on the couch.*

Mia texted back with a goofy shot of her and Eric rocking out in the car. Blue sky and sunshine shown through the window. Mia's text said: *Perfect day for a road trip :P*

Alexis smiled and put her phone away. Reaching over, she ruffled Prince's ears. He wagged his tail happily.

She closed her eyes for a moment and frowned. "I'm letting myself get distracted," she told the dog.

Prince yawned.

Alexis couldn't help it; she yawned too. One long, lazy stretch, reaching her hands high above her head, and then she snuggled into the couch. She settled the laptop more firmly on her lap and tried again. There might be a photo or two that would work for her portfolio, and she'd want to leave Terra a couple of good ones.

"Doing the small things right sets you up for success when the big things come along," she told Prince sagely and then laughed at herself.

Forcing herself to put all of her attention on Photoshop, she worked her way through one image at a time. She rubbed her forehead, fighting the ache from too much frowning at the computer.

A crack of deafening thunder yanked Alexis upright. Prince sprang off the couch like he'd been bitten by a horsefly. Light splattered across her vision as if a flashbulb had exploded in her face. Rubbing her eyes, she tried to make the starbursts go away. She opened her eyes. The light from the lamp was wavy, the way sunlight danced across the bottom of a pool. The effect faded between one shallow breath and the next.

Shaking her head, she filled her lungs and gave her heartbeat a moment to even out. *Did a tree right outside get struck by lightning?* Alexis rubbed a hand over her face, breathing out slowly and trying to bring herself back to the present. At least her eyesight was back to normal.

Prince whined.

Alexis patted the couch beside her. "It's okay, boy. Just a bit of thunder."

He barked.

"Enough. You're okay." She rubbed her arms, trying to ease the fuzzy, panicky cloud gathering around her that usually meant she was coming down with the flu.

Prince jumped onto the couch and tried to lie on her.

"You're over a hundred pounds, not a lap dog." But she hugged him close.

The rain still gusted against the house. Alexis tensed with each flash of lightning, but the thunder followed slowly, with a distant rumble. Tightness dripped out of her shoulders.

Prince jumped to the ground and went to look out the window.

This is silly. It was just an afternoon thunderstorm. She was safe and sound, indoors.

Her imagination nagged at her. *What if it wasn't lightning, but some kind of terrorist attack?* Washington, DC was less than an hour away. She didn't want to be like that character in a movie who ignored the obvious. It was a crazy idea, clearly, but it would take a while to find her editing zone again. She connected her computer to the cabin's internet.

A quick scan of the news sites showed nothing but the usual crap. *The world isn't coming to an end any faster than normal.* She rolled her eyes at her own joke. The weather site merely warned of flash flooding from scattered thunderstorms.

Social media called to her, but she disconnected from the internet before she could give into temptation.

The contrast wasn't right on a shot she'd taken. The village of toadstools growing up a dead tree was dull. If she increased the saturation of the warm tones, would it have more life?

Prince barked.

Alexis rolled her stiff shoulders. "We just went out. You're fine."

With a long whine, he started to pace.

"I have photos to work on."

He pawed at the door.

Alexis closed her eyes and took a deep breath. She shouldn't reward his impatient behavior. *Toadstools!* She was focused on toadstools. Now the green moss behind them looked washed out. She was going to have to add another layer. Not that it mattered; her composition was crap. *Maybe if I'd gotten down lower to take the shot?*

Prince put his head on her knee and did that short, whiny beg that could get him any table scrap he wished from campers.

She cringed. "I'm ignoring you."

Prince heaved a sigh and sprawled across the mat in front of the door. His chin resting on the floor between his front paws, he watched her with the saddest brown eyes in the world.

Alexis's fingers twitched to reach for her camera. It wouldn't be useful for the competition, but he looked so dejected. His expressive canine features made it easy to imagine how sad he felt. It would contrast well with her photos of him playing. Terra would like them. Alexis gratefully picked up her camera and got in several shots before Prince started to pace again.

"Is there something wrong?" Her gut twisted. Nothing looked wrong with him, but his behavior was concerning. He was probably just playing her, but if he was honestly upset, she should do something. "You're not sick, are you?"

He whined.

Her frown deepened.

Maybe it was Prince or maybe it was her own restlessness, but Alexis was craving a walk too. The rain had slowed to a light drizzle. The thunder and lightning had moved on completely. By the rules of afternoon thunderstorms, it should be sunny soon.

Alexis closed her laptop and got up. Crossing her arms, she frowned at Prince. "I'm not giving in or rewarding bad behavior."

He wagged his tail, clearly not listening.

Alexis rolled her eyes and picked up the leash to tie around her waist. Prince bounded around the small house with enthusiasm while she pulled on her boots and Terra's windbreaker, which came down to her knees. She settled for taking her phone instead of her nice camera. She was still saving for a waterproof one.

Outside was cooler than she'd expected. The air was dense with wet leaves and earth. The fall colors looked muted in the gray light. The last of the misty rain sank a chill past her skin. It wasn't as good as actual mist, but maybe it would add depth and mystery to her photos.

Prince stood on the porch, his nose in the damp air.

"Aren't we going for a walk?" she asked.

He snorted and then took off toward the path. At the entrance, he looked back at her with a whine, clearly telling her to hurry.

Alexis snapped a quick photo of his expression before following. *Is he alright?* He had none of his earlier exuberance, but at least the pace he was setting helped warm her up.

He took the path in the direction opposite to the one she'd taken earlier. It rambled its way to a T with the path that hugged the shoreline. Trees gave way to marsh grass that reached high above her head. As the sun came out from behind clouds, it gilded the flat blades with slanting, afternoon light.

Alexis wished she'd grabbed her real camera as she tried to capture the richness of textures and colors. Seeds clustered on the end of thin stalks, beads of water clinging to the fluffy down. She tried several angles. There was something worth capturing here, a sense of connection with a world so much bigger than herself and a warm gratitude at being present at this exact time and place.

Prince barked.

"Yes?" she asked, annoyed he'd pulled her out of the moment. Then she caught sight of him and smiled. He looked so goofy, standing in the mud by the boat launch, his head cocked to the side, watching her. The gold light highlighted his dark fur. She snapped a photo of him before joining him.

When she got close, he put his nose to the sulfurous mud and barked excitedly.

Alexis squatted beside him. "What is it, boy?"

Crisp in the black muck was a fresh set of tracks. She didn't know much about animal footprints, other than what she'd learned in arts and crafts with the campers, but they appeared to be deer prints. Except for one small problem. Each print was larger than the palm of her hand. Way too big to be a deer. *Are there moose around here?* Didn't seem like anyone had said anything about moose. The tracks came out of the water and led through a gap in the tall grass.

As she studied them, Alexis got a blurry, black-and-white image in her head. As if she could see a shot she wanted to take, a particular look on a friend's face, a contrasting reflection on a surface, or anything that she imagined photographing. But this was different. This picture didn't feel like it came from her. She'd been thinking moose, but the animal stepping out of the water looked like it belonged on the cover of a fantasy novel. A unicorn.

It should have been unnerving to have her imagination take such a leap forward without her. For a moment, though, it was absolutely right. The next minute the sensible part of her brain kicked in, and she almost laughed out loud.

First, she was double-checking that lightning wasn't a terrorist attack, and now she was picturing unicorns. Maybe spending a long weekend alone wasn't such a good idea after all.

She chuckled to herself. *Somewhere in the back of my mind, I must have remembered that classical unicorns were cloven hooved, like deer.* Terra loved entertaining campers and counselors with classic legends. Spending time at camp, it wasn't a surprise Alexis was thinking about them.

Prince barked.

She ruffled his ears. "Was I ignoring you?"

He licked her cheek, then took off into the grass. Following the prints.

"Prince, here, boy. Come on back."

This time his bark sounded dangerous.

Alexis's stomach shifted. *He couldn't have found a moose, could he?* Somewhere in her mind was the idea that moose were surprisingly dangerous.

She froze. He'd never run off on her like that. *What am I going to tell Terra if something happened?* Fear tasted sour in the back of her throat.

He barked again.

Alexis shook herself and swallowed back her panic. It wasn't nearly as bad as rappelling off a rock wall. Ignoring the squelching mud and the scratchy grass, she pushed forward. The path of bent leaves and trodden ground was slimy, but not impossible to see.

A moment later, Alexis tripped and nearly tumbled into a flattened spot in the marsh. She caught herself, found her footing, and looked around. The area was approximately ten feet wide and walled in by marsh grass nearly that high. Protected from the wind, with slanting light gilding everything, it seemed like a perfect hideaway.

Maybe she was busy looking at the structure of the matted grass because her mind couldn't quite comprehend what was lying in it. Her breath caught on the sulfur scent of marsh; she coughed.

Storm gray, with faded dappling, the creature almost, but not quite, looked like a horse. It was on its belly, legs tucked under it, head turned toward her, watching with dark eyes and curious ears. Its smoke-colored mane contrasted sharply with the dark mud. Its tail was long and lion-like. Fine lines, reminiscent of lightning, streaked down from the white dorsal stripe marking its spine.

All of that would have been a bit unusual, especially here in a marsh, but it was the long, white horn coming out of the center of its forehead that really made it hard to process.

Prince leaned against Alexis's hip, his growl reverberating through her. As cheerful as he usually was, Alexis knew he would do his best to protect her. She'd seen him do it for Terra. One minute friendly, the next, ready to take the hand off a man who'd been threatening Terra while trying to pick up his kid after he'd lost a custody battle. Of course, that was a human and not a mythical creature the size of a horse.

There was a guy sitting on the far side of the unicorn, gaping at her, probably in the exact same way she was gaping at his steed. He collected himself first and somehow got his jaw to work.

"Hi," he said.

Alexis tore her attention away from what her eyes were telling her was a living, breathing, mythical creature and took in the details of the man. He wasn't exactly Greek hero gorgeous, but he was rather attractive and close to her own age. Looking as if he'd swum across the Atlantic Ocean during a hurricane didn't detract from his dark, wavy hair, green eyes, and strong nose. He leaned forward and rested his arms on the unicorn's back, as if that was a normal thing to do while waiting for someone to get a grip.

What did he say? "Hi," Alexis answered, fighting for the self-control that had gotten her through three summers of camp and ropes courses.

"How did you get on the film set? And have you seen my camera guy? This horse isn't going to wait forever for this shot."

For a minute Alexis almost believed him. She couldn't remember ever having been so blatantly lied to before. A hint of a British accent added to his air of confidence. *And really . . . Who can honestly accept the existence of a mythical creature, even when staring it in the face?* But the golden sunlight was strong and true. Her interest in photography had overlapped with an interest in special effects once or twice, and there was no way special effects were this good in person. There was something not quite of this world about the animal in front of her.

Besides, this was camp property, and Terra would have told her if there was going to be a film crew mucking around in a protected wetland. *Ah, a mundane truth to hold on to.*

The warm glow of adrenaline spiked her blood. The kind of energy that allowed her to clean up vomit at three in the morning or remain calm when a camper broke an arm or just sing a happy camp song after a fifteen-hour day in the rain.

"Nice try, but no dice." Seeing his concern, Alexis guessed why he might have lied. "Don't worry. I won't tell the world." She wanted answers; hopefully, an outward appearance of casual acceptance would get her that. It was a technique she'd learned from Terra, and it had served her well. Kids were willing to explain a lot more if she didn't freak out, no matter how confused or scared she was; she assumed adults were similar.

The guy pushed his damp hair out of his face. "You really can't tell anyone about this."

"Who would believe me?" Alexis pointed out with the tried-and-true logic she'd seen in more than one movie. She patted Prince's head, needing something familiar to ground her.

The man grinned, and Alexis's chest tightened. She suddenly wished she wasn't wearing an oversized windbreaker.

"That's true." He sounded relieved. "Any idea where we are?"

A black-and-white photo of a unicorn being born of wavy energy and a lightning strike slid through Alexis's mind. It was a spectacular image, and for a moment, she wished she could paint, since she'd never catch something like that with her camera. *What did he just ask? Right.*

"This is Camp Cattail on the Western Shore of the Chesapeake Bay, not far from Annapolis." She wondered if she should add USA, Earth, and the date, but decided to hold back unless he asked. If he needed to know that, she'd have a different set of questions.

"It felt farther." He stood up and stretched his arms over his head. His dripping clothes showed off an athletic build. He wasn't quite average height, but still taller than Alexis by a good six inches or so. "Are there a lot of people around?"

That didn't seem like an answer she should give a stranger. "You're soaked."

He looked like he was suppressing a smile. "Well, there was a storm."

The unicorn pushed itself to its feet. Something about the movement was off, but Alexis couldn't put her finger on it. The unicorn shook itself and walked toward her. Prince stopped growling to sniff curiously. The unicorn put out its nose, and Prince touched his to it. Wagging his tail as if he'd heard the word *treat*, he sat down.

The unicorn nickered, at first sounding horse-like, but then shifting into a sound closer to a cat's purr or distant, rumbling thunder. Goosebumps rippled down Alexis's arms at the mix of impossible and familiar. The unicorn sniffed her. Reflexively, Alexis put out a hand. Warm breath tickled her skin, and then the creature nuzzled her with a large velvet nose. It was unnervingly real. *Freak out later. Experience now.*

"Aren't you gorgeous?" Alexis cooed, though inside she was dancing like Mia at a rave. This had to be a one-in-a-million-lifetimes experience.

Prince whined and then hopped over to the man for his fair share of attention.

The unicorn rubbed the side of her head against Alexis's torso. She was a large animal, but gentle. Alexis ran her hand up the face to the horn. It was definitely solid, warm to the touch, and smooth like glass. A YouTube video stirred in her memory. The unicorn had gotten to its feet back-end first like a camel, not front-end first like a horse.

She glanced up at the guy, who was dealing with an affectionate Prince. "What's her name?"

"Down, dog," he told Prince firmly before looking up at her. "I don't know. Just met it."

Prince sat on command, but looked up at the man with an adoration he usually saved for Terra or Alexis. Some of the tension eased from Alexis's shoulders. Leaning over, she peeked under the unicorn. Not male, so probably female?

"Storm isn't very original, but it feels right," Alexis said.

"If you have to name it, Storm works for me," he said. "That work for you?" he asked the unicorn as an apparent afterthought.

The unicorn glanced his way but didn't seem to object.

Alexis ruffled her mane. "I'm Alexis, and that's Prince."

"Nice to meet you," the man said.

Riding the wave of adrenaline, Alexis rolled her eyes but didn't press him for a name. Besides, burying him with questions while he was standing soaking wet in mud didn't seem like the best way to get answers.

She found an itchy spot behind the unicorn's ears. Storm leaned against her to get a deeper scratch. Trying to keep her footing, Alexis contemplated what to do. Prince was an excellent judge of character, and she usually had good instincts about people. So, the guy *probably* wasn't dangerous. Besides, it wasn't as if she could just walk away and never look back. She'd wonder for the rest of her life if she'd just dreamed the whole encounter. Maybe she and Prince could walk him to his house. "Do you live nearby, or are you planning to spend the night in the marsh?"

He ran a hand through his unruly hair and looked around. Nothing to see but a rapidly sinking sun and marsh grass, but he seemed to study it for inspiration anyway.

"I haven't gotten that far in my plan yet." He sighed, sounding frustrated. "Can I borrow your phone?"

Alexis blinked at the normalness of that request, giving herself a breath to collect her thoughts. "Somehow cell phones and unicorns don't seem like they go together. You're not calling another dimension, are you? My phone plan doesn't cover that."

He gave a surprised laugh. "No. This dimension only."

Glad alternative dimensions were still something to be laughed about, Alexis pulled her phone out of her pocket, unlocked the screen, and handed it over.

Prince playfully bowed at the unicorn. In response, she made a sound like a wave breaking on the shore and tossed her head. The two of them started a game of tag in the small space, pushing Alexis and the man to the edge of the flattened area. Alexis watched, not even trying to process what she was seeing. It was like rock climbing or dealing with a camper's broken arm, the only way to keep from freezing up was thinking solely of the next step, the next sentence, and never, ever looking down.

"Shit, voicemail. Hey, it's me," he said. "Umm. Try calling me back on this number when you get this." His mouth was tight as he stared at the phone for a long minute, apparently thinking hard before looking up at her. "Sorry. I don't know how else they could reach me. Can I try another number?"

"Go for it."

Brian left two more messages and then handed the phone back with a deep frown. His frustration helped steady her. In her experience, it worked best if only one person freaked out at a time.

"No magical speaking mirrors or anything?"

He grinned briefly in response to the question disguised as a joke; but his lips quickly shifted back into a thin line, and he muttered, "I really just need to talk to them."

Alexis wished the frown hadn't returned. Mia often teased Alexis about her need to nurture. Looking at the man standing in the mud, just asking for hypothermia, it was all she could do not to try and help. Maybe he had some magical ability to keep warm. She looked at him carefully as he ran both hands through his hair.

The dark stain on the bandana around his torn left sleeve looked wrong. "Is that mud on your arm?"

He looked down at it, as if surprised he had a forearm. "Oh. Crap. I thought I got the bleeding to stop."

Alexis sighed. The world seemed to shift from fantastical to normal in a heartbeat. "Roll up your sleeve."

He shrugged. "It's fine."

Alexis gave him her best camp-counselor stare.

He wavered before pulling off the sopping bandana and rolling up his sleeve. Starting at the leather cuff on his wrist and running nearly to his elbow was an oozing gash.

"Oww!" he said, clearly feeling the pain now that he was looking at the cause.

She couldn't tell how bad the cut was, but it was the bay water and mud that really concerned Alexis. Just the thought of all the bacteria invading his bloodstream at this very moment made her shudder. Reaching for her pack, she realized she wasn't wearing it. There was a first-aid kit at Terra's.

Storm made another crashing-wave-sounding whine as she played with Prince, making Alexis look up. The impossibility of the situation hit her again. *How the hell did he end up here, hurt and with a unicorn?* It wasn't worth asking aloud though. He wasn't in a sharing mood. *How the hell do unicorns even exist?!*

"Can you use magic to heal that?" she asked, wanting to know if magic was real, too, almost as much as she wanted to know if his arm was going to be okay.

He looked at her as if she'd just asked if he could pull a rabbit out of a hat.

"If you have a unicorn, I assume you have magic," she pointed out. Maybe unicorns were just animals that hadn't been discovered yet, but one look at Storm and Alexis found that hard to believe.

He looked at Storm, too, before shaking his head. "No. It'll be fine."

Alexis tried to figure out if he was saying no to magic or no to healing, but she winced as he tied the bandana back on with one hand and his teeth. Looking away, she wondered if she'd accidentally ended up on some reality-TV show. Any minute, someone with perfect hair was going to show up and laugh at how gullible she was. But in her gut, she believed what she was seeing. Prince trusted them, and there was no way that wasn't a real unicorn.

If the unicorn was real, so was that cut. If he couldn't magically heal it, then he needed help. He had goosebumps on his arm as well, and the temperature was dropping.

In the back of her mind, her mental clock was ticking away her time left to find the right photo for her competition. Guilt hit her. This guy was in serious danger of hypothermia and blood poisoning, and here she was worried about her five-year plan. There was still time.

Besides, she wasn't going to get any information about magic out of him while he was standing in the mud bleeding, and it wasn't as if she was ever going to run across a mythical creature again. It had to be like getting struck by lightning—not likely to ever be repeated. Otherwise, everyone would know about unicorns.

Alexis went with her gut. "It's going to get cold as the sun sets, and you're going to want to know when the people you left messages for call back. Might as well come with me."

He looked up, as if not having considered that. "I've got Storm."

"She'll be safe enough with us. It's just Prince and me at the place we're staying, but if you try to hurt me, he'll tear out your throat," she added, just to be safe. Her vicious protector wagged his tail and came to her side at the sound of his name. Storm followed and rested her head on Alexis's shoulder.

Four

Brian
Thursday, 6:01 p.m.
Camp Cattail
Western Shore, MD

Brian stared at the woman and the freaking unicorn. His training was a bloody joke. He was no more prepared for magic to be back in the world than kids playing with plastic swords were prepared for war. He needed to talk to his family. *How the hell is what's-her-name—Alexis—not freaking out?* The tightness in his chest made breathing hard.

"I'm just going to sit for a minute and think." He sank to the sulfur-scented mud. It wasn't like he could get any dirtier. His arm hurt, he was stupid cold, and he couldn't reach his family. Mom had said they'd get away when Nick chased him, but Brian needed to talk to her. To his dad and sisters, too. Hear the sound of their voices and know they were all right. Swallowing hard, he reminded himself it would take time for them to get a phone and call the message system.

What he should do was call the Guard, but what was he supposed to say? *Sorry, we handed over the First Knot to a wack job, who actually cut it. Thought that was next to impossible. Oops, guess all that work to keep the world safe from magic is down the drain. I got away with the Compass, but had to get a lift from a unicorn. No, I don't know why it hasn't killed me yet. And guess what? I brought an outsider into this mess.*

The oversized dog circled Brian, then tried to sit in his lap. When Brian realized what was happening, he broke out laughing. It was a little weak, but it helped calm his spiraling thoughts.

His mom would call the Guard; she'd keep Elliot from having an aneurysm when he found out. There was no point in him dealing with them yet. Without the Compass, Nick wouldn't be able to find any more Knots to cut. It couldn't get any worse than it already was.

Besides, Alexis was right. He needed to be close to her phone. He had no idea how far away a store was to buy another. And he didn't have any money on him. He rubbed his left shoulder, trying to warm up. He glanced at Alexis. *What if Nick finds me here?* He didn't want to bring the mercenaries down on anyone else. Not to mention magic. If half the old stories were true, dangerous was an understatement of epic proportions.

In college, Brian had concluded magic was actually a scary version of Santa. A story adults passed on to children that he'd swallowed hook, line, and sinker. He'd seen through the logic holes of flying reindeer and chimney entrances about the same time most kids did. It had taken him considerably longer to doubt the Guard's versions of Alexander the Great, Merlin, and magic trapped in knots. He couldn't be reeling any harder now if he'd walked smack into Santa's sleigh instead of witnessing the cutting of the Gordian Knot.

Actually, Santa would have been better. The jolly old man wasn't known for devouring civilizations. The unicorn wasn't living up to the warnings, but maybe it was like a rainbow; even the most deadly and destructive hurricanes probably produced a few around the edges.

It wasn't a good idea to bring this short woman, who might not even be a full-fledged adult yet, into this shit storm. She'd ask questions he had no idea how to answer. But he needed to get back to his family. He glanced at the unicorn, who'd clearly bonded with Alexis; there was no way to know if that was a good or a bad thing.

The dog licked his face. Brian gently pushed Prince off his lap. The dog looked like a darker version of Shepherdess, Elliot's dog, who traced her lineage back to the Shadow Hounds protecting King Arthur's Court. Magic was supposed to attract magic. Maybe this dog was a distant relative, and if the breed was good enough for King Arthur, maybe it was a good sign. Maybe all magic wasn't bad. Maybe he was just coming up with stupid reasons to agree to Alexis's offer so he wouldn't sleep in a stinky, wet marsh tonight.

He sighed. "Thank you. My name is Brian."

Alexis smiled and offered him a hand up. "This way."

Brian fell into step with her when they reached the path. Prince scouted ahead, and Storm followed behind without encouragement.

"So," Alexis said, sounding casual, "are you going to explain how unicorns exist and no one knows?"

Brian ran a hand through his hair. It stayed out of his face for a mere moment before falling back into place. "I'm not supposed to talk about it?" He hoped rather than believed she'd accept that answer.

"Not going to work. Now that I've seen a unicorn, don't you think it's safer if you satisfy my curiosity, so I don't try to figure it out on my own?"

He had to fight a grin. He couldn't help it; she was rather adorable, and her casual acceptance of magic made him feel as if the rules of reality hadn't just been shattered into a million pieces and then put back together by Picasso. "That's not bad logic."

"It's beautiful logic. Seriously? How could they have escaped the notice of scientists and social media all this time?"

He thought for a moment, trying to find a way out of explaining, but his arm was throbbing, making logic difficult.

Storm snorted and butted Alexis playfully.

"See? She agrees that you should explain everything," Alexis said.

"I shouldn't believe anything I think a unicorn is saying," he muttered. *Nothing good comes from magic.* Or at least that's what Elliot always said.

Alexis crossed her arms and frowned at him.

Brian used his steps to pace his breathing until his thoughts cleared. "Okay. The answer is simple. Science hasn't found any trace of unicorns, because as of an hour ago, they haven't existed in hundreds of years. Storm is probably the only one. She spawned fully grown from magic and the elements. I'm not exactly sure how it works. Magic has been more or less locked away since the time of Merlin, and before that, on and off since the rise of mammals. Some of it was spilled this afternoon. I don't think it means the whole world has magic or even the entire US or that there is that much out there, but it's here now."

He watched her in his peripheral vision as she tried to absorb that. Maybe she wouldn't have too many questions after all. He was able to take a relaxed breath before she interrupted his peace.

"My mom always says that when you're not understanding someone, check to make sure you're defining words the same way. What does magic mean?"

Brian desperately wished Vicky were here. Or any of his family. They'd all do a finer job explaining. Or better yet, *not* explaining. He searched through his memory, trying to find something useful.

"Simplest definition I've been taught: Magic is a terrible toxin that, when not contained, devours the world. It connects all things within its reach and can be channeled by some and manipulated by others. It's been contained more or less since Merlin locked magic in its solid form. When the form is untied, the bonds no longer hold it in place, and it becomes a gas—that's when it's dangerous."

Brian let her chew on that for a while, grateful for a moment. His muscles were stiff, and his teeth were chattering. *How much further is a heater?*

"Why was it released?" Alexis asked.

Brian shoved his hair out of his face with his right hand and then dropped his hand to cradle his left arm. "I wish I knew." Growing up, he'd thought only a villain would want to poison the world with magic, but as an adult that simple logic felt a little thin. It was too much like something a Bond villain would do if Ian Fleming had known about magic. There was a pro-magic cult that had worked against the Guard before, but they were a bunch of nuts who'd run out of support before Brian was born.

What Brian did know was Nick was planning on cutting more Knots. With magic in the world again, the Compass would be functional for the first time in hundreds of years. A little magic might be manageable, but a lot . . . Brian shuddered at the memory of Elliot's stories.

"We're almost there. I'd offer my jacket, but I don't think it'll help much," Alexis said.

Brian glanced at the oversized jacket. It might fit him, but it seemed pointless over his wet clothes. "I'm fine," he said, even though his toes were numb in his soggy sneakers, and his left arm throbbed every time his heart beat.

"How come magic isn't in the history books?" she asked.

That was an easier question. "My people, the Guard, have done their best to remove accurate descriptions of magic from the written record. They were able to completely shift Merlin and King Arthur to the realm of legends. A lot of others were labeled as philosophers and scientists. If people don't believe in magic, they won't go looking for it."

"And magical creatures? How have they stayed out of the fossil record?"

"They have too much magic in them and aren't made the same way normal vertebrates are. They don't fossilize."

Alexis raised a laughing eyebrow at him. "Convenient."

He shrugged. No reason to convince her of something that would put her in danger.

"I can't seem to dismiss the existence of Storm," she said.

"Pity."

Alexis laughed. "This is really crazy cool!"

"No!" He took a deep breath before trying again. "Sorry. But this isn't that happy magic you've heard about. This is the real thing. Magic is most closely related to a radioactive substance. You know how humans figured out how to eliminate the plague and smallpox? Well, we learned how to do the same thing with magic. King Arthur and Merlin were great leaders in the fight. They sealed the last of the major magic away. Their acolytes finished the job and more or less managed to keep the world safe from magic. Until today."

"So . . ." Alexis said slowly, clearly not sure she was following, "That unicorn is going to spread death and darkness to all the world?"

Brian eyed the unicorn suspiciously. He couldn't get his head around how the creature that had saved him from the bay was the same type of creature the Guard was so worried about. "She probably won't eat your face, but I'd be careful."

Storm gave a snort that sounded like waves on a beach.

Alexis ruffled her mane. "Maybe she's like Prince. Won't hurt you unless you hurt her or her people."

Brian looked at the dog rolling around in the yard ahead of them and shook his head at the comparison. Alexis was as naive as she was adorable, in her oversized jacket and hiking boots. Despite her short stature, the intelligence in her eyes and steady demeanor were making him reevaluate her age as closer to his.

"Here we are." Alexis led the way up the steps to the porch of a log cabin.

Brian heaved a sigh of relief.

"Storm, what are we going to do with you?" Alexis asked.

The unicorn sniffed at the grass in the front yard before taking a tentative bite. She chewed for a long minute. Then went back for more, ignoring the rest of them.

"Well, that settles that." Alexis opened the door.

Prince bounded in and headed for his water bowl, tracking muddy prints. Brian followed Alexis and stood on the welcome mat, looking down at his soggy sneakers. The warmth of the cabin sank into his damp clothes, but untying his shoes would be a herculean task.

"Leave your sneakers there." She pulled off her own boots. "I'm going to get the first-aid kit."

Her matter-of-factness helped him step on the back of his shoes to slide out of them. He was no doubt damaging them, but after everything he'd put them through today, what did that matter?

"I'm sure my arm is fine," he called, trying to ignore the throbbing.

She pulled her head out of a closet and brought a large pack to the bar counter. "Good. Then you don't mind me looking at it. Come on over. Let's see how much mud you can clean off in the sink."

Brian was too tired to argue, but as water stung and pushed the mud free, adrenaline jolted through him. *What do I say to keep Alexis from taking me to the hospital?* Showing up at the emergency room without an ID, insurance card, or money was bad enough, but he had to find his family and get to the Guard before Nick found him. A man who solved his problems with hired mercenaries would surely check hospitals looking for Brian. The risk was too high.

"I'm fine." He didn't have a choice, he had to be fine, but no one should see that deep below their own skin. Looking away, he swallowed hard. "I don't need a hospital." It sounded better than saying he couldn't go.

Five

Alexis
Thursday, 6:12 p.m.
Camp Cattail
Western Shore, MD

Alexis pulled on gloves as Brian washed the blood and mud off his arm. Though she'd been first-aid trained, Terra or the summer camp's nurse had always been around for anything a superhero Band-Aid couldn't fix. For really bad accidents, the hospital was close.

She breathed easier when the whole cut was visible. It was long and painful looking, but she couldn't see bone or any major damage. "Keep it under the water a bit longer. You could use stitches." But if she wrapped it well and it healed okay, he wouldn't need them. If he didn't mind a scar. The bleeding was down to a slow ooze, and other than looking cold, his color was okay. He probably hadn't lost too much blood. Infection was still a concern.

"I'm fine," he repeated.

She glanced up at his face. He sure as hell didn't look fine, but she refrained from saying so. "How did you get cut?"

"Fell on a piece of metal." He shrugged.

Alexis raised an eyebrow, but ruthlessly forced her curiosity back. *Concentrate on the cut.* "Have you had a tetanus shot recently?"

"Yeah." He seemed to think about it. "Two years ago."

"It's still bleeding some, which should help clean it out, but I'm worried about infection. Can I give you a ride to the hospital?" There had to be keys to a camp vehicle around here somewhere.

"I'll watch it for infection. I don't need a hospital today."

Alexis frowned, but didn't argue. "Fine, but if it shows any sign of infection, you need to get it looked at right away. And it's not my fault if it scars."

"Thank you." He sounded like he meant it.

Alexis met his green eyes. Cheeks warm, she dropped her gaze to his arm. "Okay, turn off the water. Let me see what I can do." She patted his arm dry with a paper towel. "Your bracelet is in the way."

"Right." Brian shifted his feet uncomfortably.

"Leather cuff or whatever manly thing you want to call it."

"I got it." Brusquely he unsnapped the cuff and put it on his right wrist.

Alexis blew out a long breath and reminded herself to be patient; he was in pain. Alexis made sure the laceration was clean and thoroughly disinfected before applying antibiotic cream. Using butterfly bandages, gauze, and an enthusiastic amount of medical tape, she managed to close up the wound.

She leaned back and tried to hide a smile. Just because she was happy with the job she'd done didn't mean he could assume it was all taken care of. "You should really see a doctor."

"I will. As soon as I've got some stuff sorted. Thanks, it looks great. Has anyone called back yet?"

Alexis checked her phone then shook her head. "Sorry. You're having a crap day, huh?"

That surprised a laugh out of him. "That's for sure."

"Why don't you get cleaned up before you catch a chill? The owner of the house keeps a lost and found here before donating the unclaimed items to Goodwill. I'll see if I can find you something dry to wear. The shower is over there if you want to get cleaned up. Just don't get your bandage wet." She handed him several plastic bags and duct tape.

Brian groaned. "A shower and dry clothes sounds awesome. I didn't mean to dump this mess on you."

Alexis shrugged. "I'm offering." She couldn't very well throw him out into the cold, and she needed answers about magic. As soon as he was gone, she could think about her real life again. "While you're waiting for your friends to call back, how about frozen pizza? I find there's not much in life pizza can't make better."

He took a deep breath and his shoulders relaxed. "Sounds awesome. Seriously, thank you." He headed for the bathroom.

Alexis turned on the oven, wiped paw prints off the tile, and went in search of clothes. She found sweatpants, a sweatshirt, and a camp shirt that were around the right size and left them outside the bathroom door. Then she retreated to the kitchen. Frozen pizza didn't take nearly enough brain power. Even tossing together a side salad wasn't distracting enough.

She checked her phone, just in case her ringer was turned off and Brian had missed a call. The ringer was on, and there was a text from Mia.

Why is Eric soooo hot?! It's not fair.

Alexis smiled, grateful something in the world was normal. She texted back. *What did he do this time?*

He knows all the words to Dancing in the Dark.

Alexis resisted the temptation to point out that it wasn't a lyrically complicated song. *There's no resisting that.*

It must be fate.

Alexis heard the shower turn off. Her mind flickered to Brian. If magic existed again, might fate? She almost laughed aloud at the thought. For some reason, believing in unicorns was easier than believing fate had brought Brian to her. Prince had just happened to bring her along at that particular moment. Besides, she didn't have time to daydream about a guy. She wouldn't have time for a romantic relationship until she'd put in at least six months at her dream job.

She took a chance anyway because Mia would like it: *Best of luck. I've got a bit of possible fate unfolding here. Will text you when I know more.*

Can't leave me hanging like that!

Prince and I met a cute guy while out for a walk. Probably nothing, but I'll keep you posted.

You'd better!

:-)

Alexis put the phone away before Brian saw her on it. She didn't want him to think she was texting the world about magic. Prince made a sighing sound from the living room rug, where he'd retired after making a mess of his water bowl. Rolling her eyes, she refilled his bowl and gave him a scoop of food from the bin.

Realizing that the unicorn might want water, she filled a large bowl and took it outside. Storm accepted a drink before returning to grazing. It was weird seeing a magical creature cropping grass. It seemed to her as if unicorns should eat rainbows or something equally impossible.

Alexis leaned against the railing and watched the beautiful creature in the twilight. *How can one absorb such a thing?* Storm was otherworldly and unquestionably magical. The timer inside beeped. Alexis chuckled at the juxtaposition.

After going back inside, she opened the oven. The cheese on the veggie pizza wasn't quite melted in the middle. She set the timer for another two minutes. Going to the cabinets, she found plates and cups and set them up at the bar that divided the kitchen from the living room.

Brian, in the rather oversized, borrowed clothes, joined her just as the first pizza was coming out of the oven. He was attractive in an athlete-who-just-finished-the-most-challenging-game-of-his-life kind of way. Alexis took one look at him and got a second pizza out of the freezer and slid it into the oven. If there were leftovers, she could always eat them tomorrow.

"Anyone call back?" he asked.

"Not yet, but dinner is ready. Water, milk?" Alexis checked the mostly bare fridge. "Yeah, that looks like it for options."

He took a deep breath, as if trying to gather himself. "Thank you. Water would be great," he said, as if civility was the only thing keeping him together. Or perhaps it was one thing that didn't take overthinking on his part.

"You're welcome." She set a glass of water in front of him and took a seat. "Okay, so I still don't understand. Magic was trapped, and now it's a gas? How far does it spread? Does it dilute into nothing?"

Brian cut into the pizza. It really needed to be given another few minutes for the cheese to set, but Alexis knotted her hands in her lap so she wouldn't point that out.

"Magic spreads at a rate . . . based on"—Brian fought to keep the melty cheese on his slice as he moved it to his plate—"the old writings . . . I don't know. Maybe my brain will work better after I've eaten." He picked up a piece of cheese and blew on it.

Alexis was glad that he at least had the sense not to burn his mouth. Giving the pizza its due time, she focused on the side salad.

"Is the sound on your phone turned up?" Brian asked.

"Yes. I double-checked. Do you want to try another number?"

"No, it's fine."

Alexis didn't think he sounded fine, but she chose to get herself a slice of pizza instead of saying so. "Are you trying to reach someone around here?"

Brian inhaled his slice, now that the cheese was out of the way, and cut himself another. "Sort of. What is this place?"

"Camp Cattail. It's mostly a summer camp, but they do a few retreats and field trips year-round. I've worked summers as a counselor." Alexis savored the pizza. It was the good kind of frozen food, not the kind that tasted like cardboard.

"It's not summer now."

"I'm dog sitting. It's a three-day weekend at college. Yes, I'm talking about you," she told Prince, who perked up. "And no, I'm not feeding you human food."

Prince watched her another minute, as if to see if she was serious, and then with a heartfelt sigh put his head back on his paws.

"What do you do as a counselor?" Brian said, taking another slice of pizza.

"I'm a ropes-course specialist. I still look after campers, but my best friend Mia and I share responsibility for a cabin of them, and she leads most of the regular activities. I spend most of my time leading rock-wall and climbing-tower activities for the whole camp."

"Why do you like the ropes stuff?"

The timer beeped, and Alexis got up to check on the oven. *Good enough.* She moved it to the table. "I could say I love the excitement of climbing things or the adrenaline boost from the heights, which are great, but honestly, I stay on the ground most of the time. It's the peace and quiet that calls me. I love camp, but it's an overload. Getting to the rock wall or zip line early, making sure all the equipment is safe and set up correctly and then taking it all down again at the end of the day is . . . peace." She set the second pizza on the table, curious to see if he'd zoned out. But Brian was watching her, not the food.

"You don't get bored?" he asked, sounding genuinely interested.

"Maybe if that's all I did, but the days are full of excitement, so it's nice to take a break and coil rope, tie knots, and check equipment. There's something really satisfying with getting everything just right, not just because it has to be or someone might get hurt, but because it is. Like taking just the right picture."

"You take photos?"

Alexis smiled. She could talk photography all day long, and Mia, as amazing as she was, had been listening to Alexis talk about it for years. Brian was a new audience and seemed interested. But something nagged at her. "You're trying to distract me from asking about magic!"

He shrugged. "A little, but I'm enjoying listening to you. I'd much rather hear about your life than worry about my problems. You sure the ringer is up on your phone?"

"Yes." She checked it just to be sure and then took another slice of pizza before it was gone. Somehow, he could listen and make hot pizza disappear at the same time. "What does magic do, besides make unicorns?"

"Hopefully just one unicorn. Do you mind if I have the last slice?"

Alexis waved a dismissive hand and took a bite of her own slice, waiting for an answer.

He inhaled half the slice. "I honestly don't know much. My group's job is to keep magic out of the world. What to do now that it's here—" He covered a yawn. "I'm sure the Guard Council members know more."

"How have you not asked them a million questions?"

Brian shrugged and yawned again. "Can I help clean up?"

Alexis fought to contain her curiosity. He looked so tired, and she could only guess at what he'd been through before she'd found him. She glanced around the room. There were a half-dozen camp cabins a five-minute walk from Terra's, but it was late, and it seemed like a lot of work to open one up and set it up for a guest. Besides, she had Prince to protect her.

"I'll do the dishes in the morning. Let's get you settled on the couch. You won't be able to properly deal with any of your problems if you don't get some sleep."

"Thanks. You'll wake me if they call?"

"Yes."

She stacked the dishes by the sink and handed him the extra blankets before stepping outside with Prince to let him mark a few more trees before bed. She checked on Storm, who was curled up beside the porch, her head up, apparently star gazing. Alexis glanced up at the now-clear sky. "It's a good night for it. Sleep well, Storm."

There was a soft rumbling purr in reply.

Everything settled, Alexis climbed up the stairs to bed. Prince settled in at her feet. Alexis pulled open her laptop and returned to the photo of the toadstools. Brian and magic were interesting, but the competition wouldn't wait for her to sort them out. She'd be in that dream job long after they were gone.

She yawned, and anxious energy started to leach out of her body. Her brain grew foggy and craved an escape. Her body was heavy, as if she'd been kayaking in turbulent waves all day.

Carefully, she worked through one photo after another, looking for something spectacular hidden beneath the surface, battling back her disjointed thoughts at every turn.

She rubbed her temple and shifted her stiff back. Nothing was flowing, and her mind kept slipping to the man on the couch and the unicorn by the porch. Ruthlessly she kept bringing her attention back to the task at hand. Only when she leaned back to look at a photo of Prince she'd been working on and saw the terrible banding of light and shadow did she finally admit she was too tired to be photo editing. Closing her laptop, she settled into bed.

Lightning haunted her dreams. Tangled, sticky webs kept trying to trap her.

Her cell's ringtone jarred her awake. At first, she thought it was her alarm, but it was still dark outside. Her second thought was that

Mia must be in trouble. She answered it without checking the caller ID. "Hello?"

"You're not Brian," a jarringly pleasant voice answered.

Alexis tried to sort out what that meant. She turned on the bedside light and concentrated on sitting up.

"Is Brian there? I would very much like to speak to him. My name is Nick."

Right. Brian. The guy with the unicorn. That hadn't been a dream. Unless she was still dreaming. Didn't really matter at the moment. "Just a minute."

She headed for the stairs.

Brian must have heard the phone ring because he'd turned on the light by the couch. Her eyes must not be awake yet, because for a moment, in the harsh light, she saw the room in black-and-white. But there were more people in the image. A tall, light-haired man stood with a child held close to his side. Energy cracked around the man as he came for Brian. Alexis shook her head to clear it. Warm tones saturated the room and the ghost images faded, but she was going to have to get her vision checked.

"Phone," she said, offering it to Brian.

Six

Brian
Friday, 5:26 a.m.
Camp Cattail
Western Shore, MD

Brian tried to rub sleep out of his face before reaching for the phone. Relief coursed through him. He couldn't believe he'd fallen asleep when he still didn't know what had happened to his family. Well-fed and out of adrenaline, he'd not been able to keep his eyes open. Thank God, they were finally calling him back.

"Hey," he said.

"Hello, Brian. This is Nick," the voice on the other end said.

Brian froze. When they lived in Seattle, he'd been showing off on his bike and hit a low wall. Flying over the handlebars, the world had flipped. Air punched out of his lungs, pavement hard against his back. That excruciating wait for his breath to return, praying nothing was broken. This was worse. This time he didn't trust the air to return.

"Nice of you to leave that voicemail," Nick continued after the empty pause where Brian should have said something. "I wasn't certain how I was going to contact you. Your family hasn't been particularly cooperative. But they've finally admitted that the Compass is in your possession."

Breathing hurt, but Brian found his voice. "What the hell? What have you done with them?"

"They're perfectly fine. For now. Here's Emily."

"Brian! You're okay!" Em sounded relieved and anxious at the same time.

"I'm fine. You okay? Everyone okay?"

"So far. But Brian, I think you're going to have to give Nick the Compass. It's like Avery always says. We don't stand a chance against him."

Brian shoved his hair out of his face. Avery was code for "Get help and don't give 'em what they want." He shouldn't have left. His instincts screamed at him to take the Compass straight to Nick. Brian wanted his family safe. *To hell with the consequences.*

He looked out the window to where they'd left Storm. There was a goddamn unicorn out there. This was way bigger than he was, bigger than his family. He needed help. He needed the Guard. That was the help Em meant.

"Brian?" Em asked.

He fought to control his ragged breathing. *Time.* That's what running got his family. Time to get help. The Guard would fix this, but they couldn't do it overnight. Brian's mind raced. He had to buy more hours, days. *It wouldn't take days to get them back, would it?* "I will," he promised Em.

Nick took the phone back. "So, it's simple, if you haven't already deduced. The Compass for your family."

Brian imagined punching the bastard across the jaw.

"Who answered the phone earlier?" Nick asked.

"Some chick who's letting me crash on her couch and borrow her phone." He gave Alexis an apologetic shrug. She shrugged back and returned to patting Prince.

Brian didn't want to put her on Nick's radar. *One problem at a time.* "I don't have the Compass on me. I hid it. I won't be able to get it until the day after tomorrow—or today? After today, so tomorrow—I guess it's early morning?" he added, glancing at the clock on the phone. He wanted to kick himself for rambling, but it was hard to think and talk at the same time.

"Why?" Nick said coldly.

Err . . . "I time locked it with magic." Brian tried to sound like it was a perfectly reasonable thing to do. *Thank you, improv.* "Gave it forty-eight hours before it could be retrieved. Safety measure." The silence that greeted Brian's words was one of the most uncomfortable ones he'd ever heard. Finally, he couldn't take it. "I didn't know you were going to ransom my family."

"Did you tell the Guard?"

"No. I didn't want to get them involved until I knew more," Brian said truthfully. He felt like an idiot now. *But really?* What would the Guard have been able to do to help when he didn't know anything yet?

"That's good at least. Do *not* contact them. Or the police . . . Or the FBI," Nick said, sounding like he was also making this up as he went along. It wasn't a reassuring thought. "Then meet me at the Inner Harbor in Baltimore with the Compass . . . Saturday afternoon. We'll do the exchange there."

Brian closed his eyes and tried to think through his options. Usually, he could just wing stuff and it all worked out, but this was too important. *Time*, he reminded himself. Nick wanted the Compass enough to hold them at gunpoint in the middle of the afternoon. Brian had to hold his ground. "I don't think I can get to Baltimore before sunset. My wallet and phone were on the boat. I can figure something out, but it'll take time."

Alexis started to say something, but Brian waved her off then put a finger to his lips. He'd forgotten she was standing there.

I can help, she mouthed.

He waved her off again. *Not now.*

"Seriously," Nick said, "do you want your family or not?"

"I want them. Unhurt! I'll get your Compass as fast as I can! If it was up to me, I'd bring the damn thing to you right this minute! But it's stupid time locked, and I have no idea where Baltimore is from here. Negotiating with a kidnapper isn't something they cover in any of my classes!" Brian let his frustration and desperation come through loud and clear. "I'll get there by sunset Saturday."

Nick sighed. "Fine. Going to have to make it Saturday evening then. I'll call with an exact time and place. If you change phones, call your father's cell and leave a message with the new number."

"I'll be there."

"And Brian, don't try anything stupid." Nick's voice turned as hard as granite and lost all uncertainty. "I'm perfectly willing to brutally murder one member of your family after the other, until I get what I want or you're alone in the world." The line went dead.

Brian stared down at the phone. Numb. Nick's threat sounded crazy enough to be believed. Brian set down the phone; he couldn't feel his fingers.

"I guess we're not going to get any more sleep tonight. Dawn isn't far off anyway. Coffee or tea?" Alexis asked.

"What?" Brian blinked. He'd forgotten she was standing there again.

"Coffee or tea? Hot beverage and then we can make a plan."

"A plan?" It was like his brain was scuba diving. Everything was muted and slow. Except his heart, which was loud in his ears.

"Coffee or tea?"

That at least was a concept he could wrap his head around. *Two choices.* "Coffee."

Alexis moved to the kitchen and started puttering around. "Milk or sugar? There's no cream."

"Both." *How could she sound so relaxed?*

Prince licked Brian's hand. Brian started and then patted the dog's head. Patting a dog was also in his ability range at the moment. And he could sit and drink coffee when Alexis set it in front of him at the bar. It was hot, sweet, and had a generous serving of milk in it. Focusing on the large pottery mug, warm between his hands, the wafting scent of freshly brewed coffee, and the dog, whose fuzzy head was on Brian's knee, gave him something to grasp.

Slowly his brain started to function again. He wanted to yell at Alexis for not understanding. He wanted to throw something heavy. He wanted out of the cabin with its mud-colored interior. But none of that would help his family. He took another long sip of coffee.

"Okay," he said at last. "I should have known they were in trouble. But when the boat chased after me, I thought they got away."

"Spilt milk."

"What?!"

"Principle is the same. It's already happened. No point second-guessing what's already been," Alexis said crisply. "So, your family has been kidnapped by some guy who wants to trade them for a magical compass? At least I assume it's magical?"

Brian gaped at her. But she was making sense. Far more than his brain was. "I need to call the Guard."

"Didn't he say not to?" When he shot her a look she added, "The sound was up pretty loud. I could hear most of what he said."

"I shouldn't drag you into this. It's dangerous. And there's magic."

"You must know more about magic than you were letting on. Time lock?"

"Oh, that." Brian smiled despite himself. "Hopefully that gives me enough time to figure out where he's keeping my family and get them out. I saw that in a crime movie. The vault was locked. Chances are Nick knows approximately as much about magic as I do." An old line popped into his head and almost made him smile. "Which is in the neighborhood of diddly squat, right next to the sprawling city of nothing at all. Sure, there are vague stories. Shadows and Shiners and Spell Casters, but very few specifics."

"Okay." She grinned at his joke, but sounded as if she was still trying to get a grasp on what was going on. "So, magic exists, but the chances that it will be of any use to us or to Nick is pretty small."

"I come from two separate lines of magically gifted. I should have the ability to use it. Even if it's dangerous, I'll do what it takes to get my family back. Hopefully, figuring out what I'm doing with it is one of the things I bought myself some time to do." It wasn't reassuring that everything he knew about hostage rescue came from TV and movies.

"Do you think Nick probably comes from a similar line? Since he knows about magic?"

Brian frowned. "Hadn't thought that far. But yeah, fair assumption."

"What else did you buy yourself time for?"

"To contact the Guard. That's what they're there for. Helping with stuff like this. I wonder how Nick knows about them."

"Could he be a member?"

"Of the Guard? No, of course not. Everyone in the Guard knows how dangerous magic is. Besides, I grew up in it and know everyone. He's probably with the Searcha, a pro-magic nut cult."

"What if he knows you called?"

A shiver traced down Brian's spine. He shook it off. "He can't seriously know if I've talked to the Guard. He just doesn't want me showing up to the exchange with them. I won't. But it would be stupid not to ask for help. Can I borrow your phone again?"

Alexis handed it over. "It's still really early."

"I should have called hours ago."

It took him a long minute to remember the number, but he'd been expected to memorize it for just this kind of thing. The phone rang three long times before a concerned female voice answered.

"Alexis, what's wrong? Is Prince alright?"

Brian pulled the phone away from his ear and looked at it for a moment. *What?* Had he gotten the wrong number? He hit the speaker button. "Terra? It's me, Brian Weaver."

"Brian? Sorry. I thought I recognized the number as my dog sitter," Terra said.

"I'm here too," Alexis said. "Prince is great. Sorry to be calling so early."

"Okay. You two have met? Um . . . Okay. Why don't you start from the beginning?" Terra said, sounding as if this wasn't the first time she'd been awakened for an emergency.

Brian opened his mouth to explain, but nothing came out. His family had failed to protect the world from magic. It would sound far-fetched if he hadn't just lived through it.

"So, you said how I shouldn't bring home any unicorns?" Alexis said.

Terra gave a half laugh before turning grave. "The magic breach was that bad?"

He let out his breath. That gave him a place to start. "Yes. How did you know? They had guns. The First Knot was completely severed. Should we be talking in front of Alexis?"

"It's going to be okay, Brian," Terra said. "Sounds like Alexis is already in the middle of this. Besides, she's someone I want on my team in a crisis. As far as how I know about the breach, our equipment sensed it. Realized that your unit was in the approximate area. When we couldn't reach you, we sent Russel to investigate. His last report says the magic is spreading rapidly. He's at a hotel in Annapolis and will continue his survey tomorrow, well, later today I guess, getting us a better map of what's been affected. He also said the last time anyone saw you and your family, you were out on your boat. Are they with you?"

Brian looked at Alexis. She sipped her coffee, clearly not going anywhere. "No. They're being held hostage. A guy calling himself Nick has Alexander the Great's Dagger and some kind of mercenary group working for him. I got away with the Compass, but he has the rest of my family. He wants the Compass in exchange for them. We have until Saturday night to come up with a plan. Alexis found me after I got away."

"Great job getting away. If they'd gotten the Compass, the consequences . . . You did the right thing."

Something eased in Brian's chest.

Terra sighed. "I want more details, but now's probably not the best time. We've got a lot to deal with. Alexis, can you drive Brian to DC in my camp truck? The keys are on a purple p-cord in the drawer next to the silverware. We're going to need him here."

"No problem, but is it just me or is this one crazy coincidence? Prince finding Brian," Alexis said.

"Prince found him? Oh, that makes sense." Terra sounded relieved to find logic. "I told you, he's descended from King Arthur's Shadow Hounds. Brian comes from several strong magic lines—of course the two of them would be drawn together. Anyway, I'm going to see about moving the council meeting up to this morning instead of tomorrow. Brian knows where we'll be. Let's say ten a.m."

It was a little like being caught in a whirlwind. Brian looked at his empty cup; he was going to need more coffee. "Okay. We'll see you soon."

"What do we do with the unicorn?" Alexis asked.

"Unicorn? Right, you said something about that. You actually brought it home?"

"Yep." Alexis walked over to the window. "There's a real, live unicorn sleeping by your porch."

"It actually helped me get away from Nick," Brian added. "Then it followed us home like a stray cat."

"That's really interesting. See if you can get some pictures. He should probably be fine at camp. Magical creatures are supposed to have some sort of invisibility ability, and there's no one there this weekend. He should be safe enough," Terra said.

She, Alexis mouthed while holding up the coffee pot in question.

Brian rolled his eyes at her. Yet, it was oddly endearing that she cared about the gender of a mythical creature. He shrugged off the thought and held out his cup for her to refill.

"Sorry, I know you wanted a quiet vacation, Alexis," Terra said. "But this has gotten out of hand. I think it's best if you and Prince stay in DC with us until this gets sorted."

"I don't mind dropping Brian off, getting some of my questions answered, and coming back here to stay with Prince. I've got that photo competition."

"Or I could drive myself," Brian put in.

"It's not that simple," Terra said. "Alexis, just knowing about magic might be putting you in danger. I'd rather have you with the Guard. Bring your stuff, we can talk about it when you get here."

Alexis looked torn, but she seemed to think better of arguing. Instead she asked, "Are we worried Nick knows about the Guard?"

Brian poured milk into his cup from the personal-sized milk carton. It was amazing to him how quickly Alexis was processing. He added an extra scoop of sugar from the tiny Tupperware container.

"The Guard isn't the best kept secret in the community of magical artifacts. But as long as he thinks he's getting what he wants, we should be okay."

He opened his hands palms outward to ask if Alexis had any more questions. She shook her head.

"Then, I guess we'll see you soon," he said to Terra.

"Good," she said.

Brian ended the call and leaned back on the kitchen stool. It was still barely dawn outside; they had more than enough time to get to DC, but if he didn't keep moving, he might start thinking about his family. Terra would have the answers, and everything would be alright. He should have called her sooner. He tried to take a deep breath, but the tightness was coming back to his chest.

"So, breakfast?" Alexis asked. "I don't think either of us is going back to sleep."

His stomach hadn't really woken up yet, but he'd be hungry soon enough. "What do you have?"

"Prepackaged bowls of cereal from the dining hall," she said, checking the cabinets and then standing in front of the open fridge for a long moment. "And . . . that looks like about it."

"Then I'll take a . . . bowl of prepackaged cereal." He picked the chocolate one, peeled back the top, and sloshed in the carton of milk. Hopefully, his family was getting to eat at least as well. *Nick will feed them, won't he? Crap.* Worrying wasn't helping, but it was easier to do than playing flip cup sober. He glanced down and realized he'd eaten half the bowl without noticing or tasting anything. Shrugging, he polished it off and reached for another one. The serving size was tiny after all.

"Do you live around here?" Alexis asked between bites of Chex. "Since we've got time, do you want to swing by and get some of your stuff? Maybe a change of clothes?"

He glanced blankly at his borrowed sweats. Not the best impression for a Council meeting, even if they would understand. Mom would be bummed he hadn't gotten his hair cut. He pushed the thought away. "Um, yeah. Thanks. I've got stuff at the Airbnb we were staying at in Annapolis." Plus, he could grab the backup cash.

"Would you mind straightening up the kitchen? I'm going to get ready and then grab stuff for me and Prince."

"How are you so cheerful?" He knew it wasn't fair to take his mood out on her, but she was acting like this was no big deal.

"Camp training." She must have seen his skepticism, because she crossed her arms and added, "I've found that when I get thrown a curveball, being positive and calm helps. At least neither of us is throwing up or has a broken bone."

Brian knew he didn't look any more convinced than he felt, because after a pause she continued.

"Would you prefer I freak out, though? I could throw a fit right here. Just sit on the ground panicking, expressing all the ways this is nuts and could all go terribly wrong. I could even make it all about me? It would be easy. This is supposed to be my vacation. I'm trying to get on the right path for the next five years of my life. The world does revolve around me after all." She raised one finger in the air to punctuate that last part and then crossed her arms, waiting.

Brian tried to take that in. A laugh in his chest caught him by surprise.

It would all work out. Things always did. Feeling more like himself helped. Being surly wouldn't rescue his family.

She uncrossed her arms and smiled back.

"Okay. You're right. Sorry," he admitted. "I'll clean up the kitchen."

"I'll be right down."

Washing mugs, spoons, and the dishes from last night didn't take long. Putting away the extra milk was even faster. He wiped down the counter and bar, just to keep his hands busy. The off-white laminate was worn and just a bit stained from years of hard use. It contrasted with the brightly colored cereal bowls. Building a tower out of them didn't hold his attention for long.

He heard the shower turn off. Judging from his sisters, it was still going to be a while.

Prince whined with his leash in his mouth.

"Where'd you get that?" Brian asked.

The dog whined again.

"Okay. Let's help out more and get your stuff. Help me find it."

He'd never had a dog, never had more than a fish. Animals were awesome, and they'd always gotten along well with him, but it hadn't made sense to own any with all the traveling and moving they'd done growing up. He'd been fifteen when they'd housesat for his aunt, though, and she'd had three dogs. Em had been in heaven. Brian had enjoyed it more than he'd admitted, and it had been surprisingly hard to say goodbye to all the dogs, especially to the year-and-a-half-old boxer. He still made time every Thanksgiving to take the dogs for a walk. So, it wasn't hard to put together a traveling kit for Prince. Everything, including the purple ball Prince had brought him, was all neatly stacked when Alexis came down the steps.

She'd changed out of her yoga pants and oversized T-shirt. Like yesterday, she was wearing jeans, a tank top, and a flannel shirt—this time a brown one that almost matched her pretty eyes. It seemed like a weird thing to notice, so Brian turned his attention back to getting ready.

"Does he have treats?"

Prince reacted by bouncing around the room like a puppy.

"I guess that's a *yes*. Anything else he needs?"

She went to one of the high cupboards and pulled out a bag of treats and a dog bone and looked over the rest of the pet supplies. "I hope that's good. Thanks for packing his stuff."

He shrugged and waved a hand at the tower he'd made on the counter. "I ran out of cereal bowls."

She grinned at him. His stomach shifted. Probably too much sugar before sunrise. He was not getting a crush on a girl while his family was being held hostage, he told himself firmly.

"Anything else we need?" she asked.

"Do you know how to get to Annapolis from here?"

She set down her backpack and checked her phone. "I do now. Looks like it won't take too long. We should get those pictures of Storm before we go. Do you think she'd let me ride?"

"We don't have time for that!" *Has she forgotten that my family is being held hostage?*

"If we get to DC early, it sounds like all you're going to be able to do is climb the walls until the meeting starts. Please! How many chances will I have to ride a unicorn, right?"

Brian frowned at her. He was tempted to point out that magical creatures were dangerous, but it felt silly to say that about Storm. He shrugged. "Just because she found me doesn't mean she's mine."

Alexis grinned. "Good enough." She left her bag by the door then headed out.

Prince bounded out with enthusiasm, as if this morning was the best of his whole life.

As much as Brian didn't like it, Alexis was right. There was nothing the Guard could do until they were all together. And she was so . . . cheerful.

Birdsong and crisp air greeted Brian. It really was going to be a gorgeous day. He shrugged off an uncomfortable desire for unrelenting clouds and a cold rain.

Storm had bedded down by the porch, but rose fluidly when Alexis approached.

Prince gave Storm a lick on the nose, as if in greeting, before bounding off to mark his trees.

Alexis offered both hands with an apple in the right palm, letting the unicorn come to her. Storm didn't hesitate. She nuzzled the free hand before taking the apple in one light bite. Alexis scratched her neck while cooing, "What a beautiful lady you are. May I ride you?"

Storm snorted, glanced at her own back, then seemed to shrug. Alexis looked at the wide back. Turning to Brian she said. "Mind giving me a boost?"

Brian put his hands on his hips. "How are you going to steer?"

"She's a unicorn. I'll just ask her to go where I want, and if that's okay for her, we'll go there. That'll work, right, girl?"

Storm seemed to lose interest, turning her attention to munching grass.

"Have you ever even ridden a horse before?"

"Sure," Alexis said in a way that didn't inspire confidence.

Brian rolled his eyes. Riding Storm didn't feel real to him, as if it had happened to someone else, but he could understand why Alexis wanted to. He rather wanted to ride again too. Magic was supposed to be toxic, but at this point they'd already been exposed to it. What harm could a little more do?

Might help me understand magic better, he told his guilt. His guilt was as unenthusiastic about that logic as a pro baseball team upon being handed a wiffle ball and told to "make it work." Still, Nick wanted more magic in the world. If Brian was going to keep that from happening, every piece of information he could learn about magic would be invaluable. *How better to learn than from a magical creature?*

"Fine," he said, walking over and lacing his fingers.

Alexis put one hand on Storm's shoulder, the other on his. She put her foot in his fingers and he counted down from three. Alexis jumped with his boost and landed rather neatly on Storm's back. "I can't believe it! I'm on a unicorn!"

Storm stopped grazing, looked back at Alexis and nickered, sounding like purring thunder.

"Is that a good sound or a bad sound?" Brian asked.

Alexis giggled. "Would you mind taking me slowly around the yard?"

At first Brian thought she was talking to him, but Storm managed quite alright on her own. It was a very slow walk. At least Alexis wasn't in any danger of falling off. "Looks like you're on a pony ride at a festival."

Storm pounded the ground with one big, cloven hoof.

Brian put up his hands in apology. "I wasn't calling you a pony."

The unicorn neighed and arched her neck, as if she was pulling against a bit.

Alexis patted her neck. "It's okay, girl. I'm not much of a rider."

Storm made that thunder purring sound again.

Alexis stuck her tongue out at Brian.

He chuckled and watched as they made another snail-slow loop around the small yard. Prince lay down by his feet and heaved a heavy sigh. "I hear ya, boy," Brian commiserated; but he was really enjoying himself. Alexis looked like a princess from a fantasy movie crossed with a western. The sun was just starting to rise, sending light through gaps in the fall foliage and bringing warmth. The smell of damp leaves somehow made the moment solid, reminding him that all of this was grounded in reality.

"Okay," Alexis said, taking two large handfuls of mane. "Can we try just a bit faster? But only a bit?"

Storm arched her neck again, and she picked her hooves up higher. The white on her seemed to glow a soft blue, as if someone had changed the filter on the CGI. She stepped into a slow, controlled canter, like the dancing Lipizzaner stallions he'd seen in Austria. Alexis slipped first right and then left. Caught herself and laughed jubilantly.

After one circle, something shifted, as if a watery sheen rippled around Storm, starting at her horn and enveloping her and Alexis. The sheen got thicker. The next moment, woman and unicorn looked like nothing more than a heat mirage.

"Alexis!" he shouted.

"Whoa, girl," she told the unicorn. Storm slowed. The sheen lifted, then dissolved completely when they stopped in front of him.

"You okay? What the heck was that?" His panic receded as fast as the image, but concern was left like an afterimage in its wake.

"I'm great! That was awesome!"

"But what happened?"

"Um, at the end there? I don't know, everything got kind of wavy. I feel fine though."

The smart thing would be to get her off the unicorn and get on the road. "May I join you?"

"Sure. There's plenty of room up here. If that's okay with you, Storm?"

Thunder purring was their answer.

"Could you come over to the railing?" he asked. "Please."

Storm did. He was about to use the porch as a mounting block when he froze. For a moment his mind was in the middle of the bay. Battling for air in turbulent waters. Clenching his teeth and taking a deep breath through his nose, he fought to bring himself back to the present. Breathing out slowly, he tried again. This time, he landed squarely on Storm's back. No waves, no lightning, he was all right. He took another deep breath to be sure.

There might be plenty of room, but the slope of Storm's back either had him sliding off her rear or settling right against Alexis. He accepted the latter as the practical choice. He tried to figure out where to put his hands. On his thighs was fine but wasn't going to work when they started moving.

"Mind if I?" He waved his hands.

"Hold on if we're going to try that again," Alexis agreed.

He wrapped his hands around her waist. She was curvier than her loose clothes let on and fit well against him. Her hair was still a bit damp from her morning shower and smelled mildly of cucumber. Not usually a smell he associated with erotic, but if he didn't get his mind on something else, he was going to find himself in an awkward situation.

"Ready?" she asked him, sounding unaffected by her nicely shaped rump wedged between his thighs.

"Ready."

Storm didn't need to be asked. She picked up a walk that shifted into something faster, but not quite a trot. Brian tried to steady Alexis as much as she was steadying him. After a minute they got used to the rocking rhythm, but he held on, just because he could.

He suspected Storm was using some sort of magic to keep them from sliding off.

Brian had just started to relax when Storm surged into her slow canter. Everything around them got hazy and marred by ripples of light. The world shifted. Time seemed to slow, and the forest and cabin—even the ground and sky—faded to a mirage. Then evaporated away. What was left looked like white ribbons or vines of . . . magic? They threaded through the trees, cabin, earth, and sky, as if they were analogous to the iron skeleton of a skyscraper, but with the soft edges of a natural thing.

In front of him, Alexis gasped.

Brian held her closer.

"What the hell?" she whispered.

Storm slowed. Brian wanted her to keep going so he could get a better grasp of what he was seeing, but he had to check on Alexis first. The light around them shifted, and the world settled back to a reality he was familiar with. Storm stopped, almost tumbling them off. She stood still in the middle of the field, sides heaving. Sweat and lather glistened in the early morning light.

Alexis leaned forward and patted Storm's neck. "Are you okay, girl?"

Brian slid to the ground. "She's breathing like she ran a race, but we're still in front of the cabin."

Alexis looked at the ground. Brian offered her his hands. She nodded, and he helped her down.

"Thanks. Maybe that shift thing she did wore her out." Alexis took Storm's nose into her hands and looked over the unicorn.

Storm butted her playfully, as if to say "Don't worry," and then went over to drink water out of her bowl. She was still breathing hard.

"Shift thing?"

"Have something better to call it?"

Brian shrugged. "No, that makes about as much sense as anything."

"Think we should give her a bath?"

Storm growled. It was clearly distinct from her purr, though it also reminded Brian of thunder.

"I think she'll be just fine." He patted her neck. "Thanks, girl."

"Yes, that was amazing!" Alexis ruffled her mane.

Storm purred and started munching on fallen leaves.

Alexis dug her camera out of her bag. "I'm going to grab a quick photo of Storm, and then let's go meet your famous Guard. Want to be in the pictures with her?"

"I'm good." He leaned against the railing. "Do you think the shift thing was seeing magic?"

"I guess so." Alexis frowned. She lifted the camera to her eye and tried another shot.

"I don't understand how I can take that and use it to help stop Nick," Brian said frustratedly.

"Seriously, what the heck?" Alexis scowled at her camera.

"What's wrong?"

Seven

Alexis
Friday, 7:48 a.m.
Camp Cattail
Western Shore, MD

Alexis lifted the camera to her eye again. Her mind scrambled desperately to make sense of something so clearly wrong with the universe. "The pictures aren't showing up on the screen. I can see her through the viewfinder, but . . ." Alexis pulled out her phone and tried to use its camera instead. Storm wasn't visible on her phone screen, either.

"See?"

Brian looked back and forth between the unicorn and the phone, clearly seeing (or more precisely, not seeing) the same thing she was.

"Here, you try." She handed him her camera, forgetting to ask him to put the neck strap on first.

"That's super weird. If I hadn't just ridden her, I'd be questioning my own vision." He gave the photo he'd taken one last look before handing back the camera.

A headache bloomed in her forehead, as if she was staring at an optical illusion and her brain couldn't process it. "Would you mind getting back on her?"

"Okay."

Storm kind of rolled her eyes at Brian, but let him lead her back to the rail and hop on.

Alexis's frown turned to a scowl as she kept playing with buttons and angles. She dug different lenses out of her bag and tried those. Having her whole view of the world shift when she was on Storm's back was cool, but this . . . *this* just made everything feel unreal.

"I give up," she said at last. "Flash, aperture, shutter speed—nothing made a difference."

"Am I invisible?" Brian asked, sliding off Storm and coming to look.

"No, you just look badly Photoshopped into the air. Great, no way to prove we're not nuts."

Brian laughed. "Just as well. Makes it easier to keep magic a secret."

An answering smile came unbidden to Alexis's face. She took a deep breath and tried to let her frustration go with her next exhale. "I guess that means it's time to go. I'll just fill up Storm's water bowl. She should be fine without us for a few days, right?"

"She might look more or less like a horse, but she's not a pet. She'll be fine."

"Alright. Let's get you to DC so you and this Guard can rescue your family." She shouldered her bag. After that she could get back to her normal, solidly real life. She'd be back here before dinner. Maybe even get some good shots in the golden hour before the sun set. Terra wouldn't keep her from that. There was nothing Alexis could do to help rescue kidnap victims, and Terra would understand how much this photography competition meant for Alexis's future. Understanding the value of a good plan was something they had in common.

Brian carried Prince's supplies and followed her to the parking lot. The camp truck was old, a bit rusty around the edges, and smelled of mulch and sweat. It was, however, transportation. The cabin had a tiny back seat, just big enough for her belongings and Prince's crate. Thankfully, the crate was already there; it looked like it had taken real skill to get it wedged into place. Prince bounded in without having to be told twice, but curled up with a martyred look on his face.

"I'm sorry. That's the rule. Around camp you can ride shotgun, but out on the big roads you need to be in your crate. Safer that way," Alexis told him, closing the wire mesh door.

He didn't look convinced.

Alexis rolled her eyes, fighting guilt.

"He'll be fine," Brian said. "He jumped right in there, no problem. And I'm sure he'll be glad to see Terra."

Prince's ears perked up at the sound of his owner's name.

"Soon," she told him and handed her phone to Brian. "You get to navigate."

He fiddled with it for a moment. "Okay. Out of camp you're going to make a left."

Alexis nodded and put the car in gear. Part of her mind kept returning to reasons she should give the keys to Brian and let him go without her. Sure, Terra had asked her to drive, Brian didn't have his driver's license with him, and Alexis still had a lot of unanswered questions, but this was probably one of those times curiosity could kill a cat. What if getting mixed up in this could somehow put her own family at risk? Luckily, they were on the West Coast at her younger brother's robotics competition, which seemed a safe distance away.

Alexis glanced around for something to distract her brain before it started calculating how long until the zombie apocalypse or some other absurd eventuality.

Brian gave a big stretch, drawing her attention. He was muscular without looking like one of those guys who lived at the gym. At least she was going to have a good story out of this brief detour from her plan, though it would need some serious editing.

Taking a deep breath, she brought her attention back to the road and the moment she was in.

"What do you think that shift thing was?" he asked.

"I don't know—super weird though. I've been seeing a few flashes of stuff like that since yesterday afternoon. Like when I brought you the phone, I could have sworn there were two other people in Terra's living room. But saying it's probably magic doesn't actually explain anything." She'd been trying to work through it, but everything had been moving too fast. Her temples still had a mild throb. She was tempted to dig her thumb into her forehead between her eyes, but it would probably pass soon enough, and she was driving. Being magic wasn't part of her five-year plan either. She'd watched enough movies and read enough books to have zero expectations of it solving her problems. Besides, it sounded like Brian and his Guard would put magic back wherever it came from and get the world back to normal as fast as they could.

"It was like the white light was growing," Brian said thoughtfully. "Almost as if magic is related to salt or ice crystals that are twisted in strands along the bones of the world."

"Huh? Which image was that?"

"The white light, entwined in with everything." Brian sounded as if he thought she was a touch dense.

Alexis tried to remember a white light in particular, but there was nothing nearly that structured. Had they not seen the same things? "For me it was like someone had turned the saturation way down. Kind of like everything was lit by moonlight or we'd stepped inside a black-and-white movie. I can't remember any true white. There were people—Terra and some of the past campers—I recognized, but the rest . . . like ghost images on old film that hadn't been properly processed. There were animals, too, and a monster with lots of teeth. But all of it was moving like a merry-go-round." She took one hand off the wheel to massage her forehead for a moment. "What did you see?"

"I saw . . . Well, the best way I can think to describe it is what would happen if a digital artist had crossed the structures of a beehive, snowflakes, and tree roots, and used the result to build the bones of the world out of white light," he said slowly. "How can we not have seen the same thing?"

Alexis tapped the steering wheel thoughtfully. "Maybe it's like color blindness, but when it comes to magic. Apparently, everyone experiences the world a little bit differently. Some people eat cilantro and taste cucumbers and some people taste soap."

"That's weird. The cilantro thing, not what you're saying. But, what does that tell us? Darn, now I'm hungry for Mexican food."

"We just ate breakfast."

"Mmmm. Breakfast burritos."

Alexis laughed, but she wanted to stay on topic. "You're the guy with the magic heritage. Didn't you grow up learning about that?"

"I'm a study-just-to-get-by-with-decent-grades kind of person. I enjoyed the stories, but never had any interest in actually reading the old texts."

"What about the shadow-light-spell-person thing you mentioned before?" Alexis glanced over just long enough to see him roll his eyes at her.

"Shadow, Shiner, and Spell Caster. Shadows and Shiners are able to channel magic. They're supposed to work together. Shadows see the truth in shadows, and Shiners wield the strands, whatever that means. Anyone can be a Spell Caster, because they build spells. Look, all I know is the classic definitions. They're like the Preamble to the Constitution, you memorize it as a kid without knowing what half the words mean."

She gave him a *quit-playing-the-idiot* look.

He tossed his hands up. "You get what I mean. As kids, we played imaginary games. Shiners would throw lightning like the Star Wars villains, Spell Casters used magic wands like Harry Potter, but I think we were about as accurate as kids playing Cops and Robbers."

Alexis tried not to smile, then turned serious as she worked through what he'd said. "Do you think what you saw are strands?"

"Oh." He seemed to think that over for a few minutes.

Alexis did a quick check of her mirrors to make sure she was paying attention to the road. At least she'd had enough caffeine that she was wide awake. Maybe she could snag a nap this afternoon, after she met this magical guarding council. It wouldn't count as procrastination, because taking a photograph that would set her on the path for her next five years probably shouldn't be done on less than six hours of sleep anyway.

"But," Brian said, "if I'm a Shiner and I can somehow use the strands, why could I only see them when Storm shifted?"

"Maybe it just takes practice. I've been seeing flashes of those weird image things when I'm not on Storm. Just in much shorter bursts. I thought I was just imagining them. Like I'm pretty sure I saw Storm born out of magic and a lightning strike. Maybe you can see the strands also."

"Does that make you a Shadow?"

She shrugged uncomfortably. "It doesn't make sense for me to have magic. I'll leave that to you and your Guard people."

"Why not?"

"It's passed down through family lines, right? Then it would be genetic. I don't know about a single magic ancestor. Maybe magic reacts with everyone differently. Or maybe I just need to get my brain checked."

"You don't need an MRI. There are plenty of people from magical lines that won't know it."

Her cell phone chirped. Alexis let out the breath she was holding, grateful for the distraction.

"You've got a text from someone named Mia," Brian told her.

Since the text was displayed across her phone for him to read anyway, she asked, "What does she say?"

"Out all night, exclamation point. This city is awesome, exclamation point. Why the F aren't you here, question mark and like a dozen explanation points," Brian said. "Wow, she's enthusiastic. Want to reply?"

"Can I tell my best friend about magic?"

"Not a good idea, but you can always ask Terra."

"Then no. She'll assume I'm still sleeping like any sane person on fall break would be. I'll text her back when we get there."

"Why aren't you wherever all these exclamation points are being made?"

"I graduate in December. Mia doesn't graduate until May, so she still has the spring to get her life after college sorted out. Terra offering to let me dog sit was a chance I couldn't pass up."

"Dog sitting will sort out your life after graduation?"

Alexis laughed at the incredulity in his tone. "No, I'm trying to get the right photo for a competition. It's a long story."

"Right. Sorry. Sort of blew that plan out of the water."

Alexis shrugged; her problems seemed petty when compared to his. "I've still got time to get the photo."

"Now that I'm not avoiding answering questions about magic, can you tell me about your photography?"

Alexis hesitated at first, just glossing over it, but Brian kept asking questions and seemed to listen to her answers. Before she quite knew how it happened, she was giving a detailed outline of her five-year plan. Thankfully, the navigation got tricky before she could over-share more, and they were at his Airbnb before she noticed the time had gone by.

Annapolis was a touristy small town with a historic air to it. Alexis and Mia had visited a few times when they worked at camp. It was home to the US Naval Academy, which had students with perfect posture who took their football seriously. Main Street ran right by the water and had a small marina, an old-fashioned market, cutesy shops, and cheerful bars.

Brian's family's Airbnb wasn't far off the beaten track, in one of the high-priced, tightly packed neighborhoods.

The parallel parking gave her trouble, no surprise, but it was more annoying than usual because she kind of wanted to impress Brian. On the fifth reverse, she finally nailed it. Well, there was like half a foot between the passenger door and the sidewalk, but good enough. Any more attempts and she'd reach *flat out pathetic*.

"Trucks are a pain to parallel park. Almost no one drives pickups around here," Brian said.

Alexis let out a breath and grinned at him. "Spatial awareness isn't one of my many talents."

"Well, if you can manage one of your nontalents so well, I look forward to learning more about what you'll admit to being good at."

She laughed at his mock-serious tone. It might not be her plan, but she was having fun.

He led the way up to a remodeled brick house. "This is the one." The door swung forward when he started to punch in the code. "That's not good." He pushed it the rest of the way, revealing a house in shambles. It was like one of those shows where an apartment had been searched. Furniture was turned upside down, the few belongings in the place were strewn around, and disorder was everywhere.

Alexis swallowed hard. "Really not good."

"Yeah. What do you want to bet Nick and his guys were here looking for the Compass?"

"Do you think they're still here?"

"I doubt it. Nick knows I have it now. Or that it's safely time locked." He tried to grin at her, but his joke fell flat.

Alexis knew logically that it was just a few things out of place and none of it belonged to her, but her stomach turned uneasily, and prickles itched up the back of her neck. She put a hand on Brian's arm to steady herself. Her vision shifted.

Everything went gray. Ghostly images of people in dark clothes searched the house. One of them made a call to a tall, light-haired man, who was somehow both in the room and standing beside a hospital bed. They hadn't found what they wanted and were long gone. The world spun; she staggered to keep her balance. Just as suddenly, everything shifted back.

Except Brian had his right arm around her. She indulged for just a moment in leaning against him, but quickly pulled herself together. When she was standing steadily on her own feet, she looked up at him.

"You okay?" he asked.

"Yes. It happened again. They were here, but couldn't find anything. Some guy with light hair, blond maybe? Is in charge," she summarized before she could second guess what her gut was telling her was true.

"I'd say it's a pretty safe guess you're a Shadow." There was a smile there for her, but concern, not joy, marked his eyes.

She pushed away the fact that he was probably right and took a deep breath. "I'm really okay. Should I call the police?"

"Call Terra. This place is rented in my parents' name. I don't know how I'd explain it to the police without admitting they're missing. I'm going to grab my stuff. Wait here."

Alexis was tempted to argue that she should go with him, just on principle. She was perfectly capable of anything he was, but then took a deep breath and nodded. It wasn't like there was anything she could do to help him pack anyway.

Terra picked up on the second ring. "Everything alright?"

"Mostly. We're fine. Just stopped by Brian's family's Airbnb so he could pick up a few things. Looks like Nick's people were here last night. The place has been tossed." *Seriously?* She'd seen way too many crime dramas if she could use a simple word like *tossed* to describe something seriously messed up. "Brian figures we shouldn't call the police, because the Airbnb is in his parents' name."

"This isn't good, but Brian's right. We'll deal with the break-in after we get his family back. Hopefully there is no serious damage. Just make your way here. I got the meeting moved up to ten this morning. Most of the members are going to be able to make it."

"Can do."

"How are you holding up?" Terra asked.

"It's like working the climbing tower—one foot in front of the other and don't look down. I'll process later."

"I'm glad you're the one who found Brian and that unicorn. Not many people can keep their heads like you can."

Alexis was surprisingly touched by the casually given compliment. "Thanks. See you soon."

Brian wasn't back yet, and Alexis didn't want time to think too hard about what she'd gotten herself into, so she read over Mia's earlier text and thought about a reply. Deciding the truth was too unbelievable to be a breach of her promise, she went with: *Glad you're having fun. I was up at the crack of dawn riding a unicorn. Wait until you meet the talk, dark, and handsome man I found.*

Brian was shorter than Mia, but he was definitely taller than Alexis.

Mia texted back: *Hahahahaha. If only! Eric and I are going to Central Park today! Good luck hunting your perfect photo!*

Thanks. Have fun! Get sleep.

Sleep is for the weak!

:P

Alexis smiled. Eric was a better choice for Mia on the trip. Alexis would have dragged them home by 2 a.m. and refused to leave until noon. She valued sleep and quiet too much for that kind of nonsense in an overstimulating city like New York. Sounded like Eric was managing.

Of course, when Alexis stopped to think about it, she probably hadn't had a whole lot more sleep. She was really going to have to find time for a nap.

Since her phone was out, Alexis texted her mom. Nothing like what had happened to Brian's family was likely to happen to hers, but it was better to send a few quick texts than worry. Besides, her mom would appreciate the check-in, despite the time difference. Alexis got the usual busy, happy reply from her mom and put the phone back into her pocket; breathing was just a bit easier.

She let Prince out to stretch his legs and mark some wrought-iron light posts. Prince had just settled back into the truck when Brian returned with a backpack over his shoulder. "I've got enough to get by. What did Terra say?"

"Get to the meeting."

"Alright, let's go."

Alexis handed Brian her phone before concentrating on maneuvering the truck out of the parking spot.

When Brian was done setting her phone's map to take them to Guard HQ, he leaned back in his seat and asked, "How come you saw magic again and I haven't?"

She shrugged. "No idea. It's like it's tapping into my subconscious and throwing a raging frat party. Not my favorite."

"How do you think I could get it to work? I could probably throw a raging party."

Chuckling, she said, "Well, that might work, or it might do the opposite."

Brian sighed. "Did you see anything useful?"

Traffic was light, giving Alexis room to think through what she'd seen. It was like a dream, she could no longer tell what she remembered and what her brain was making up on the spot. It was uncomfortable, but glancing at Brian, she knew she had to help if she could. "I think the blond guy, the one in charge—"

"Nick," Brian supplied.

"I guess. He was at a hospital. I don't think he was actually here," she said thoughtfully, seeing the image again in her mind. "Or maybe he was thinking about the hospital while he was here?"

"Did something happen to my family?"

Startled, Alexis took her eyes off the road to look over at him. "No, nothing like that." She returned her attention to the road. At least, she hoped she was right. "I think it had something to do with him. Maybe he's sick?"

"That's no excuse for kidnapping people. Or putting the world in danger by letting magic loose."

"I don't know that he is. I'm not even sure it was Nick I saw. It could be like at camp, where I was seeing people from the past."

Brian blew out a long breath. "Fine. We're not going to help my family that way. Just as well, I guess, with magic being so dangerous."

"Am I in danger if I'm a Shadow?"

He looked surprised. "Well, no. Merlin was a Shadow. He used magic to stop magic. I just wouldn't let the power go to your head."

"You sound like you're making it up as you go."

"I'm not! All that's true. King Arthur was a Shiner. It's a cool story. They just understood that we've moved past magic, like we've moved past black death and leprosy."

Alexis concentrated on accelerating the pickup truck to merge onto the highway. Once she was comfortable in a lane she said, "We'll be in DC soon enough. What's your major?"

He accepted the change of topic, and they settled into an easy conversation about college. He shared his thoughts and experiences readily, but also asked his fair share of questions and seemed to actually listen to her answers. He was interesting, funny, and smarter than he apparently liked to let on. His athletic streak made sense given his rather nice physique, but she was surprised by how little he seemed to care about winning. In turn, he somehow got her talking about the time when she was eleven and her grandfather had shown her how to use his camera.

Alexis sat up taller. "There was this moment . . . We were having a picnic in the park, perfect golden-hour lighting, and my Uncle Mark said something funny. Everyone was laughing and I got the shot. The composition was total beginner's luck, but it was almost perfect. I was so proud when my grandfather framed the photo and hung it on the dining room wall. It was the first time I thought about being a photographer. My grandmother still says it makes her smile every time I visit."

Brian's whole attention was on her; she was barely able to stop herself from oversharing.

"Sounds like fun," he said into the silence that lasted a little too long.

"It's my passion. It's a long shot to be a professional, but I'm so close. My younger brother is way more practical—his passion is robotics. And my little sister—" Alexis stopped mid sentence. Brian had stiffened and was staring out the passenger side window; she'd cut too close to home. "You'll get your family back."

He pushed his hair out of his face with both hands. "Why can't I see magic? I should be able to use it."

"Why? You want black death or to start losing pieces of skin?"

"That was an analogy. King Arthur and Merlin were fine. Alexander the Great let it out on purpose. If this stuff is so terrible, I want to use it against Nick."

Alexis frowned at the road. *There has to be some way to help with his pain.* "Maybe you could try to get in touch with a different part of your brain. There was this free meditation class offered at school for a few semesters—was supposed to help with stress and studying. Maybe something like that could help you approach it from a different angle."

"Humm . . . I've never been very good at meditation."

"I can walk you through it. I attended classes as often as I could."

"Sitting still and not thinking requires a class?" Brian scoffed.

"It can't hurt."

"Fine." Brian closed his eyes.

Alexis gently talked through a restful meditation she'd particularly loved. She kept an eye on the clock and tried to make it last at least ten minutes. Before she reached the end, though, he'd fallen asleep. Poor guy must have been way more tired than he'd realized.

Alexis smiled. Figuring out magic was important, but he needed rest even more than she did.

Taking several deep breaths, not enough to get sleepy, but enough to center herself a little bit, Alexis tried to let everything but driving go. The roads were mostly highways, and the traffic was heavy, but at least it was moving, so she let herself simply be. Watch the road, check mirrors, be aware of other vehicles, monitor her speed, and mindfully pay attention.

Her thoughts kept trying to drag her back to the events of the last twenty-four hours. This time yesterday, she'd been helping Mia do last-minute packing. It was a clichéd line, but it really was amazing how much could happen in a day. But if that was true, how much of her time was she wasting? The perfect photo wouldn't take itself, and then she'd need to edit it.

She hadn't thought about that photo in her grandparent's dining room in a while. She watched the road more carefully than necessary and swallowed hard. Uncle Mark had been one of those fun, big-hearted people that was everyone's favorite relative. Then one day, when Alexis was a junior in high school, he was gone. There was still an ache in her chest when she thought of him. After the funeral she had been in her grandparents' dining room, and there he was, still laughing in the photo. Her grandma had noticed the picture, pointed it out, and everyone had started telling their favorite Mark stories. Laughing and smiling with their tears. It was in that moment, Alexis knew, not only did she want to be a photographer, she *needed* to be one. To capture and share the emotions, not just the images.

Alexis shook herself, trying to bring her attention back to the present. The sky was clear and blue. Her breathing was even. An eighteen-wheeler with fruit painted on the side of the trailer passed her.

What did Brian think of her? Did he have a girlfriend? He hadn't mentioned one while they were talking, but that didn't mean a lot.

A gray SUV jumped into the gap between the camp truck and the car in front. Alexis slowed as quickly as she could without slamming the brakes. She wasn't sure the truck could handle it, and she didn't want to wake Brian.

She glanced over at him again. If her last twenty-four hours had been crazy, what did that make his? How was he still functioning with his family being held hostage? It was too nuts to fully grasp. Like magic. She just couldn't quite get her head around any of it.

Alexis wanted to groan aloud. She wasn't supposed to be trying to understand magic, or Brian, or even her own feelings. She was supposed to be present in the moment, to be giving her brain a rest. Every time she brought her mind back to the moment she was in, it would hang out for a few minutes, pretending to be perfectly content, and then it would sneak away again as soon as she let her guard down.

Thankfully, the roads got more complicated, and she had to start paying closer attention. Questions like *Why does this roundabout have traffic lights? Doesn't that defeat the purpose of a traffic circle?* replaced questions like *What does it mean to be a Shadow? What will it mean for my life? What makes magic so dangerous? Does Brian like me as much as I'm growing to like him, or is he just a nice guy? Why am I thinking about him like that when his family is in danger? What's wrong with me?* Pondering traffic circles and crosswalk use was far less worrisome.

Magically, if that word could still be used casually, there was a big parallel-parking spot just around the block from the address Brian had put into her phone. The signs saying where and when she could park were confusing, but after close inspection, she decided it was fine.

Brian was still sound asleep, his head at a less than ideal angle, propped against the window and his shoulder.

Prince was watching curiously but seemed in no hurry to go anywhere.

She checked her cellphone. They still had a bit of time before the meeting. She set an alarm for 9:45, double-checked that it was set for a.m. and not p.m., pulled her jacket from the back to use as a pillow, and listened to the sound of her own breath. It flowed slowly in and out.

Alexis's alarm screeched.

"What?!" Brian came awake faster than she did.

Yawning, she switched off the alarm. "Time to head to the magical meeting."

"How . . . what?"

"We got here early. You fell asleep on the way. I needed a nap. We've got fourteen minutes to walk half a block. It's all good."

He yawned and rubbed sleep out of his eye. "Right."

"Your hair is sticking out weird."

He snorted with laughter, pulled down the mirror, and tried to fix it by running his fingers through it. There was something a little distracting about watching him. She was tempted to fix it for him, but clasped her hands together instead.

Focus! Alexis told herself sternly while pulling down her own mirror and doing a quick check. Terra had seen Alexis at her worst, but there would be new people she'd probably have to meet. There was something intimidating about the idea of people who guarded magic. At least her straight, boring hair was behaving itself like usual.

"Ready?" Brian asked, as if it were the two of them against the world.

She grinned at him. "Ready."

Prince was excited to stretch his legs, but he walked well enough at Alexis's side when she asked him to heel.

Warm sunlight brightened the crisp air. The sidewalk was wide and tree lined. The townhouses on this street were friendly looking and made of brick. A few nicely dressed people were walking dogs, and joggers were out getting exercise, but this wasn't a touristy part of town. None of the buildings were allowed to be built too high, which gave the city a comfortably open feel.

"This is it," Brian said, stopping before a house about halfway down the block. Unlike its neighbors, this house was built of uneven gray stone. It had a tower, big windows, and an entryway that could almost be called a porch. The word *castle* came to mind.

"I would have expected a secret organization to try to blend in a little more." Alexis tilted her head, trying to picture the best angle to photograph it.

"It was willed to the Guard, along with a trust that funds our branch of the organization, by a rather eccentric woman who took a fancy to our work. The Guard uses it as a front for collecting interesting artifacts and paying for a few post-grads, who write papers on the historically relevant stuff. Not a terrible cover. Helps that most people don't believe in magic."

"I still have a lot of questions about that."

"Me too."

Prince whined and tugged at his leash, straining towards the porch steps.

"Okay! We're going." She rolled her eyes at Brian.

He grinned.

"Brian!"

Alexis jumped. Turning, she saw two men walking toward them.

The shorter man, radiating anger, waved at them. "What the hell happened?"

Prince moved to Alexis's side and pressed close. She patted his head reassuringly.

When the two men reached them, the taller one smiled. "You must be Alexis. I'm Seth. I'd shake your hand, but I was sent to get pastries for everyone." He indicated the large, flat box he was holding. "Terra speaks highly of you. Thank you for bringing Brian."

"You're welcome," Alexis said, returning his smile and hoping there was something in the box without too much cinnamon. She probably shouldn't turn her nose up at free food, but the over-used spice was all she could smell.

Seth was a neat-looking man in his mid-thirties with easy confidence. He had brown hair, white skin with only a nod at a tan, and wore a dark-blue suit, which made his cartoon dolphin tie stand out.

"And this is Elliot." He indicated the frowning man beside him.

"How the hell did we end up with a magic breach?" Elliot demanded of Brian, not sparing Alexis a glance. He looked like a man in robust health despite his obviously advanced years. His short, snow-white hair contrasted nicely with his deep-brown skin. He wore tan slacks and a light-blue button-up shirt rolled up at the sleeves.

"There were a dozen men with guns," Brian snapped back. "They threatened us. They threatened Em. What the bloody hell were we supposed to do? Besides, we couldn't have known he'd have Alexander's Dagger. None of us expected him to cut it."

Seth glanced around. "Maybe we shouldn't do this out here." They were alone on the street, but clearly out in the open. "Elliot, meet Alexis."

More than willing to help defuse the situation, Alexis offered her hand. "It's nice to meet you."

"Right. Thanks for helping keep the situation contained." Elliot moved the tray of coffee cups he was carrying to his left hand so they could shake.

The world tilted on Alexis and tried to invert. She shifted her weight, fighting to stay upright, though she wasn't sure which direction that was. Brian grabbed her upper arm, steadying her. The world shifted with an audible snap, like cracking knuckles. Color drained from everything around her, and the shadows danced. A dark silhouette of a man stood in front of her, feet wide, blocking their way and holding a dagger that was dripping crimson blood.

Elliot let go of her hand. The world snapped back into place.

Alexis blinked as if she'd stepped out of a cave and into the light.

"You okay?" Brian asked, letting go of her arm and looking her over.

"Um, I think so," she lied. She glanced at the sidewalk. No signs of blood. She turned her attention to Elliot. He looked perfectly normal, but Prince was glued to her side. The soft rumble she could feel rather than hear was his growl. "Probably just need some coffee. Been quite the twenty-four hours." She rubbed the goosebumps on her arms. *What the hell?!*

"You two have been through a lot," Seth said kindly. He waved them towards the castle-like house.

Elliot scowled at her. "Are you showing signs of magic channeling?"

She shrugged. Her five-year plan was no longer the only reason she didn't want to admit to being a Shadow. Something wasn't right here, and Prince was upset; that seemed like evidence enough to watch her words. Or perhaps Prince was just feeding off her fear.

"I don't really get what that means." Brian shot her a confused look, but she continued, "Let's get inside before we're late."

"Terra likes things on time," Seth agreed.

Alexis took the steps up the porch carefully, making sure her balance hadn't been affected.

Brian was watching her with concern, but she shook him off with a *not now* look. He didn't appear convinced, but he let it drop.

The door was big and old-fashioned. The inside was dominated by cherry wood, including the floors, walls, and furniture. The entryway had a little reception desk. Terra was sitting on it, chatting with a woman who had short, curly, brown-and-gray hair, and laugh lines on her golden face.

Prince acted as if he didn't have a leash on and threw himself at Terra. Alexis didn't even try to hold him back. Terra, tall and a bit overweight from years of camp food, stood her ground easily as he jumped on her. Her business-casual floral blouse and gray pants looked nothing like anything Alexis had ever seen her wear.

"Hey, boy! I missed you too," she cooed to her dog. He licked her face and then sat, tail wagging frantically, waiting for her to finish with the humans so he could have her full attention. "Alexis!" Terra exclaimed as if they hadn't seen each other in years, not months.

Alexis hugged her warmly. Thankfully the shadows, muted by the indoor lighting, stayed exactly as they should have.

Terra gave Brian a hug. "I'm so sorry about your family. I don't know how we could have seen this coming, but I feel like I should have."

"I'm just ready to get them back," Brian said when she let go.

"I agree with you on that." The older woman pulled Brian in for a hug too.

"It's good to see you, Camila. Meet Alexis."

Alexis offered a hand to shake, but was given a warm hug instead. The world shifted a little. Flickers of light and shadow from a long, interesting life, but nothing that caught her attention.

"Nice to meet you, Alexis." Camila smiled warmly. "So glad you were there to help Brian. Thank you, gentlemen, for getting supplies. Is that going to be enough coffee?" she asked Elliot and Seth.

Terra cleared her throat, gaining the attention of the room. "There's enough coffee. Everyone has arrived for now. More people are en route, but it'll take a while. Shall we begin?"

"I could take Prince for a walk," Alexis offered.

Terra looked at her with surprise on her face. "You're invited to the meeting."

Alexis shifted uneasily, sensing everyone's attention on her. "I'm not one of the Guard though. And I don't know anything about magic or hostage situations." She was happy to leave those problems to the professionals.

"You're one of us now," Terra said. "Come on."

Alexis wanted to protest further, but not when there were so many people looking at her. Plus, she didn't want Brian to think she didn't want to help. It was probably a dumb reason to let herself get dragged along, but there it was. And she did want to see him back with his family, but no one could expect she'd be any help making that happen. She had skills, but none of them applied here. Seeing a few dancing shadows didn't count. They were decidedly unpredictable, and she was untrained.

They filed into a warm-toned meeting room with a long, cherrywood table. Terra took the seat at the foot of the table, Elliot at the head, and Camila beside him. Seth put the pastries at the center and took a seat between Terra and a pretty woman with hay-blonde hair, who was already sitting in the room with a stack of papers and a laptop. She was introduced to Alexis, but Alexis already had too much on her mind to remember another name. Just the woman's Scottish accent registered.

Alexis took a seat next to Brian on the empty side. Prince curled up happily at his owner's feet, forgetting all about Alexis. She pushed away the twinge of jealousy. After all, he wasn't her dog, but with all that was going on she'd appreciated having him close.

"We all know why we're here," Terra said. "There has been an attack against us. Someone calling himself Nick is in possession of Alexander the Great's Dagger and used it to cut the First Knot. Magic is back in the world. And Nick has taken the Weavers hostage in exchange for Merlin's Compass."

Everyone looked at Elliot, clearly expecting him to say something, but Alexis was distracted by the table. Something weird was happening in the reflections on the highly polished surface. For starters, the colors had faded.

"We, of course, can't let him have it. I'm proud of you, Brian, for coming to us," Elliot said.

"So, what are we going to do?" Brian asked.

Alexis found his hand under the table, trying to reassure him. A static-like spark jumped between them; the reflections on the table sharpened but still weren't decipherable.

"We'll figure it out. I was on the team that got magic back into its stable Knot form in 1979," Elliot said, taking a bear claw from the box.

"That was just a leak, yet how many people died? This is full breach," the blonde woman with the Scottish accent said. "Nothing to this level has happened since our ancestors finished Merlin's quest."

"Eight people died." Elliot gave her a cold stare, cleared his throat, and set down his pastry. "But this strain of magic is considerably less toxic. As long as we contain the breach, that won't happen again."

The Scotswoman turned to Brian. "Was there anything left of the Knot?"

"I wasn't asking about magic! I was talking about my family," Brian said.

Silence. Alexis didn't lift her eyes from the table.

"Of course, we need to rescue them." Camila offered Brian a pastry.

Brian shook his head. Alexis wrinkled her nose at the cinnamon rolls.

"We'll do everything we can, but I'm afraid our first priority is going to have to be making sure we contain the breach," Elliot said. "I know it wasn't your fault, Brian, but this much magic in the world is a serious problem, no matter what strain it is. Once magic is in the world, artifacts such as Merlin's Compass start working, pointing the way to more magic. If another Knot is found and cut . . . Well, let's just say we'd be looking at far more than eight funerals."

Crimson liquid pooled onto the table and spread in all directions. Alexis touched a finger to it, only to find it was all in her head. But she wasn't crazy. The images in front of her clicked in her mind. They weren't going to help Brian's family. They were going to put stopping the spread of magic before all else. Even before the lives of their own. She was seeing something awful happen if the Guard got their hands on the Compass. Not the Guard, specifically. The silhouette with the knife was back.

"It'll take a while to figure out how to trap the magic that's already loose, am I right? Perhaps we should concentrate on more immediate concerns," Seth said. "Let's get the Compass to the vault. It'll be safe there, even if this Nick tries a direct attack. Then we can focus on getting the Weavers back."

"You have a point," the Scotswoman said. "I've been looking through my notes, but I can't find the pertinent information we need for trapping magic in our collection. I can send out requests to the other branches. Maybe someone else has what we'll need. Or maybe someone in the rare-manuscript community in DC."

"Good, but in the meantime, if that man knew about the Guard, he'd know where we are. Brian, let's get the Compass to the vault," Elliot said.

"It's already safe, in the marsh. Time locked," Alexis blurted out. *Crap. Mia is supposed to be the impulsive one.*

Everyone looked at her. Pulling in on herself, she wished she could take the words back. The images lost focus the second Brian let go of her hand, but there was still invisible blood splashed across the table. Brian's family's lives were at stake. She met his green eyes. *No.* She wouldn't take her words back.

Eight

Brian brightened when Seth said, "Then we can focus on getting the Weavers back."

It was a relief that someone was bringing the conversation back to his family. It wasn't a surprise that Seth, wearing a goofy cartoon tie Em had given him for Christmas, was the one to do it. Brian gave him a grateful smile.

Seth tilted his head in an acknowledging nod. Beside him the blonde and Scottish Sadie droned on about resources for trapping magic. *How can she act like a cut knot is the most important thing right now?* As if his family's lives weren't hanging in the balance.

Brian looked to Terra for help. She'd taken them on hiking and kayak trips, swapping endless magical creature stories with Vicky and teaching Em how to safely traverse rock scrambles. But at the moment she was taking notes, not looking up.

Camila's usually warm, smiling face was wrinkled with concern as she followed the conversation.

"Brian, let's get the Compass to the vault," Elliot said. He was the man who had brought Vicky in as his apprentice in orchestrating his intricate treasure hunts, who was always Em's first choice as partner in improv games, and he had known Brian's mom since she was an infant. Yet he cared more about an inanimate object.

Brian fought the tension building in his chest. Seth was right; once the Compass was in the vault, they could concentrate on saving his family. Brian let go of Alexis's hand so he could unclasp his leather cuff.

"It's already safe, in the marsh. Time locked."

Brian turned to Alexis, not quite able to believe he'd heard her right. Her shoulders were hunched, and strands of hair slid forward, hiding part of her face. She looked as if melting through the floor wouldn't get her far enough away. Her gaze met Brian's, and something stubborn crystallized in her expression.

He had no idea what she was doing. *This is the Guard. They are going to fix everything. At least as soon as they get their heads out of their asses about the Compass being the priority.* But, shaking hands with Elliot had discomposed her more than meeting a unicorn or learning the truth about magic. She'd collected herself quickly, but something had happened. *Is there something wrong with the vault?* Whatever it was, her eyes told him it was bad.

Magic was suspect, but Alexis wasn't. He, Terra, and Prince all trusted her. The Compass was nearly as safe with him as it would be in the vault, especially since no one knew where he kept it. Brian would find out what Alexis was thinking; then he could decide what to tell the Council. Fake time locked or in the vault, either way it was safely out of the way, so the Council could focus on the most important thing: getting his family back. Taking a deep breath, he followed the rules of improv and accepted Alexis's created reality, starting with why she looked so uncomfortable.

"It's not your fault. I'm the one who was worried Nick would find us." He turned to the rest of the group. "Nick has enough connections to hire a whole squad of mercenaries. I was worried he'd be able to trace Alexis's cell phone and find us. He has the number. The movies make it look pretty easy. I couldn't risk the Compass falling into his hands before we made contact with you guys." That scenario had crossed his mind earlier, but he'd dismissed it on the basis of tiredness and paranoia. *Thank heavens we know next to nothing about magic.*

Alexis gave him a grateful look that might be read as gratitude for him taking the blame, but he knew it was for backing her up. They needed to have a conversation soon.

Sadie frowned. "Time lock? Where did you learn that?" She was on loan from the Great Britain Guard Office while doing graduate work at George Washington University. Brian's mom had recruited her, since Sadie was the only one in her branch that believed there was anything more to the stories than a useful sales gimmick. She'd pulled her blonde hair back in a bun, making her look a bit older than her twenty-four-years.

"When we were in Kenya, we visited a Guard Post there, or maybe it was the trip to Paris, in the Egyptian section of the Louvre. I can't remember exactly. But Dad and I realized there was a safety measure thing built into the Compass. Of course, it could only be activated after magic was back in the world. Weirdly easy to do, but it seems to have worked well." Brian felt like the tailor in the tale of the Emperor's New Clothes, asking people to believe in something even though it clearly didn't exist.

"I wish you hadn't messed with magic. Are you sure the Compass is safe?" Elliot asked.

Brian folded his hands carefully in his lap. "As sure as I can be of anything."

"Okay," Terra said noncommittally. "Why don't you start at the beginning and tell us what happened? We have time to hear the details now."

From the boating trip through calling Terra, Brian explained what'd happened, only making up the part where he time locked the Compass after Nick's call.

He was good at cherry-picking his truths and being flexible with facts to put people at ease. It had helped him adapt quickly to new places and make friends every time his family moved. But he hated outright lying, even if it was to outsiders about the Guard, and could usually come up with creative ways around it. His stomach turned sour at lying to people he'd known his whole life.

Finishing up his narrative, he drew the group's attention back where it belonged. "How are we going to rescue my family?"

Everyone looked around the table at anyone else.

"We can't give him the Compass," Elliot said, sounding a bit defensive.

Brian took a deep breath. "I'm not saying that, but he threatened to kill my family. So, how do we save them?" he said with painful patience.

"It was a good thing, putting off the exchange time until tomorrow night," Terra said.

Brian caught himself fidgeting with his leather cuff and folded his hands back in his lap. "Thanks. I figured we'd need the time."

"We will. It will give Zach Marsile time to get here. He scored high on our Shadow aptitude test. Hopefully he'll be able to get us a better reading on the situation," Terra said.

"You didn't tell me you were calling him," Elliot said. "That's like fighting fire with a flamethrower."

"Fighting magic without using all of our resources would be like trying to find our way out of a cave without a flashlight," Terra countered.

"Can he even tell if he has the ability?" Seth asked before Elliot could reply.

"He said there is no sign of magic in Florida, which is good," Terra said, taking the redirect and running with it. "We're hoping magic doesn't spread nearly that far. But it means we won't know if he can help until he gets closer," Terra said.

"When's his ETA?" Seth asked.

Terra shrugged. "Just got ahold of him about twenty minutes ago. He said he'd leave as soon as he can, so maybe he'll be here late tonight or tomorrow morning. I should have a better idea in a few hours."

"How's Russel's mapping of the magic spread going?" Sadie asked.

Brian tried not to shift impatiently in his seat. *You're getting bloody sidetracked!* he wanted to yell. He pushed his hair out of his face. *Mom wanted it cut.* He brutally shoved the thought away and took a deep breath.

"Last report, slowly. I don't think it will provide helpful information before tomorrow night," Terra said.

Seth frowned. "Can we send someone to help?"

"It's like taking the barometer, sextant, thermometer, and captain's log out of our maritime exhibit and trying to predict the path of a hurricane. Russel said more people would just get in his way."

Brian rolled his shoulders. They were tight, as if his shirt was too small. His breathing was shallow.

"Besides," Sadie said. "Now that magic exists again, secrecy is going to actually matter. None of the post-grads on staff have given the oath." She gave Alexis a suspicious look.

Alexis reached for his hand again under the table. He took it and squeezed it reassuringly. Sadie was as off topic as the rest; Alexis was one of them. Sadie would see that soon enough—she was usually a nice person. She had worked closely with his family during their time in Britain. Alexis laced her fingers with his, and he was able to take a deep breath. The conversation would turn to his family soon enough.

"Let's schedule another meeting to talk about that and the future of what the Guard will look like going forward after lunch," Terra said.

"I like it," Camila said. She was a middle-aged woman, originally from Costa Rica, and had been in the States on and off since childhood. Her kids were around Em's age and were serious Capture the Flag players. "We've been a Guard in peacetimes, now we have to figure out what a Guard during a time of magic looks like."

"And we need to figure out what we want to say to the other branches," Seth said. "If anything."

"That's not going to be simple," Sadie said.

"Okay, after lunch we'll talk about it," Terra said. "Meanwhile, who else in our branch do I need to get in touch with?"

"Zach's older sisters?" Camila asked.

"Currently in Australia. His parents have been notified but are keeping their distance. We don't need any more kidnappings on our hands."

Seriously? Brian thought. *Figuring out who to call isn't going to fix our problems now.* To help his sanity, he zoned out through the rest of the list. The Guard was like a sprawling extended family, one where most people could no longer quite remember how they were related. Only there were a lot fewer people. It was challenging to keep an active membership when it wasn't a religion and there was so little proof magic existed. Elliot liked to say the reason he ran the place was the great food they always served at the yearly picnic; but no one believed him, because he was the only one left who'd seen magic firsthand.

Maybe it was Brian's skin, not his shirt, that was too tight. Rolling his shoulders, he tried zoning back into the conversation.

"I think we can count the Steele family in the 'no' column," Seth was saying. "I send them a note or give them a call during our annual fundraisers, but never hear back. Shame, we could use a wealthy backer."

"Don't they have two sons? The older one must be getting close to college age," Camila said.

"I'll put them on the list anyway. If you're right about the kids, they might be noticing magic and be more willing to hear us out," Terra said.

Grinding his teeth, Brian glanced at Alexis to see if she was as frustrated as he was, but she had her head tilted at a bit of an angle and seemed to be listening hard. Her eyes were fixed on the highly polished table, or rather, they seemed to be looking *through* it. Her hand held his tightly. Awareness prickled down his spine. She was trying to read the shadows and reflections. He wasn't sure how he knew, but somehow it was perfectly obvious.

"Brian?" Terra said, as if she was repeating herself.

"Sorry. Long few days. What?" he said, glad they were finally back on topic.

"You scored well on the aptitude test."

Not following, but understanding which test they were talking about, he said, "I don't know. No one ever said."

Terra included Alexis in her explanation. "We don't like to give people the results in case they're wrong. Designing a personality test based on descriptions written hundreds of years ago in dead languages isn't exactly a science."

Brian nodded, trying to unclench his jaw. He already knew this, but he understood she was using the chance to explain more to Alexis. *Patience is a virtue.* He almost gagged on the old saying. "But you're going to tell me now?"

"Have you been able to tap into any magic?" Terra countered.

"A little. I'm probably a Shiner, but I haven't been able to do anything useful yet. Well, the time-lock thing was more of a spell-slash-built-in-safety-measure thing. But nothing res-cue-my-family related."

There was an uneasy murmur around the table.

"That's what your aptitude test pointed toward," Terra said; her delight didn't quite ring true.

Brian frowned. "I can't even see magic most of the time."

"Good," Elliot grumbled.

"I think the reasons you can't hold on to it are several fold," Sadie said. "First, there just isn't much magic available for you to tap into. Second, it is supposed to take practice, and third, Shiners are stronger when they work with a Shadow."

A flicker of hope lit in Brian's chest. "Are you going to teach me how to use it?"

"Like hell we will!" Elliot growled.

Brian looked around for help.

Terra spoke into the resonating silence. "We don't know how to teach you."

"Then why are we talking about it?" The frustration in Brian's chest simmered into anger.

"We don't know," Terra repeated calmly. "But the Shadow-Shiner bond is another reason I want Zach up here. I'm hoping he'll be able to *see* a plan for saving your family. And that the two of you will be able to work together to do so."

Elliot's scowl deepened. "Magic isn't the solution to any problem."

Terra gave Elliot a hard stare. "Until you have a better idea, we need Zach."

Brian ignored the tension in the room and tried to remember Zach. The older, red-headed and long-legged Marsile sisters he remembered. It had been a few years since they'd attended the annual picnic, but they'd left a bit of an impression. *Their brother, though?* Vaguely, Brian remembered a tall, auburn-haired kid near his own age, who always took his sketchbook and walked away from the fun. Brian pushed his hair back from his face, and then Terra's words sunk in.

"Wait! Let me get this straight. Unless someone comes up with something better between now and tomorrow night, Zach and I are going to save my family?! What about the rest of you?"

He let go of Alexis's hand. Rage was radiating off his skin like heat off a furnace. Fighting for control, he spoke through gritted teeth: "The Guard is supposed to be there for its own. These guys have guns. This isn't some problem to be fixed by waving a wand. This is a hostage situation. I came to you, not the FBI, because magic and my oath are mixed up in this, and the government isn't equipped to deal with that, but this isn't the Middle Ages. This is real life. If you're going to treat this like a game . . ." He couldn't breathe. His skin was too tight. At some point he'd gotten to his feet.

"Brian," Alexis said softly, touching him on the arm. "You're glowing."

He looked down at his hands. Surprise shifted his thoughts and loosened his chest. Geometric swirls of green light appeared to be painted on his skin. They traced across the back of his hands, accenting his veins, and ran up his arms in hard-edged swirls. They radiated heat across his whole body.

"You *do* have magic!" Terra said, sounding pleased.

Brian glared at her. Glancing around, he noticed she was the only one of the Guard smiling; the rest looked uncomfortable, almost scared. These adults—even at twenty-two he still considered them adults compared to himself—they didn't know what the hell they were doing.

"You're right, of course," Terra added with what he realized was forced cheerfulness. "Magic isn't enough, but from what you said, I think Nick might be a Shiner also. He glowed blue, right? Shadows and Shiners are rare—if Zach is a Shadow, that gives us an advantage on the magical end of things. Meanwhile we'll use more-modern means to see if we can figure out who Nick is and where he's getting his resources from. Things will look better soon."

They were afraid of him. Sinking in on himself, Brian swallowed hard. The magic faded from his skin like a drop of dye diffusing into a lake. Hollow, he sat down.

Alexis laced her fingers with his. Brian glanced at her. She met his eyes, and he didn't see any fear there, only empathy.

If I need a Shadow to help figure out what Nick is up to—

She gently kicked him under the table, as if asking him not to finish the thought. Maybe she didn't want to be partnered with him. But her hand was still in his.

"We should have you take the aptitude test," Seth said to Alexis.

She shrugged. "Cool. Even after seeing Brian with magic like that, I'm still struggling to accept it actually exists. Do you all have powers?"

There was a slightly awkward silence. Brian didn't bother saying anything; his skin was itchy, and the walls seemed to be getting closer. Part of him noticed Alexis had shifted the attention of the room away from him, and he was grateful.

Terra was the first to step into the breach. "According to the literature, magic is strongest in people in their late teens and early twenties. If you're about that age when magic is released, then you are most likely to connect with it. The less magic in the world, the more pronounced this phenomenon. There's barely any magic in the world, comparatively. It's supposed to be like learning a language. There's a certain period, when you're young, when it's easy to learn. After that you can maintain the skill—it's much harder to pick up from scratch as an adult. As of yet"—she looked around the table as if to confirm—"none of us have shown signs of magical ability."

There was a general murmur of agreement.

"Not this time, thank God," Elliot muttered.

"What do you mean?" Alexis asked him.

He shuddered. "I had a touch of Shadow abilities during the magic breach in 1979, but it cleared up as soon as we got that mess sorted. Haven't had any symptoms this time."

"Well," Camila said, "I don't know about the rest of you, but I think we've yammered enough for one meeting. Besides, my stomach says it's lunchtime."

Brian sent her a grateful look. Camila winked.

Terra checked her watch and grimaced. "That work for everyone? We'll take a break now. Those who want to, meet back at one o'clock to discuss the structure and function of the Guard moving forward and our first steps for getting magic back where it belongs. We won't be able to make any major decisions though until we have more members present."

There was another murmur of agreement, and everyone dispersed. Brian let go of Alexis's hand before getting up. It wasn't like they were dating or anything, and he didn't want anyone drawing conclusions. She let go easily. *Good, one less thing to worry about.* That should have made him feel better; it didn't. He pushed away the stray thought before it could trouble him. What he needed was to get out of there.

He tilted his head to indicate she could follow if she wanted. Camila cornered them before they left the conference room, wanting to know their pizza topping preferences, but then they were free.

"I need some air," he said. His skin was still too tight.

Alexis nodded. "Me too."

The town house had a backyard—it was tiny, but it was his favorite part of the headquarters. There was a small, overgrown pond in the corner. Big-leaf bog plants had conquered three sides. In the middle, water lilies and duckweed battled for surface area. There was a soft trickle coming from the mostly clogged fountain. The tiny leaves of the ornamental maple on the pond's bank had turned maroon. The large sycamore tree at the other end was dropping burnt-yellow leaves as big as a dinner plate. Around the uneven brick terrace were faded patio furniture and four of the best rocking chairs Brian had ever met. He led Alexis toward them.

She sat in one. "These are great."

"My favorite part of the whole place." He sank onto the one beside her, feeling as if he'd spent last night downing energy drinks while pulling an all-nighter studying for three midterms the next morning. He was both exhausted and jittery. "Why was I glowing?"

"Magic," Alexis said, but she must have seen the look he gave her, because she added quickly, "You had the same markings as Storm, only green instead of white. It was really cool."

Brian studied her. "The same as Storm? Oh, down her back." He tried to visualize them. She was right, but he wouldn't have connected the two if she hadn't said it. "You weren't worried?"

"That you were upset, yes. That you were going to explode, nope. You were drawing on your own energy, not the energy around you. I can't really explain it. But you're going to have to watch your temper. Probably don't want to start glowing like that in public."

Brian ran a hand through his hair. "I can't remember the last time I was that mad." The reason he'd been so mad came back, and he clenched his jaw. "I can't believe they aren't even trying to save my family."

"They're trying. Terra called Zach. In some ways it's a magical problem, but I get what you mean. It isn't magic that took your family, it's some crazy guy with guns. You sure you don't want to call the FBI?"

"What would I tell them? And Nick said not to. He knows about the Guard—there's no guarantee he doesn't have someone in the FBI who might tip him off. Bloody hell, I can't believe I'm talking like this." Brian fought to sort out his thoughts. *Zach*... "Why don't you want the Council to know you're a Shadow?"

Alexis bit her lip and played with a strand of her hair, almost hiding behind it. "I just don't."

He looked at her, lost for words. That wasn't the only thing they had to discuss. "And what about the time-lock thing?!"

She shifted her gaze to the pond, and her shoulders hunched. "Thanks for covering for me."

"I followed your lead, but what the hell were you doing?"

Alexis's chest rose and fell slowly before she looked him full in the face. "It's the magic. I saw things. I don't understand. But something doesn't feel right. Maybe it's just my imagination or maybe I'm going crazy, but ..." She looked back at the pond and took another deep breath. "It's stronger when we're holding hands."

Brian let out a long breath, trying not to take his frustration out on her. This was all as new to her as it was to him. Newer, since she'd not been raised with the stories of the Guard. He offered her his hand. "What exactly did you see?"

She took it, and this time, maybe it was just his imagination, but a tiny spark of energy crackled between them.

She met his eyes again briefly before looking back at the pond. "There was blood on the conference table and a shadow blocking the way and—" She took a long shuddering breath. "Sorry. Let me try again." Sitting up straighter, she tucked her hair behind her ear.

"I'm not sure exactly what I'm seeing, but it's like a really good photo—sometimes I don't have to know exactly what it's a photo of to understand how it makes me feel. What I'm seeing around here makes me really uncomfortable."

She took another deep breath, then spoke in one tumbling rush. "Don't give them the Compass. If you can't find another way to get your family, you'll need it. I don't think they are going to let you use it, even as bait. I feel like they're going to put stopping magic before your family. They don't know how to save them. They're not trained hostage negotiators or a SWAT team, they're just regular people with day jobs. And there's something else, something big, but I can't see it!" She took another deep breath before plunging back in. "I can usually trust my gut. So, I just went with the time-lock thing without even thinking about it. I don't see how it does any harm. Them thinking you don't have the Compass," she added, sounding defensive. "If everyone thinks it's safely time locked, including Nick, no one has a reason to look for it on you."

He let her breathe for a moment and let himself try to digest what she'd said. "What makes you think you're missing something big?"

Alexis looked around her. "It's like this pond. When I first look at it, I see plants and water, but if I shift my focus and look harder, I can see the reflection of that little tree on the surface. It's so cluttered with floating plants and fall leaves, I didn't notice it at first. And even now, I only know it's the reflection of the tree because I can see the tree. In the magical shadows I can't see what's being reflected, only the reflection, and it's mostly black-and-white, except the red, the red was—well, red."

"Do you think that means something happened to my family?"

"No! I don't think it's something that's already happened."

"But something might?"

She looked at him pleadingly. "I don't know! I don't understand any of this. I'm supposed to be taking photos."

Brian raked his free hand through his hair and forced himself to take a deep breath.

"Actually." She suddenly sounded thoughtful. "Do you think you can do that glowy-green magic thing again? I want to see if it can be photographed. Storm couldn't be, but maybe—"

He groaned. "I have no idea what I did, but now I feel like crap."

Alexis tilted her head to the side as if trying to figure out why.

The backdoor opened, and he let go of her hand. They both turned to see Terra and Prince stepping out of the house. Brian set his shoulders. Maybe away from the rest of the Guard he could get a straight answer out of Terra.

Nine

"I thought I might find you two out here. Mind if I join you?" Terra asked.

Alexis looked to Brian. He was the one who'd chosen this spot to—she assumed—get away from everyone.

"Please," he said.

Terra took one of the empty rockers and turned it to face them. "How are you holding up?"

"How am I supposed to be holding up?" Brian snapped. Alexis watched him draw a deep breath and try again. "Sorry, I'm doing my best."

"I'm the one who's sorry. I really wish we'd been able to stop this from happening," Terra said.

"What I care about is fixing it. I thought that meeting was supposed to help us figure out how to save my family. Instead, you're discussing old group members and talking about raising money."

"I really think Zach will be able to help when he gets here. I can only imagine what you're going through, but we'll figure this out," Terra said, but in that voice Alexis recognized as the one Terra used when a situation became a shit show and she was being extra calm to wade through it. Not a reassuring sign.

Alexis hoped Brian couldn't tell. He was already upset enough. And talking about the shadows couldn't have helped. *My fault.* For a newfound superpower, she would have rather done without it. *Why couldn't I have gotten invisibility or teleporting?* With that thought came a mental picture of her riding Storm, invisible, along a DC street. Hysteric giggles bubbled up in her throat; she fought them back.

A big leaf dropped from the sycamore tree and fell slowly, rocking back and forth as it moved toward the ground. She gave it her full attention. Her breath came back to normal before she turned to Terra.

"This Compass," Alexis said, hoping she was wrong, hoping for a moment that she was crazy after all. "When all's said and done, it's not more important than Brian's family's lives, is it?"

Terra looked over at Prince, who was marking the backyard fence. She frowned. "I wish I could say it's not. But . . ." She sighed. "This is so much bigger than us. With Merlin's Compass Nick could find more Knots and spill their magic with Alexander the Great's Dagger. We don't even know how many Knots are out there. There could be dozens or hundreds. The old stories are full of tales of terrible monsters and horrible powers. The possible damage to the world is catastrophic. Your family is important, but—"

"What if we just use it to lure Nick out? With my family in the open we could surprise him and get them back," Brian said.

Terra frowned. "I don't know. Maybe? That will be a decision for the whole Council, but I don't think it will come to that. With Zach helping, I'm sure you'll find a way to save your family. I know we're against magic being set loose into the world, but now that it is, I can't see the harm in using it against people like Nick. We've got the history and knowledge behind us, and, clearly, you've got plenty of magic to work with."

It wasn't a straight out *no*, but it was close enough. Alexis didn't look at Brian; it wasn't an *I-told-you-so* she wanted to claim.

"How did you time lock the Compass?" Terra asked.

Alexis winced at the question and tried to hide it with a roll of her shoulders.

"Well." Brian shrugged. "Honestly, I'm not sure how to explain it. It was kind of like what happened in the conference room. Do you think the pizza is here yet? I'm starving. Mind if I go look?"

Terra spread her palms in surrender. "Go for it."

"Thanks." Brian walked away without looking back.

Alexis tried not to feel hurt that he hadn't invited her to join him.

Terra cleared her throat. "You're sure you're not sensing any magic?"

"Me?" Alexis asked, trying to sound surprised and hide her guilt. "I think I'm better off without it, honestly." That, at least, was true.

"I'd hoped . . . oh, never mind." Terra cleared her throat. "And how are you holding up?"

Alexis shrugged. "So many questions. I don't even know where to start." Frowning, she looked in the direction Brian had gone.

This was her chance to explain to Terra that there was no need for her to stay in DC. That going back to camp to finish her vacation and get her perfect photo was really the best thing for everyone. Especially if no one but Brian knew she was probably a Shadow. *Probably.* Hysteric giggles started to rise up. Hopefully, her college was outside the reach of magic. Seeing things in reflections and shadows would make it difficult to focus on her schoolwork. Besides, the stuff sounded dangerous—she half-expected to be showing signs of sickness or poisoning already from the way people talked. Graduation was so close; she didn't want to mess it up now.

She reached for the first question that popped into her head. "You didn't really mean not to bring home any unicorns, right?"

Terra laughed. "It was just a joke. Well, mostly. Alexander the Great and the Gordian Knot isn't just a story. That's the same Knot that Nick cut yesterday. It's probably the most documented one we know of. It's also the least toxic. Some magics spawn city-eating monsters. This magic spawns unicorns, which are supposed to be on the less dangerous side of the spectrum. When you joined the ropes-course team, the association came to me."

"Any rainbows with those unicorns?" Alexis asked.

Terra laughed before turning serious. "Nothing about magic is sunshine and rainbows. Don't ever forget that. It's a force of destruction."

Alexis opened her mouth to say *okay*, when she realized something. "But if this stuff is so dangerous, why are you okay with Brian and this Zach using it?"

Terra sighed. "I wish there was a better way. I really do. It scares me how much we don't know."

Alexis's eyes widened in surprise.

"Yes, I'm scared," Terra said in reply to the unasked question. "King Arthur was a Shiner like Brian is. Merlin was a Shadow like we hope Zach is. Yet, despite that, they put humanity first. They chose to lock the last of the known magic in Knots, and their followers locked any that was found afterward. The First Knot is just a crack in the dam holding magic back from destroying the world. One crack we can hopefully mend, but any more than that . . . we'll be drowning in magic so fast we won't stand a chance. If Arthur and Merlin used magic to stop magic, I don't know how else it can be done."

"But the question is kidnapping, not magic. Can't we just call the FBI?"

"Even if Nick isn't a Shiner, he could still be a spell caster. Getting the Weavers, Brian's family, back is a magic problem. The FBI can't handle that. Plus, I don't know what would happen to Alexander the Great's Dagger if Nick ends up in police custody, and we really do need to get that into the right hands."

Alexis massaged her forehead and right temple. "Okay."

Prince came over, tail wagging, clearly hoping *okay* was a cue for him to get a reward.

She patted him on the head. The reflection on the pond shifted. Swirling darkness consumed the maroon leaves. She glanced up at the tree; it looked normal, but that just made the image in the water creepier. Maybe her imagination was having a party with Terra's words, because when she glanced back at the pond it was normal.

But her gut said things were going to get a lot worse before they got better.

"I'm sorry this isn't simple," Terra said.

Alexis's phone chirped, and she checked it, grateful for something normal. "Mia, texting to check in," she explained to Terra.

Central Park is AMAZING! I can't believe you are missing this!!

Alexis wished for a moment that she was there, where she understood the rules of reality. She replied: *Sleep, don't forget.*

I napped in the sun. Eric is taking good care of me! You're free to look after your tall dark and handsome.

Alexis texted back with a smiley face sticking out its tongue, and her mind turned to Brian. Zach would help him. Terra wouldn't be wrong about something like that. But as little as she could figure out from the shadows, there was something not right here. Maybe she'd just stick around until Zach got here. Once Brian was with another Shadow, he wouldn't need her anymore. She'd still have a day or so to find that photo. It wasn't as big of a buffer as she'd like, but that was nothing compared to what Brian was going through.

Mia sent back an emoji of a burger and *Yummmmmm.*

Mind made up, Alexis looked at Terra. "Maybe you can explain more about magic to me over pizza."

"Food makes everything better." Terra stood up and led the way toward the door.

Alexis glanced back at the pond, and goosebumps prickled her skin. *Making everything better might be asking a lot out of a few slices of pizza.* She looked resolutely away from the pond, which seemed to be producing dark fog, which was spilling out into the back yard. Hugging herself and rubbing her upper arms, she stepped into the headquarters; her vision shifted back to normal.

Alexis looked around, disoriented by the indoor light, but the world stayed normal. Breathing easier, she rolled tension out of her neck. A flicker of curiosity nagged at her, but it wasn't strong enough to overcome how uncomfortable she'd been a minute ago.

"You okay?" Terra asked.

Alexis looked away from the shadow cast by a hall table and shook herself. "Peachy."

Terra laughed.

The pizza had arrived. Everyone was digging in and eating around a long table that was more well used than the conference one. Alexis vaguely realized she'd eaten pizza the night before, but it felt like so long ago that she didn't mind. Besides, it was pizza.

Grabbing a slice, Alexis took the open seat between Brian and Elliot. Terra took the spot across, beside Sadie.

"Seriously, though, what was the unicorn like?" Sadie was asking Brian.

Brian shrugged, clearly not wanting to be in the conversation. "I don't know. Like a unicorn. Alexis knew what it was right away, even when I tried to say it was a horse dressed up for a film crew. You explain," he said to Alexis.

Wishing she could have stayed in the background watching everyone, Alexis took one look at Brian and knew that wasn't what he needed. He needed the focus to be anywhere but on him. Taking a deep breath, she forced herself to step into the spotlight with enthusiasm. "She's amazing. She's mostly like a horse, but with a bit of deer, cat, and thunderstorm—and smarter. Her horn feels like glass. I named her Storm."

"You named it?" Elliot said, sounding appalled.

Flinching at his tone, but curious, Alexis turned to him. "Why not? She seemed okay with it."

Elliot opened and closed his mouth before finding words. "It's not alive."

Alexis looked at him blankly.

"Mythical creatures," Sadie said, sounding like she was lecturing a classroom of students, "are just an echo of the world. We say they're 'born' from magic and the elements, but that's not an accurate translation. They do not grow or reproduce and are composed of magic, with only a touch of matter. They are not alive."

"Thank you, Sadie. Well put," Elliot said.

"But she eats and drinks," Alexis said, completely lost. She looked to see if Brian had understood any of that nonsense, but he was intently wolfing down the four slices of pizza left on his plate. And Terra was up answering a phone call.

"An echo of life. The best modern analogy would probably be a robot toy. It might be programmed to pretend to eat and drink, but it's all just for show," Sadie said.

"But she's smart."

"It's not a female," Elliot said.

"You call your car a female," Camila said mildly. "Everyone have something to drink? I think there are a few sodas left in the fridge."

Elliot grumbled something before saying, "Mythical creatures are dangerous. That unicorn isn't a pet—it's got as much sense and as much benevolence as the thunderstorm it came from. You'd do well to stay as far away from it as possible."

"Storm's a sweetheart, and she's a friend, not a pet."

Elliot stood up from the table. "That's bullshit."

"She was totally okay with me riding her."

"You did what?!"

Alexis really wished she'd kept her mouth shut, but this was unfair to Storm. "I asked if I could, and she was cool with it. I wasn't going to miss a chance to ride a real-life unicorn."

"You're lucky it didn't tear you both to shreds," Elliot snapped. "And Brian, your mother was a damn fool for letting that wack job have the First Knot. Any more magic let loose and we can kiss this world goodbye."

Alexis watched, jaw literally hanging down, as Elliot marched out of the room. Part of her realized she should be hurt or angry, but his words were simply too different from her experiences with magic so far. They sounded like nonsense.

"Magic is a bit of a sore spot with him," Camila said mildly. "But your mom, Brian, clearly didn't have another choice. It wouldn't have been such a big deal if Alexander the Great's Dagger hadn't surfaced again."

"Maybe most magic is bad, but Storm is good," Alexis said, then flinched. She was now the center of attention again, and who was she to argue with these people? Clearly, they knew a heck of a lot more than she did.

"Maybe you've seen too many unicorn T-shirts," Sadie scoffed.

Brian cleared his throat and looked up from his empty plate. "The unicorn saved my life when I was getting away from Nick. For whatever else it might be, that part is fact."

"Maybe it was saving the Compass and not you," Sadie said.

"You just said it's not alive, now you're saying it's got motivations?" Alexis asked, trying hard to keep up.

"It's an echo of life. Even a computer has programming."

"Fine, whatever. You're the expert," Alexis said, wishing her headache wasn't getting worse.

"Sorry," Terra said, sitting back down. "That was Russel. He's picking up magical readings just south of Richmond, but not any further. Not great, but not terrible. He's headed west now."

"It's probably still going to expand more," Sadie said.

"I'm hoping you can put together a team to look at growth rate. There should be some way to use rate-of-travel-minus-radioactive-decay equation of some sort and see if we can project how much farther," Terra said to Sadie.

Alexis watched Brian as the others talked about how to use scientific methods with ancient artifacts to monitor magic. He looked like he wasn't comfortable in his own skin. She wouldn't be surprised if he started glowing again. He needed to get out.

"Alexis," Seth said, "since you're new to this magic stuff, would you be interested in seeing the vault? You can see where the Compass will live once we get it out of that time lock. Seeing our relics might help answer some of your questions. Elliot usually gives the tour, but..."

"That would be great," Alexis said, accepting that she wasn't going to get more out of Terra at the moment.

"Brian, would you like to join us?" Seth asked.

"I've seen it a dozen times," Brian said.

"Terra?" Alexis asked, jumping into a thoughtful pause between Terra and Sadie. "Does Prince need a walk? Maybe Brian could take him. Looks like you have a lot on your plate, and since he doesn't want to see the vault..."

Brian sent her a grateful look.

"That would be awesome. You don't mind?" Terra asked.

"Not at all." Brian leaped up from the table almost as fast as Elliot had.

"Which way?" Alexis asked Seth. She hadn't eaten much, but she wasn't really hungry. "Do you want help cleaning up?" she added, looking at Camila.

"It's all good. I'm sure people will be hungry on and off this afternoon. But thank you. Here, Seth, you're going to need my keys."

Seth led the way down a long hallway, the scent of cinnamon following him like cologne. He opened the door to a room set up like an art gallery. There was only one other door out, but Seth seemed in no hurry to lead her toward it. The art was mostly old-fashioned-styled oil paintings with modern composition.

"Alexander the Great and his Shadow." Seth pointed to a Roman soldier standing hands-on-hips with a hooded figure half hidden behind him. "King Arthur and Merlin." The two stood back-to-back, Arthur with Excalibur drawn and Merlin with his staff swirling magic. "And these are famous spell casters throughout history, Euclid, Isaac Newton, and so forth."

I'm going to need new history lessons. Or a refresher of ones she'd already taken; many of the names on the plaques next to the paintings sounded vaguely familiar.

A security camera drew her attention; maybe because it was solid and real, not something she had to fight to understand.

"Is that painting especially valuable?" She pointed to a rather mediocre oil of what was probably Napoleon, though it could have been George Washington—he was riding a white horse.

"No. Good spot. The only one here not of a magical person," Seth said.

"It's also the only one the video camera is pointing at," Alexis said.

Seth looked disappointed. "True. That's because it's the entrance to the vault."

He swung open the painting and punched a code into the second door behind it. There was a ledge and a narrow flight of poorly lit stairs.

Alexis kept a hand on the wobbly banister as Seth led the way, talking over his shoulder.

"Originally this was used for the Underground Railroad and then was turned into one type of secret space after another. Eventually, it was reinforced into a bomb shelter during the Cold War and finally became the home of our branch's vault. There are many Cosantor branches."

"Cosantor?" Alexis interrupted.

"It loosely translates as *the Guard*. It's the name for the organization Merlin founded. Sadly, near the end of the nineteenth century it evolved into a corporation headquartered in England that sells antiques and artifacts, using the lore for cachet. Our branch, which we simply call the Guard, is one of the few that is privately funded and still upholding Merlin's charter. Elliot is a big reason we're still strong."

I bet it's because of his diplomatic approach to people, Alexis thought, but didn't feel the need to say something so sarcastic out loud.

At the bottom of the stairs Seth used two keys to unlock the next door. "We're hoping different kinds of security will help prevent different kinds of thieves. Elliot even considered Shepherdess to be part of the security, but that poor dog is getting senile. Oh, you haven't met her yet, have you? He left her in his quarters when we went for coffee."

He swung the door open, and Alexis blinked in the bright fluo-rescent light. The room looked sterile and was unnervingly white. The only break from the painfully bright walls and ceiling were the stainless-steel tables, shelves, and filing cabinets. The shadows had sharp edges and stayed perfectly normal. Alexis straightened her hunched shoulders.

"Is this a lab?" Alexis asked.

"Basically. This room is climate controlled so we can translate these volumes without damaging them. Besides research, we also do restoration. Rare books and maps are worth a lot of money, and finding treasures like that helps keep us funded beyond the limits of our foundation. But of course, we only sell things with no relevant magic information in them. Camila runs the day-to-day of this world, and Sadie is one of our experts."

"Really interesting," Alexis said, meaning it, but also craving alone time to get her bearings. The room was claustrophobic, despite the bright lights.

"Over here is the really interesting stuff," Seth said, leading the way to a blank wall. He pulled the case off what looked like a ther-mostat and typed in another code. "I want us to upgrade to an iris scanner. Maybe now with Searcha making bold moves, we finally will. Historically, most artifacts stayed with individual family lines, but as we saw yesterday, that's not safe anymore."

There was a click and a section of the wall, nearly a foot thick, swung open. Inside was more comfortable; dark wood tones, inlaid bookshelves, and warm lighting reminded Alexis of a small old-fash-ioned library. There were several pedestals holding glass cases, and the far wall housed a line of cabinets with drawers.

"What's that?" Alexis asked, pointing at the center pedestal. Under the glass was what looked like a pile of seaweed the size of a grapefruit.

"That," Seth said with a dramatic pause, "is the reason we've had such luck building our strength, and why we understand the dangers of magic so well. That is the Fifth Knot. Merlin tied the Knots and passed them onto his most trusted apprentices and Arthur's most trusted knights. Most have been lost. The Weavers, Brian's family, were responsible for the First Knot. All the other Knots have been lost to time.

"The Fifth one was lost until 1979. Louise, who passed away a few years ago, and Elliot rescued that one from a bunch of government scientists. You should have Elliot tell you the story some time. Thank God they recognized what it was and were able to get it out. The Cold War was enough of a mess without adding a magic race to the arms race."

Alexis tried to listen to what Seth was saying. It was interesting, and she doubted she'd be able to get the story out of Elliot, but the hairs on the back of her neck were standing on end. The Fifth Knot warped the air around it, like a heat mirage. She didn't think it was releasing magic, just somehow bending the energy close by. It was both pulling her in and giving her the creeps.

Alexis studied the shadows, but they all stayed resolutely normal. Perhaps if Brian was there and she could hold his hand something would shift, or maybe not. *How could something so benign looking hold such power?*

She glanced around and noticed Seth was watching her carefully. If he figured out she was a Shadow, he'd tell the others. "So, tying the Knot traps the magic?"

He grinned. "Exactly. Hopefully, we can figure out how to retie the First Knot before anyone is hurt."

"Why is magic so dangerous?" she asked, hoping he had a more helpful answer than she'd gotten thus far.

"It's like plutonium, but echoing the destruction of nature and life. Set it loose on the world, and not only are you changing the laws of science, but poisoning us at the same time. Heck, it's even the real reason dinosaurs went extinct."

Alexis wasn't sure she completely understood his metaphors or how they could know about dinosaurs, but she got the point. "Why would anyone want it in the world then?"

"The idiots of Searcha think it's alive. Like a caged animal, pacing its tiny space, trying to get free. They think it's a natural part of the order of life, and it belongs in the world. You should see their website. Bunch of nut jobs."

Alexis glanced at the Fifth Knot. An angry, caged breast was an apt description for its energy. "How do we know it's not alive? Just out of curiosity."

"That's like asking how do we know gravity, thermodynamics, or plutonium aren't alive."

Alexis thought of Storm. And thought of how scientists were finding that animals were a whole lot more intelligent than humans gave them credit for even twenty years ago. *Sounds like Searcha has a point.* Magic lived and breathed in a way gravity didn't. *Might the Guard be missing something? There is so much they don't know.*

Seth didn't seem to notice her doubts. "We figured out how to contain magic, just like we figured out how to use fire or the wheel, but it was too dangerous for people to control, so we got rid of it. Alexander the Great might have been able to handle a little magic, but look what happened to his empire after he died. Eventually magic got so out of hand humanity ended up in the Dark Ages. Locking away magic allowed us to thrive, to build great civilizations, and get the world to such a great state."

She was tempted to point out just a handful of things that needed serious work in the current world, but she understood what he was trying to say. Humans, at least, had come a long way since the Dark Ages. She looked around for something else to talk about.

"What's this?" Alexis nodded to a case that held an animal hide with weird writing and beautiful imagery on it. Most of the leather was taken up by a forest, with magical creatures among the trunks and spider webs lacing through the branches. The image had an underlying structure that echoed the marks on Storm, and Brian, too, when his magic flared up.

"Merlin's charter for the Cosantor. Isn't it amazing?"

"It is." Alexis tried to study it, but the Fifth Knot was like a guy she had a bad crush on; she was too aware of its presence to be comfortable in the same room.

She shifted her attention to the next case; it contained what looked like an abacus.

Seth's phone rang. "Sorry—work. I should take this. Dr. Murphy," Seth said into the phone.

Alexis wandered around the vault to give him privacy. There were old crystals, a bulky rock, something that looked like a protractor, and other weird objects. Some bent the light a bit, others didn't, but none of them had the magnetism of the Fifth Knot. Part of her was nauseous just looking at it, but another part yearned to see if she could untangle it. It was like a puzzle, begging to be solved.

Thankfully, Seth's conversation was short, and she could give her attention back to him.

"Sorry. Bit of an emergency. I'm going to have to go. Mind if I walk you out?" he said.

"No worries. You're a doctor? What do you do?"

"I'm a PhD, not an MD." Seth gave a modest shrug. "I work in a lab that does epigenetics research, and I do a bit of consulting. Mostly that means paperwork."

"A paperwork emergency?"

He smiled. "Paperwork is no laughing matter. If you let it go too long, you can be buried under the weight of it."

Alexis chuckled and followed him out, waiting as he locked each door behind them. "Thanks for the tour."

"You're welcome. Shall I take you back to Terra or would you like to settle into your room?"

Alexis didn't hesitate. "My room sounds great. I've got a photography project I'm working on, and I could really use some time to get some editing in." Something normal was incredibly appealing, not to mention some peace and quiet.

Her room was small but nice. The green wallpaper was cozy, and light came in through the window. The sycamore tree in the backyard took up most of the view and gave her a little space from the bustle of city beyond. There was no desk or chair, but the green-and-brown quilt on the bed was welcoming. Alexis settled onto it with her computer.

As she touched up shots of Prince, her breathing deepened and clarity settled in. Curiosity about Searcha nagged at her until she gave in and saved the photos for later. A few quick keystrokes and she found the website she was looking for. Maybe the pro-magic organization would have better answers than the Guard.

Ten

Brian
Friday, 12:42 p.m.
Washington, DC

Being outside in the crisp autumn air helped ease the feeling of being trapped. Brian walked for a while, letting Prince explore interesting scents and mark light poles. DC was a pretty city to walk around, but his skin was still tight. What he really needed was a swim; that would take the edge off. Too bad he didn't know of any nearby pools.

"Can you jog?" he asked the dog.

Prince glanced at him and wagged his tail. Brian was pretty sure that was his response to everything.

"Well, I guess there's only one way to find out, just don't stop abruptly on me." He tightened the leash and started a slow jog. Prince's ears perked up, and he fell into step at Brian's side.

"How about a little faster?" It was probably silly to talk to a dog, but then again, Terra had always insisted that her dog and Elliot's came from a long line of Shadow Hounds. Maybe the mutt was magic too. Either way, Prince kept pace without hesitation, and Brian let himself embrace the movement.

There were trees, interesting houses, and other people to look at. The sidewalks were wide and comfortable. The streets were in a grid format, alphabetized in one direction and numbered in the perpendicular, so it was easy to find his way. Only the diagonal streets, named after states, were confusing. And if he got lost, well, he could always get an Uber.

He didn't have his phone.

A stitch sliced into this side. *What if Nick calls while I'm out?* Alexis had no way of finding him. Gasping for breath, Brian stopped and leaned against a tree. *What if Nick figures out I'm lying about the time lock and wants the Compass now?* His hands were trembling. His heartbeat was loud in his ears, but he could still hear his thoughts over it. *I might never see my family again. It's my fault. I ran.* Fighting to get air into his lungs, Brian doubled over, drowning above water. The world's edges darkened.

Prince licked his face.

Brian sank to his knees and wrapped his shaking arms around the dog. Holding on as he had to Storm in the bay.

"I'm panicking," he realized in a gasp.

Prince whined and licked him again.

He clung to the dog for a long time, listening to air move through his nose and feeling fur against his cheek. Slowly the pressure eased from his chest.

He sat back on his heels. "I don't panic like that," he told Prince firmly, denying reality.

He got another lick on the face in reply.

Slowly his hands stopped trembling. "I'm okay."

Prince wagged his tail.

"Nick won't call until tomorrow. The Guard will have a solution soon. It will all work out, you'll see." He wasn't sure if he was trying to tell himself or the dog, but it had to be said. The words didn't really help though.

He stood up, glad no one seemed to have taken notice of his . . . well, whatever the hell that was. His cheeks were hot, his family was in danger, and here he was clinging to a dog for support. Fighting off shame, he ran one hand after the other through his hair. There wasn't time for useless emotions, especially anger at himself for not being stronger than he was. Easier said than done, of course, but he had to try.

Looking around, he picked up his bearings from the nearby street signs. They'd come further than he realized. "Thank you, Prince, you're a good dog. We need to get back now. Not that there is any hurry, nothing for us to do until tomorrow." His breathing grew shallow. "This doesn't help anything."

Prince tugged on the leash.

"Right. Jogging." Brian picked up his long-distance-run pace, leaving everything else behind. A rhythm was set by each footfall, resonating with every breath. Warmth and coolness danced across his skin as the sun reached through the branches of a lanky maple tree. His stride lengthened. Aromas of fried food wafting from a restaurant made his mouth water. His shoulders loosened, allowing his arms to relax into the song of the run.

Slowly, he grew aware of his connection with the wider world. How the sidewalk, and the earth below it, connected him to all those who'd walked on it before. To L'Enfant, who designed the roads with the support of George Washington. To the scent of city air, and how he shared it with the people, animals, and plants around him.

When he noticed the fine, white strands glowing faintly, Brian had no idea how long they'd been there. As when he was riding Storm, they were around him, like the tendrils of a watermelon vine spun by a drunk spider, most sections no thicker than a strand of hair.

He slowed his pace to examine them, but they faded.

"What the hell?" he asked Prince.

Prince wagged his tail.

Brian rolled his eyes.

Prince tugged at the leash.

"Aren't you tired yet?" He was a little worried he was going to overheat the dog.

Prince wagged his tail and tugged again.

Brian took another look around. No sign of any glowing strand things. "Fine." He picked up a jog again.

As he settled back into the movement, he spotted the strands again. Maybe he had to be moving to see them? But as he focused on them, they faded, no matter how fast he ran. Finally, he slowed to a light jog, his breathing coming in hard gasps.

As soon as he stopped looking for the magic and got lost in the movement of the run, the strands came back. This time, Brian tried to look at them without really focusing. As if they were an optical illusion where the image jumps out at you if you don't look too hard at it. Slowly, Brian was able to get the strands to stabilize as he came to a stop. They were everywhere, tangled, and seemed to be growing slowly. He could move through them without trouble, but unlike the laser fields in the movies, he couldn't see which direction the light was coming from. Among the strands were little flecks like glitter.

Approximately three feet above a rain puddle was an especially large cluster of glitter, about the size and shape of a marble. Very slowly he extended a finger to it. It flickered and then held. It was warm, like sunlight.

"What do you think?" he asked Prince.

The dog wagged his tail.

"Would you growl at it if it was bad?"

Prince sniffed the glowing-orb-magic-thing as if he could see it too. And then, of course, he wagged his tail.

"You silly dog." Reassured, Brian gently plucked the magic-marble-like-thing out of the air. Like a tiny kiwi it was fuzzy and a bit squishy. "Super weird."

Prince sniffed it again, but kept his distance.

Brian closed his hand around it. It stayed warm in his palm. Maybe there was some way to use it to rescue his family. What a sparkly marble of magic could do, Brian didn't have the faintest idea, but it seemed like the best idea he'd come across all day.

He looked around, but the strands had faded from view again. Frowning, he checked the street signs and then grinned. He was just over a block away from HQ.

Since the strands were invisible again, he double-checked his palm. He could still feel the warm marble of magic, but there was only the merest shimmer where it should be. It was disconcerting.

"I'm going crazy," he told Prince.

Prince was clearly bored by the invisible marble of magic; he sniffed a trash can before claiming it as part of his territory.

Brian rolled his eyes and set a light pace back to HQ. He took the front steps two at a time and found Terra, Elliot, and Elliot's dog, Shepherdess, in the front hall. Brian could tell he was interrupting a serious conversation, but he was too energized to wait—besides, they'd stopped talking when they'd seen him.

"Did I miss anything important here?" Brian asked.

"We're making progress, it's just slow," Terra said. "We moved the one o'clock meeting back a couple of times, it'll be tomorrow morning now." Terra checked off her fingers as she went. "Zach is on the road, but he won't be here before tomorrow. Sadie is out talking to several of her rare-book contacts, trying to track down some volumes. Camila has gone to the grocery store for food. Says she's making empanadas and could use help if you have time when she gets back. Seth had something at his job to deal with, but he should be back tonight. Alexis is in her room working on her photography. And last, but not least, thanks for walking Prince."

Brian shrugged in acceptance of the gratitude. "Look what I found." He opened his palm. The magic was no more than a slight shimmer, but it was still solid in his hand. He rolled it between his thumb and forefinger. "It's sort of a lump of magic."

"I don't see anything," Terra said.

Elliot scowled. "I don't think you should be messing with that stuff."

"It's basically invisible. Do you think there's some way to use it to help my family?" Brian asked.

Terra reached out a finger to touch it.

"I wouldn't do that if I were you," Elliot started to say.

Terra yelped.

Brian almost dropped the magic in surprise. "You okay?"

Terra shook out her hand. "Yes. Just felt like a bad static shock. Surprised me." She looked at Elliot. "What do you know?"

"Not much." Elliot patted Shepherdess on the head. "Saw something like that a long time ago. You're lucky as hell it wasn't bigger. Terra might have been knocked unconscious by that spark. You're playing with fire, kid. I don't know how you could use it to help your family, but I'm well aware of how that toxin could burn down the world."

"If we don't use magic, how are we going to rescue my family?" Brian asked.

"We'll be able to make a better plan when Zach gets here," Terra said, sounding like a broken record.

Elliot started to say something, but Terra continued as if she hadn't noticed, "Elliot and I are working through the logistics for the trip to get the Compass tomorrow. How about I see you at dinner?" Without waiting for a reply, she herded Elliot toward the front office.

Brian scowled after them. They were no help. Even Prince said *hi* to Shepherdess before wandering off in the direction of the kitchen.

Maybe Alexis could see the invisible magic. If she could do the same things Zach could, maybe she'd seen a plan by now. Besides, he wanted to double-check that Nick hadn't called.

Brian and his family often stayed in the guest rooms. There were several clusters in different parts of the house. Students who were grant funded, such as Sadie, were housed in the east wing. Short-term guests were upstairs. Elliot and Shepherdess were the only ones who lived on property year-round, so they had a suite of rooms next to the vault, where they could keep an eye on everything.

On the way up the front stairs, Brian paused to look at a painting. Alexander the Great, riding his famous war steed and unicorn Bucephalus. The creature was supposed to be a man-eater, and Em had used the image to inspire a short story she wrote for school about a terrible monster. Vicky had been horrified, insisting that unicorns were the only benevolent mythical creature. Em had enjoyed the argument and kept prodding Vicky until Mom had banned the subjects of unicorns for the rest of the trip home. *How are the girls going to react when they see a real live one?* He grinned at a mental image of their faces, but it faded quickly. He tried to stop himself from picturing them now. Locked up somewhere, hopefully together. He'd get them back, no matter what he had to do.

Elliot was wrong about Storm being dangerous to them, and he was wrong about magic burning down the world. Terra had said they should use it to their advantage, and that's exactly what he was going to do. He held the marble of magic tighter in his hand and took the rest of the stairs two at a time.

The community living room made Brian flinch. Memories clung to every surface. Hours playing with his sisters while their parents were in Council meetings, evenings listening to Mom read aloud, and big, boisterous improv games with the extended Guard family. He walked briskly through, not wanting to get bogged down; he had to keep moving forward if he was going to make more memories like those.

Alexis would be the room between Terra's and Camila's rooms. Camila would be trying to act as chaperone, somehow forgetting that he and Alexis were both adults, and he was a little too distracted by where his family was to get into any trouble. Rolling his eyes, he walked down to the closed door.

He hesitated a moment. Maybe Alexis wanted to be left alone. Maybe she was regretting bringing him back to Terra's cabin. Shaking himself, he rapped on the door. He didn't like second guessing himself, and whether she liked it or not, she had magic now. She could help him rescue his family.

"Come in," Alexis called.

He opened the door. She was sitting cross legged on the bed spread with several sheets of paper, a notebook, and a laptop around her.

"Hey," she said, smiling. "Good timing, I was about to go looking for you."

Glad he wasn't an unwanted intruder, Brian came into the room smiling. "Look what I found." He opened his palm. He wouldn't have known he was holding anything at all anymore, except he could feel the shape of the magic marble in his hand.

"Oh, wow," she whispered reverently. "What is it?"

"You can see it?"

"Yes."

"What does it look like?"

She looked at him, surprise clear on her face, then back at the magic thoughtfully. "It looks like a clear grape, filled with moving water. The light shining through it is creating beautiful ripple reflections."

"I could see it when I plucked it out of the air," he said. "It was among the strands. I saw them again, but not anymore. I can't even see this now."

Alexis reached a finger toward it.

Brian pulled back. "Be careful, it shocked Terra."

"Badly?"

"No—but weird, since she can't see it. I think they're all around in the air, but I don't think they're shocking people. I don't know what makes this different."

"I'll risk it," Alexis said. Brian held the magic out to her. Tentatively, she touched it, then gently picked it up. "This is amazing. Like liquid sunlight, moldable like clay, and"—she sniffed—"it smells citrusy."

"Really?"

"You can't smell it?"

Brian shook his head.

She tilted her head. "It reminds me of a blood-orange rooibos tea my mom drinks."

"I guess magic really is like cilantro."

She grinned. As she played with the marble, it started to take on a green color that Brian could make out. She flattened it into a disk between her hands. Resting in her palm, it looked solid.

"It wasn't green before," Brian said. "How come I can see it again?"

Alexis shrugged and offered it back to him. He took it, awareness tingling where their hands touched. "It feels solid to me, now, and smooth, no longer fuzzy. A little flexible, but not moldable." He sniffed it, but other than Alexis's shampoo and the scent of old house, he couldn't smell anything.

Alexis made a face and took it back. "Okay, that's weird, because look, even touching it, you can see how my fingers leave prints. It's super soft."

Brian took it back. There were dimples, where her fingers had been, and the grooves of her fingerprints, but other than the flexibility of a Tupperware lid, he couldn't mold it at all. "Maybe it's the same as how we see things differently. Does it still look like liquid sunlight?"

"No. As I played with the magic, it's like a bit of green dye was released and diffused through it. Now it just looks like a piece of translucent green gel, with bits of glitter. Only cooler."

"And to me it looks like . . ." Brian rooted around in his mental vocabulary for something as accurate as possible. "Unpolished jade."

"Hmm." Alexis took it back and picked up a pen. "Let's see what this does." With the back end she prodded the magic. It moved like clay.

"Okay, my turn." In his hands, the magic retained its shape. He could even make a clicking sound with the pen when tapping it, as if it really were a rock. Alexis tried tapping it with the pen while he held it and made a clicking sound. He tried tapping it in her hand, and the pen would shape it. But when he touched it, it was solid as a rock on his side, yet it molded into her hand like clay as he pushed, as if it were a mushy blob with a hard surface.

"Fascinating," he said after they'd experimented for a while. "But I still don't see how it's going to help anyone."

"Magic might not, but I've got some leads. Here, take a seat." She scooted over on the bed to make room for him.

He hesitated a moment, but there really wasn't anywhere else in the room to sit. "What did you find?"

"So . . . the Searcha have a website. Did you know that?"

He shrugged. "I never thought to look."

"It was something Seth said while showing me the vault that made me look for them."

"You're not serious? They're a bunch of nut jobs."

Alexis rolled her eyes. "Maybe, but I believe Storm is alive. That's not my point. My point is: Websites don't build themselves. I took your description of Nick and tried to find someone in Searcha who matches. I don't think I have anything yet. My friend Mia is so much better at social-media-stalking people than I am, but I have taken a few journalism classes." She handed him her laptop and opened a window. On the screen were photos, names, and a few details about each person shown.

Hope flared painfully for a moment in Brian's chest, but it was quickly followed by disappointment. "He's not any of those people. But it was a good idea. Thanks for trying."

"Okay," Alexis said, not sounding the least bit perturbed. "How about these people?"

Brian was halfway down the page when he recognized what the photos had in common. "These people are all from old Guard families, ones who don't come to meetings anymore."

"With all Nick knows, it makes sense to cover our bases and check everyone who is familiar with magic. I only got a few names during the meeting, and most of them weren't the full names. And do you know how many Steeles there are in DC, Maryland, and Virginia combined? A lot, at least according to the internet white pages. Plus, multiple ways to spell it. But it's a place to start. Maybe you can help with that? At the moment I'm looking through the message board on the Searcha website, trying to find anyone who posted a lot or who asked questions that might indicate they know enough to go after your family the way Nick did."

Brian looked at her blankly for a moment. He couldn't believe no one else had thought to use the internet to look for Nick. Or even look for him at all. "What are you going to do, even if you can find him?"

Alexis shrugged. "Knowledge is power. We know the goal is to get your family back. How we get from here to there we don't know, but at least searching for photos of people associated with magic and anti-magic organizations until we find one that you can identify as Nick seems like a decent starting place."

"Thank you." The words were inadequate, but there was no way to express how grateful he was.

Alexis smiled. "Thank me if it works. I'm just glad I thought of it. Though it's more something Terra said, but hasn't had a chance to follow through with. So, help me out with names and info on people who aren't regulars in the Guard anymore."

Brian started to say he was just grateful she was doing something—even if it got nowhere, it meant a lot that she was trying. Then her words sunk in.

"You can't seriously think it's one of our own?"

Alexis played with the magic marble, squeezing and reforming it as if it were a stress ball. "Something isn't right here, Brian. The stuff I'm seeing . . . thankfully, it's taken a break from showing me anything for the last few hours, but still. And Elliot is weirdly defensive about magic being dangerous and Storm not being a living thing. Even magic itself feels alive. Even this." She held up the green magic goo. "Feels alive somehow. It's pulsing with quiet energy."

Brian started to protest, but Alexis put up a hand as if asking him to let her finish.

"It also feels dangerous, don't get me wrong. Well, not this stuff. It feels friendly." She indicated the glob again. "But magic in general. That Knot in the vault makes my hair stand on end. And it didn't take me long on that website to see Searcha doesn't have it right either. The kind of change they're calling for . . . well, from what I've seen in the shadows, it wouldn't be good. They're almost as nuts as Seth said. And they seem to know even less than the Guard about magic, if that's even possible. How Elliot can be so convinced magic isn't alive . . ."

She closed her eyes and rubbed her forehead with her free hand. "I'm getting side tracked. My point is, it's worth covering our bases. The fact is Nick knew your family had the First Knot and the Compass and knew that you'd be in town for the Council meeting. It's worth covering our bases."

"If you think that thing is alive, should you be treating it like that?" Brian said, gesturing to the glob of magic she was winding between her fingers. It was an easier question than the others that came to mind.

Alexis looked down in surprise, as if she'd forgotten about it. "I think it's alive more like the way an apple is alive, not an animal, and weirdly, I don't think it minds. Focus. Steele's first name?"

"Peter, I think. Yeah, that's right, Peter, but I met him once. He's got to be older than my dad."

"But he has two sons. Have you met them?"

"No. But if the oldest is only just college aged, he'd be too young. The guy I met had to be at least in his mid-twenties, probably closer to thirty."

"Fine, but I still want to double check. Next . . ." She went down a list written on one of the pieces of paper.

She was wrong, probably, but she was doing something to help, so he gave her all the information he could remember about old Guard members. And he looked through the rest of the photos she'd found. None of them were of Nick.

"Can I flip through the rest of these tabs?" he asked, seeing there were at least a dozen windows open.

"Sure. You said Nick was close to thirty and blond. What about an accent?"

Brian tried to remember. "He just sounded like he was from the US, though kind of wealthy or well educated or something, but I have no idea where I got that impression."

"Okay, Southern, Texas, New England, Midwest, or something else?"

"I didn't notice one, but that doesn't mean a lot. For a while I stopped hearing if people had a British accent."

Alexis grinned briefly at his last comment. The bits of British accent that colored his speech were endearing. "Okay, we're not going to narrow down the search that way."

"Hey, what are these pictures?" Brian asked, turning the laptop so she could see the tab he'd pulled up.

"Oh, I was just looking through some of my old photos, trying to clear my head after looking at the Searcha website stuff."

"You took these? I know you said you are a photographer, but wow! They're amazing!"

Alexis grinned. "Thanks."

"Like this one, I can almost hear the laughter and the noise." He indicated an image of kids playing a game, with half of them blindfolded and throwing stuffed animals and the other half clearly yelling directions. "Fun in the chaos, but on another level . . . I'd almost say it feels like it's about communication. These two seem to have it figured out, confident and excited, while these two . . . well, that pained expression captures it all."

Alexis looked surprised and then watched him closely for a moment before saying, "It's a team building game we do with the campers sometimes."

"And this." He indicated a rainy-day shot through a window, wondering if he was reading too much into what might be casually taken photos. He continued, more to himself than to her, "Makes me feel at a distance from the world. The rain is beautiful, but somehow it makes me miss not only the sun, but something . . . well, more than that."

There was an intensity, perhaps a vulnerability, in her eyes that made him uncomfortable, not as if he hadn't understood, but as if he'd perhaps understood too well. He didn't want to know her like that. Only his family understood each other on a deeper level; everyone else stayed safely on the surface, where he could walk away from them when it was time to move on. He looked back to the pictures, trying to put a little distance between them.

"And this one." He scrolled up to one near the top that had caught his attention first. "What is that, a hawk? How'd you get a picture of it catching a fish?"

Alexis shifted a little, and the energy between them settled back to a normal level. "It's an osprey. I spent almost a week going to the same spot before breakfast. Just waiting for that shot. Their nest is a little off to this side, on a channel marker. I lucked out—the lighting was perfect."

"That's dedication."

Alexis shrugged. "Mostly just patience. Plus," she added in a conspiratorial whisper, "I had a really challenging group of campers that week, and I needed the break."

Brian laughed.

"Here, switch." Alexis offered him the lump of magic for the laptop. "I want to check on some of these names."

"Wow," Brian said, taking the magic. "Is it just me, or is this heavier than it was before? It has the weight of stone now, not just the look of it."

"Weird. I think you're right—before it was like a feather."

There was a knock on the half-open door. Brian put the lump of magic in his pocket.

Camila pushed the door the rest of the way open at Alexis's invite.

"Crap, I was supposed to help make dinner," Brian realized aloud.

"If you don't mind. Alexis, you are welcome to help or not as you'd like," Camila said.

Alexis stretched. "I could probably use the movement. I'll come back to this after dinner and be able to concentrate better."

"You can bring your empanadas up here to eat if you like. Looks like everyone is running in different directions. I'm not going to be able to herd everyone to the table," Camila said. "But I know how to pick my battles."

Brian glanced back at the mess of papers and Alexis's hunt for Nick. Unlike her, he'd go nuts running down that many dead ends, looking for someone who might not even be found among the Searcha or the Guard.

"Real food will fuel the people on our team," Camila said. "This is how you can make a difference for your family right now."

Brian pushed his hair out of his face and put on a smile. "Then let's make an awesome dinner." Maybe afterward he could work on developing patience and help Alexis hunt through the internet.

The rest of the day passed for Brian like a series of moments suspended in a web of anxiety.

In the warm kitchen, onions stung his eyes as he chopped to the rhythms of '80s Latin pop. A warmth melted in his chest as he watched Alexis, with flour on her forehead, laughing at Camila's stories. The aroma of spices and sautéing vegetables steeped him in memories of exploring a market in Costa Rica with his sisters.

A ringtone silenced the laughter and music. Camila answered her phone. Brian swallowed hard when he realized it was one of her kids calling to check in, not a helpful update on his family. The music returned when she hung up, but it took longer for the laughter to follow.

The marble rolling pin was heavy and cool as he flattened the dough. Cutting it into circles was easy; getting the filling to stay inside was a battle, no matter how many different methods Camila demonstrated. Alexis laughed every time the filling fought her. Brian scowled at first, but soon joined her. His mouth watered as the empanadas baked. Their victories grew until they had enough to feed an army.

Sadie was the first to ask if the food was ready. Brian concentrated on rolling over and pinching yet another crescent of dough so he wouldn't interrupt her progress update. The empanada grew more misshapen as she rambled about the book she wanted, *Travels of Sir Walter*, and how Seth's contacts had saved her from taking a trip to Baltimore for it. Brian's head came up; finally, some good news.

Sadie winced at his look. The book was in Old French, and it would take her a few days to translate it. She scurried out with her dinner.

Camila tossed the empanada Brian had mutilated into the trash, giving him an encouraging pat on the shoulder. His next one came out perfectly, as if that would make anything better. At Camila's encouragement, Alexis told funny stories about camp. In his gut, laughter warred with guilt. How could he have fun while his family was held hostage?

The dishes were piling up. That was something he could fix. A lone soap bubble floated up and away.

Elliot arrived next for dinner; Alexis excused herself with a pile of empanadas. Brian concentrated on placing the dried plates carefully into the cabinet without breaking them; Elliot's review of his journals for useful information was even less helpful than Sadie's progress report.

Brian joined Alexis in her room. Reading through endless message boards and social-media pages, he ate his own food and her leftover dinner without noticing. He chased down dead ends and red herrings until his skin started to glow green. Giving up for the night, he retreated to his room, but sleep was as tricky to grasp as the empanada dough.

His brain oscillated between thoughts of his family and what the hell he was going to do in the morning. Elliot was expecting him to take them to the marsh and retrieve the Compass. That was going to be bloody fun to explain.

Eleven

Alexis
Saturday, 3:05 a.m.
Guard Headquarters
Washington, DC

The light around her was a kaleidoscope of washed-out colors. She saw the passing world as Storm saw it. Tissue-paper-thin layers of past, solid slabs of present, and shifting smoke of futures, all built on a latticework of interwoven strands of light. Little jewels of energy pulsed like fireflies throughout, bringing her the warmth of joy. But anxiety clawed at her hindquarters. She followed one of the wide strands. Or was perhaps pulled along by it. Each of her long strides took her a distance impossible in solid reality.

Alexis found herself on Storm's back. *Dream logic,* her brain registered, gently enough not to wake her or interfere. She took a deeper interest in the surreal scenery gliding by. It felt detached, like the view out the window of a car in an old black-and-white movie. They were outside DC. The views had less marble, less polish. More industrial, more authentic. Commerce and industry connecting with ships and the world beyond. A tall, brick clock tower ticked away the seconds like a heartbeat.

Down a wide, well-used street, Storm slowed to a trot and left the waterfront behind. A big brick castle loomed ahead. Yet it wasn't really a castle. It was too square, too modern; but it was as imposing and powerful as an ancient king's home.

Storm held fast to the thread with her essence, and it pulled them through wide walls, sterile rooms, and bleached halls. Storm shied uneasily. It was too unnatural. Too alien to her. The shadows of pain, suffering, and vibrant splashes of grief and joy were what made Alexis uneasy.

Storm stopped at the doorway of a room, dimly lit on one plane and glowing with blue light on another. No, the room wasn't glowing. The man was. He was also somehow reflected in two places at once.

The first place was an office building somewhere else, where he was arguing with a man in a dark uniform. Storm nudged her way through one wall, where a family was huddled together. There were strong threads connecting them to Brian. His family, Alexis realized. They were scared but unhurt. Storm pulled back into the room with the arguing. Bits of conversation snuck between the gaps in the wavy lenses that separated Alexis from them.

"We didn't sign up for kidnapping," one of the men said. The shallow scar on his square jaw simmered with unforgotten pain. His shadow reflected dark deeds in dark places.

"I've doubled your pay. Deal with it," the man glowing with blue light said. "Besides, it's barely kidnapping. I'll have my Compass tomorrow, and they'll be back where they belong. Family is the best leverage."

"They've seen our faces."

"What are you saying? Kidnapping isn't acceptable, but murder is fine?" He laughed coldly. "No. Not an option. We'll do as I say. They won't go to the cops." He yanked a strand of blue energy, knocking the other man to the chessboard-patterned carpet. "Do you understand?"

Fear and resentment emanated from the scarred man on the black-and-white floor.

The world around Alexis and Storm shifted to the second place the glowing man was. He sat beside a bed, face buried in his hands, barely more than a blue silhouette of grief. On the bed was a boy around twelve. Light haired and too thin, he was solid in both reality and in the magical plane. He slept peacefully, evidently unaware of the turbulent cloud of pain, guilt, and desperation radiating off the glowing form beside him. A band of this swirling energy, like the arm of a hurricane, brushed against Alexis, stinging her skin like sleeting rain. The unicorn beneath her flinched back.

Alexis could feel Storm's yearning to help, but they couldn't get close. The man's pain shielded him from any outstretched hand. He sat alone, feeding his desperation with angry fuel. Carefully, as if walking on sharp stones, Storm shifted around the edges of the room and gently laid her head against the boy's chest. Pain and sickness flickered through Alexis's understanding, but something else, too, something important, and yet too complex for her to grasp.

"What do you want from me?" Alexis asked the unicorn.

Storm lifted her head and aimed her horn at the deep, opaque shadows behind the glowing man. She pawed the ground and snorted, as if calling out an opponent.

One of the shadows took form. A cloaked figure stood grinning, both hands on the glowing man's shoulders. "Mine," he seemed to say. Then he lifted his hands, grabbed the fabric of the world, and tore. Light, darkness, and terror poured in all directions. The stinging energy tangled around Alexis, around the whole city, around the whole of existence. Then it yanked all of them into a void of freezing, burning pain.

Alexis woke screaming.

Gasping for breath, she thrashed around, trying to get her bearings. The room, lit by moonlight, wasn't her own. Wait, that wasn't moonlight; it was Storm's horn. The unicorn was lying beside her bed, her head up and watching with large eyes. The room was in the Guard's headquarters. She was in DC. The world around her was reassuringly solid. Even Storm's nose was soft and real when she nuzzled Alexis and nickered apologetically. There was no gaping hole in the fabric of reality, just a little more magic than there had been two days ago.

Alexis sat up, crossed her legs, and tried to slow her breathing. Goosebumps puckered against her clammy, oversized camp T-shirt.

Her door banged open. Brian charged in, geometric patterns on his skin glowing green. Ready for a fight.

"I'm okay." Alexis quickly put up both hands to slow him down.

"Is she hurting you?" he asked.

"No, no. I had a nightmare. I think." She massaged her forehead.

His glow subsided a little, and he took a deep breath.

Terra and Prince arrived before he could take a second one.

"What's going on?" Terra flipped on the light, clearly not realizing that between Storm's horn and Brian's glow it was unnecessary.

The room was getting a bit crowded. Prince jumped on the bed, gave Alexis a big kiss, and then touched noses with Storm. Alexis wrapped her arms around the dog. Her trembling stilled.

"Alexis is okay," Brian said to them before turning back to Alexis. "How did Storm get in here?"

Alexis shrugged as best she could with her arms full of dog. "She wasn't here when I went to sleep." She shifted her gaze to the rest of the people gathering. "Sorry to wake all of you. I had a nightmare." As if that was a normal excuse for waking up screaming. She'd never had a dream like that before and hoped like hell she never would again.

"What is that?" Camila asked, joining the group.

At first Alexis thought Camila was asking about nightmares, but then Storm stood up with a rumbling whinny, and Alexis realized what she meant. Somehow a laugh tried to break free of her chest. Or maybe it was a sob. She buried her face into Prince's fur before she could do either.

"She's the unicorn," Brian said, as if it weren't as obvious as the horn on the Storm's head.

Storm pawed the floor and shook out her mane, acting as claustrophobic as Alexis felt.

"Let's have this conversation in the main room. It's too crowded in here," Terra said, leading the way out.

Camila followed, but Alexis wasn't in a hurry to move.

"You okay?" Brian asked.

Storm nuzzled him for attention. He gave it to her, but kept his eyes on Alexis.

Deep breath in. Deep breath out. Alexis wanted to mean it when she said *yes*. The room smelled of fresh rain, and for a moment, she was distracted by trying to pinpoint the scent. It was coming from Storm. The realization made her smile. *Of course, a unicorn wouldn't smell like horse.* "I'm okay."

"Well." He offered her a hand and a mischievous grin. "You have to admit, Storm meeting everyone is way better than getting a picture."

Alexis laughed and took his hand. "True." Storm nickered worriedly at her, so she gave the unicorn a big hug. "Come, meet everyone, please."

Storm snorted, but followed Alexis and Brian. Prince stayed close, as if Storm needed the company more than any of his humans.

"Everyone," Brian said when they reached the main room, "meet Storm. Storm, meet Terra and Camila."

Storm sniffed suspiciously from the main doorway. She was beautiful and magical looking, even in the harsh overhead lighting.

Alexis patted her on the neck. "It's okay."

Elliot charged into the room with a sword, Shepherdess and Seth at his heels, but skidded to a stop just over the threshold. "What the hell?!" He pointed his sword at Storm as if issuing a challenge. "It's a monster!"

On the floor was the cloaked shadow again, grinning like a jack-o-lantern.

Storm gave a deep growl. She shot Alexis an apologetic look, reared as high as the ceiling would allow, and came down with a clap of thunder that shook the floor. Light and energy shifted around her. She turned and cantered down the hall, fading as she went, and disappeared altogether through a wall.

Everyone stared.

Silence held for a long moment, broken only when Prince whined after his friend.

"I guess she doesn't like crowds," Brian said.

"I . . . I . . ." Seth tried. "I didn't realize. . ."

Shepherdess growled at the room in general. Alexis had met her earlier and found her to be way less outgoing than Prince.

"Is everyone okay?" Elliot asked.

"Yes," Terra said. "Alexis had a nightmare. That's why she screamed."

"But the unicorn?" Elliot pressed.

"Didn't hurt anyone. Just visiting," Brian said.

"It's okay, Prince," Alexis called to the dog, who was still whining at the wall. "I'm sure she'll be back to see you."

Prince sighed sadly and dropped to the ground, still watching the wall through which the unicorn had left.

"How can Storm be solid," Alexis asked "but also be able to go through walls?"

"More proof it's not alive," Elliot said.

Terra cleared her throat before saying, "That's a good question, Alexis. I'll put it on Sadie's to-research list."

"She went through the wall? I just saw her turn invisible," Camila said.

"Yes. She got all translucent first. Alexis and I are calling it *shifting*."

"Monsters can move between planes of reality, like molecules can go from solid to gas," Elliot said softly, as if he was remembering a long-ago time.

"We're all going to wonder if we dreamed this tomorrow," Camila said.

"At least we'll have that." Brian pointed to the cloven-hoof marks, singed into the wood floor where Storm had stamped them.

Most everyone gathered to take a closer look. Even Shepherdess went over to sniff them suspiciously.

Seth, though, came to Alexis. "What did the unicorn want?"

Alexis wrinkled her nose. He really did wear cologne with traces of cinnamon.

The shadows faded back to normal; Alexis pulled her eyes away from the ground to look at the real people in the room. "I don't know. Maybe she just came to say *hi*. She didn't hurt me. It was just a nightmare. I really am sorry I woke all of you."

"I wouldn't have missed seeing that unicorn for the world," Camila said fervently.

"More than ever, though, it's clear why we can't hand over the Compass," Elliot said, almost apologetically. "The First Knot was supposed to hold one of the smallest and least dangerous of magics. That unicorn might not mean us harm, but it's clearly powerful. Can you imagine if a swamp monster, firebird, or some other kind of terrible beast was let loose on the world?"

There was a murmur of agreement.

"The sooner we get the Compass to the vault the better," Seth said.

Alexis sensed Brian's mood shift and saw his shoulders slouch.

"Tomorrow," Camila said firmly. "It's late, and everyone needs sleep."

Terra stood beside Alexis and Brian as everyone said their good nights, gave the hoof marks one last good inspection, and then headed to bed.

"Do you want to talk about your nightmare?" Terra asked when it was just the three of them and Prince.

Alexis shuddered. "Not really."

Terra gave her a long thoughtful look before nodding. "Okay, then."

"They're not really going to choose the Compass over my family? Are they? They're going to save both," Brian said.

"I'm sorry, Brian. I hope we can. But we're making this up as we go. Most adulting is like that, but usually you can find someone who's better at it than you are and ask for advice. Here, though . . . We've got some dusty old books in dead languages and a modern world with a don't-negotiate-with-terrorists philosophy. You can see that by handing over the Compass we'd be opening up all our Guard families to attacks like this? Then there are the magical consequences . . . We're going to do everything we can to protect the Compass. Your family would understand. And Zach will be able to help when he gets here."

Brian shrugged and didn't look convinced.

"Try to get some sleep," Terra said gently. "It's going to be a long day tomorrow."

"Night," Alexis said.

Terra hugged her, called Prince to heel, and left.

"That was a nightmare?" he asked softly, not looking up from the floorboards.

Alexis tried to sort out what she'd experienced. "Honestly, I don't know. I was dreaming, but with Storm. I could almost swear she was taking me somewhere. A city different from here. I saw your family, I think. They seemed well. Locked in a room somewhere. Together and safe for the moment. The man holding them was all blue?"

"Nick. He's got blue magic, like I have green."

Alexis nodded. "He doesn't want to hurt them. I think he'll give you your family for the Compass without hesitation. The people working for him might be a problem, but at least Nick's calling the shots."

"You keep saying it's a dream, but with everything that's happened . . . Do you think it was some kind of magic?"

It was impossible not to be swayed by the hope in his voice, but she thought carefully through everything that had happened before she nodded. "I think it was. I think Storm was showing me what she could—trying to help."

"What if Elliot is right? Storm is just trying to get the Compass into the hands of someone who will use it?"

Alexis gaped at him before collecting herself. "I guess that's a fair question." Mulling it over, her forehead wrinkled, then smoothed out. "But I'm trusting my gut on this. Storm wants to help us, not magic." Storm also wanted to help Nick, but Alexis decided not to say that out loud.

Brian breathed a sigh. "At least they're okay for now."

Alexis prayed she was right as she studied the hoof marks. It felt like Storm had been sharing the memory of her trip that afternoon. Because she'd been born when Nick had cut the Knot and Brian had gotten his powers, the unicorn was tied to both men. Or at least could follow the strands that bound them? Or maybe it *was* just one terrible nightmare.

Brian took a sharp intake of breath. "But then what made you scream?"

Alexis winced and glanced up at him. "The blue man has his own problems. He's watched over by someone terrible. Someone who wants to tear the very fabric of the world apart and let magic devour all of us. I think. It's a little hard to explain. Scared the crap out of me though."

That was putting it mildly, but there was no way to describe the terrible foreboding that had scared her awake. It was like her fear of heights: Once she had both feet back on the ground, she couldn't quite remember how horrible it had been. At least until she was in the air again.

"So, the Guard is *right*? We shouldn't hand over the Compass?" Brian asked.

"I don't know!" Frustration seeped into her voice. "But something isn't right here either. The man who tore the fabric of the world. I think he's here, or his influence is . . . I don't know, exactly. I saw the same shadow here. I think that's the reason Storm fled. Did you notice she only got upset when Elliot came charging in? I don't think it was just because he was waving a sword. She showed me what would happen if magic got back into the world. I don't think she wants that, yet she clearly didn't like someone who was in that room. Handing over the Compass to the Guard doesn't feel right. I'm sorry! I wish I could see more. I wish I knew what to do." Her stomach clenched.

The frantic fear in Brian's gaze softened. "You're doing far better with this magic stuff than I am. I didn't mean to ask so much of you. You're doing an awesome job. Thank you, for everything." He shifted uneasily. "Um . . . weird question, but can I hold on to your phone tonight? Just in case Nick calls. I know he said he wouldn't call until tomorrow, but I think I'll sleep better if I know I'll hear a possible call."

Alexis hugged herself; her phone was such a personal thing, and Mia could text or her mom could call.

"I won't poke around on it or look at your photos or anything," Brian said quickly, as if reading her thoughts, appalled that such a thing was even a consideration.

Alexis did a quick inventory of what was on her phone, but other than her conversation with Mia about the tall, dark, and handsome guy she'd met, there wasn't anything more private than what Brian already knew about her. And there wasn't anything interesting to be worth digging through. Besides, she trusted him. "Okay. I'll get it from my room."

"Honestly, Alexis, thank you," Brian said.

She nodded, but something in his shadow had caught her attention, and she studied it as she led the way back down the hall. She tried to figure out exactly what it meant. Staring at it didn't help bring the smudge of a shadow into focus. After he pocketed her phone, she held her hands out to him. He took them in his. Warmth sparked between them; the edge of his shadow sharpened into an image she could start to understand. Possible futures, she realized. The hooded shadow still stabbed him in the back if he stayed. Nothing new there, but another path was taking form. A dark and winding road ahead if he tried to save his family without the Guard. On his own, there'd be no light to guide him.

Hard to know how accurate her vision was, but she realized with sharp clarity that, once again, she wasn't going to let him go alone.

Brian stepped closer and touched her chin with his free hand. She lifted her eyes to his. For all that she was seeing about possible futures, she was still caught off guard when she realized what he was doing. He was going to kiss her. He held her gaze for a moment, giving her time to catch up.

"May I?" he asked softly.

In answer, she leaned in and lifted her face fully to him. His lips were light on hers, but the power of the kiss melted through her whole body. She pressed close.

He deepened the kiss before pulling back a bit, and their gazes locked.

"You're glowing again," she breathed, tracing the winding line on his jaw with her index finger.

He grinned. "Would it be a cliché to say we're magic together?"

Alexis giggled. "Not if it's actually true."

"Hard to argue with facts." He sighed, pulling her close for a hug. "Or with time. It is crazy late. I should go."

She buried her face against his shoulder. Enjoying the warmth and strength of him for as long as she could. Reluctantly, Alexis accepted that it was the middle of the night. She wasn't tired at the moment, but he needed sleep. She let go. "Good night."

"Good night."

Alexis stepped slowly back to her room and closed the door. Her mind was spinning—and not just about the kiss.

Twelve

Even though he'd set the alarm for 5:30 a.m., Brian was awake before it went off. Breakfast wouldn't be ready until seven. He figured that would give him plenty of time to get out of the house before anyone saw him.

The Guard's loyalty was to protecting the world from magic. Brian's loyalty was to protecting his family. If he couldn't trust the Guard to save them, and Nick really didn't want to hurt them, then there really was only one answer. He'd have to go himself and hope he could trick Nick into giving him back his family without giving up the Compass. How Brian was going to pull it off, he had no idea. Well, that wasn't completely true. He had some vague notion of an Uber ride and checking out an antique store for an old compass, but he'd figure it out as he went.

It would work out. Everything always did in the end. But if it didn't, he wasn't going to drag Alexis down with him. While he yanked on clothes, he reviewed his conversation with her from the night before. When she had time to think back, she'd realize he'd been saying goodbye.

He'd thought about waiting for Zach to show, but it was hard to imagine he'd be able to see anything more than Alexis. And waiting would risk the Guard learning his plan. Or Alexis.

Her fear about what would happen if magic was released worried him. That scream would haunt his own nightmares, but magic had been released before without ending the world. If worse came to worst and he did have to hand over the Compass, well . . . the Compass couldn't be the only way to find Knots. The Searcha would find another way now that magic was back in the world. It wasn't like he was going to hand it over unless there was absolutely no other way. And there would be another way. There had to be. Sacrificing his family's lives for an old relic might be something a storybook hero would do, but despite the existence of magic and unicorns, this was still the real world. And he wasn't some damn fairytale hero.

He crept down the stairs, careful to avoid the creaky steps he'd learned as a kid playing hide-and-go-seek. He'd be in Baltimore before breakfast. Hopefully, Alexis would cover for him and send the Guard on a goose chase into the marshes.

"About time," Alexis said.

He jumped.

She was sitting, cool as could be, on the front steps. Her green scarf was pulled up around her ears, several paper-towel-wrapped parcels in her lap, and her backpack over her shoulders. "It's a bit chilly out here."

He pulled the door closed carefully. "What are you doing?"

"Waiting for you, of course. Come on. Let's walk. I need to warm up."

He fell into step with her. It's not like she would be able to talk him out of his plan or join him in this craziness. He could spare a few minutes to walk with her.

She handed him one of the wrapped parcels. "Bagel and cream cheese?"

He wanted to protest, but his stomach growled, and the bagel was still warm. He took a bite. No arguing with an everything bagel and a thick layer of cream cheese. "How long were you waiting?"

"Five minutes, maybe. Probably less. Can I get my phone back?"

Brian frowned but handed it over. "How'd you know I was leaving?"

She shrugged. "Figured it out after Storm left. There are threads between all of us, I think, even if I can't see them, but ours is strong enough that I could use it to wake me. Or maybe you woke me? I'm not sure."

"I certainly didn't mean to."

Alexis didn't seem bothered by that.

"Where are we going?" he asked.

"The park. I have an idea about how you can use magic."

"But I need to head to Baltimore before the Guard notices I'm missing."

"We've got time. Plus,"—she pointed to his shadow, obvious against the glow of a street light—"it shows us going to the park as a good thing and leaving at just this moment as a bad thing. Don't ask me why. But if we're going to make big decisions based on some dancing shadows and weird tricks of light, then we might as well make small decisions based on them," she said, sounding annoyingly cheerful.

He opened his mouth to explain why he wasn't taking her with him but took another bite of bagel instead. They were going to the park; there would be time to argue later. At least she wasn't going to try and talk him into staying. He finished the bagel with gusto, crumpled up the wrapper, and made a perfect basket into a passing trash can.

Somehow, everything felt more possible. He took a deep lungful of fall air, stretched his arms over his head, and ignored the self-satisfied grin she shot him.

The park was empty at such an early hour. The big green space was one he and his sisters had played in over the years.

Alexis pulled a battered Frisbee, clearly from the Guard's game closet, out of her bag.

"We're not seriously playing Frisbee at this hour instead of going to rescue my family?" he asked.

"The exchange isn't until tonight. In the meanwhile, we don't know where they are. Plus, like I said, I have an idea."

He shrugged and tossed it back and forth with her. She was decent at catching it, but wasn't very good at throwing it to him. He used it as an excuse to make a few dives, rolls, and leaps, hindered only by the need to protect his bandaged forearm. Terra had said he was healing nicely when she'd inspected the cut, but he was glad he was right-handed, because it would still take a while to fully heal. A reminder of how he'd been injured threatened to ruin the morning, but he ruthlessly pushed it away. In fact, he gave up thinking about everything else and just enjoyed making Alexis laugh at his antics and cheer his more-spectacular catches.

Afterwards they lounged on a picnic table, hand in hand, watching color and light brighten the southern sky. It was one of those perfect moments.

He was so enjoying himself that he didn't notice at first that the world had faded. He could see the structure of it, the lines connecting everything. He blinked, but they stayed.

"I can see them again," he whispered.

"I think exercise helps clear your mind," she said. "Can you touch any of the strands?"

He fished for a random one, but like beams of light they were impossible to catch. He looked around for a solid one. The Frisbee. He remembered all the fun times he'd had with it and the other Guard kids over the years and today with Alexis. The light got stronger, or more solid—definitely thicker. About the width of a pencil. He reached out and traced the line with his fingers. The strand slid easily over the pad of his index finger like a silk ribbon and bounced like a rubber band.

"Can you see it?" he asked.

"No. I can kind of feel it, but only in a vague way. I think Storm can see both. I saw them a bit in my dream, when I was seeing the world how she saw it. But once I was on her back, all I could see were the shadows."

Brian tilted his head, thinking. "Okay, what about this bit of magic glitter here?"

Alexis shook her head.

He plucked it from the air.

"Hey, cool. Now I can see it."

He tossed her the lump of magic, about the size of a pencil eraser, and returned his attention to the strand holding the Frisbee. It grew brighter as he concentrated. Carefully, he wrapped the strand around his hand. He tugged. The Frisbee jerked.

"Now, I saw that!" Alexis said.

He yanked harder. The Frisbee flew right at him. Alexis ducked out of the way, but he caught it neatly before it hit him in the face. Joy bubbled in his chest. He was doing magic!

Alexis laughed. "That's awesome!"

"Let's see what else I can do!"

He tossed the Frisbee. The strand stretched like an elastic string, and the Frisbee swung back around. He caught it and whooped with enthusiasm. He tossed it again, letting it hit the ground. It settled there for a moment before he brought it back.

"All hail Thor," a dry voice behind them said.

Brian and Alexis swung to see who it was. They let go of each other's hand, but the strands didn't fade away this time.

"Zach!" he exclaimed. The tall, auburn-haired guy was leaning casually against a tree, arms crossed in front of him. The strands seemed to touch him and back off and reach again, the way they did with Alexis. He was the Shadow Terra was counting on. Brian got up and offered him a handshake. "A Frisbee isn't much of a hammer."

"And no one would claim that you're blond, but that's still the coolest and least weird real-life magic I've seen so far."

"Thanks! Just learned it this morning. This is Alexis."

"Nice to meet you, Zach," she said, but seemed to brace herself before accepting his outstretched hand. She took a moment to search his shadow and then let go quickly.

Zach's eyes opened wide. "You're a Shadow too?"

Her gaze was cool and calm, but Brian could sense her tension.

"Yes."

"Terra didn't say anything about there being another Shadow."

"I think she might suspect, but I haven't admitted it to anyone but you and Brian."

"Am I missing something? I'd have come, anyway, to help. Brian's family is great, and it's awful what's happened. The Guard looks after its own."

"Not quite. Stopping the spread of magic comes first in their book. Saving my family comes second," Brian said, not bothering to keep the bitterness out of his voice. He shook it off. "Thanks for making the trip though. That's a heck of a drive!"

Zach studied him with a rather blank look.

"Have you spoken with the Guard yet? Since you got your magic, I mean," Alexis said.

"I . . . No." Zach shrugged. "I just got here. Thought I'd spend a few minutes in the park before going to HQ. Try to clear my head and all. Recognized Brian."

"How would you like a bagel?" Alexis asked.

"You have more?" Brian asked.

Zach shrugged again and joined them at the picnic table. He didn't seem quite himself, but Brian had never really known him that well.

Alexis pulled more cream cheese bagels out of her bag. "Last toasted one for you." She handed it to Zach. She handed an untoasted one to Brian with an apologetic smile. "Only had so much time this morning."

"More prepared than I was. Thanks," Brian said. He noticed Zach watching them. Their eyes met and Zach dropped his attention to the bagel, looking embarrassed.

"Thank you," Zach said.

"You're welcome," Alexis said to both of them, before turning her focus to Zach. "I hope I'm wrong. Maybe you could figure out what's giving me the bad feeling and let me know? Elliot and the others might be more on guard with you, though, since they know you're a Shadow."

"What's wrong with Elliot?"

"I think . . . Well, I'd love to be wrong. I'm still new to this whole magic thing. When I'm around him I keep seeing an image of a cloaked figure stabbing Brian in the back. Metaphorically. I think."

"Could that be because you two are running away from the Guard? Maybe you just see him trying to stop you," Zach said coldly.

"How can you tell?" Brian asked.

Zach rolled his eyes at Brian. "Your shadow."

"I don't think our leaving explains Elliot's shadow. I saw it long before we even thought about going on our own," Alexis said.

"Self-fulfilling prophecies only come true because people try to stop them from happening," Zach said.

Alexis shrugged. "True. At least according to my limited knowledge of mythology. But I don't know how real magic works. We won't know until we've experimented. But now doesn't seem like the time to try out different things."

"Isn't that what you were just doing?" Zach gestured at the Frisbee.

"With Brian's magic, cause and effect happen faster. You don't have to believe me about Elliot. Go talk to him yourself."

"So, you want me to play double agent in the Guard. Report back to you about what they're doing?"

"No!" Brian said, appalled.

Alexis shot him a look that made him think that was exactly what she would have liked, but she didn't say anything.

"We're not going against the Guard. I'm just going to get my family back. We think that Nick, the guy who has them, doesn't want to hurt them. I think I can use that to my advantage. A hostage exchange only works if the bad guy is really willing to kill the hostages, right? But I can't do it without taking the Compass with me. I need to be able to bargain, but I won't give it to him." Brian hoped he sounded more confident than he felt.

"You're willing to gamble your family's life on that?" Zach asked softly.

Tension knotted Brian's shoulders. "The Guard is ready to give up on them. Terra thinks *you're* the only hope that my family has. Can you see a way out of this?"

"I haven't even been to HQ. I've only gotten into magic territory a couple of hours ago, and I'm so sleep deprived I don't know if I'm hallucinating," Zach snapped.

"We have until tonight. If by then, you have a better plan, by all means let us know. But this is the best we could come up with."

"If this doesn't work, if you hand over the Compass, you'll be kicked out," Zach warned Brian. "And with all the magic Searcha will release, it'll be a bad time to be out in the cold."

"I know. That's one of the reasons I'm going alone."

Zach's eyes narrowed. "I feel like there is more to see, just out of sight."

"I've found physical contact, like shaking hands, often shows me more," Alexis said.

"Worth a try. If a handshake is better, how about a forearm shake?" Zach said.

The idea of Zach trying to read him made Brian uncomfortable, but he needed Zach's help. Even if that meant letting him see far more of himself than he wanted to share. He was only just starting to glimpse how much Shadows could see.

He glanced at Alexis. She gave a slight nod. *Crap.* He really didn't have much of a choice, did he? *Family first.* And in a way, Zach was family too. He reached out and took Zach's wrist. Magic crackled green around his lower arm and hand, but it didn't touch Zach anywhere, unlike how it did with Alexis.

Zach got a vague, unfocused look that Brian was beginning to associate with a Shadow using magic.

After a long, uncomfortable minute of Brian trying desperately not to fidget, Zach offered his free hand to Alexis. She took a deep breath and grasped Zach's wrist also.

Zach's forehead wrinkled in concentration.

Brian used his free hand to twiddle with a strand of energy connecting him to the picnic table, then another one to a leaf. They weren't as strong as the Frisbee, but if he thought about how they were connected, what they had in common, the strings solidified. While he explored, he stumbled across the one connecting him to Zach. They were connected through their families, through events, and through the Guard. Despite the fact that they'd rarely spoken, it was still a stronger connection than he had with most people outside his family. Curious now, he looked for the strands connecting him to his family. *Does it only work on people close by?*

Once he started looking, the strands were surprisingly easy to find. The ones connecting him to his family were strong, thick, and indestructible. He tugged gently. The strand stretched, but had almost no resistance, as if it could stretch forever. They were too tangled with other strands to lead him to his family. But he could sense them. They were alive and as well as they could be under the circumstances. But they were in danger. The unease tore at him.

He fought to move his attention to another strand—getting upset now wasn't going to help anything. *If Zach could come up with a better way . . .* He dragged his focus back to the strands.

The one connecting him to Alexis was so obvious he didn't know how he could have missed it. Shared experiences, shared goals, and a hum of awareness pulsed through the strand, built upon the foundation of things that connected all humans. He strummed the strand curiously. She glanced over at him, warmth in her eyes.

Zach let go of their hands. "Okay. I don't have any more answers than Alexis does. Less, probably. I'll talk to Elliot and see if I agree with Alexis's reading of him. I know him better, so maybe it'll be easier to read him. If I can find another way, I'll call. Or if I think she's completely wrong."

"Thank you," Alexis said. "What's your number?"

Zach gave her his and entered hers into his phone.

"Okay," Alexis said. "I'm going to stretch my legs. Maybe consider finishing those bagels?"

Brian watched her go, enjoying the way her soft brown hair caught the morning light.

"Take her with you," Zach said before taking a bite of his bagel.

Brian hesitated, but Zach seemed like the best person to ask. "Do you trust her?"

Surprised flashed across Zach's face before he seemed to consider the question. "To have your back, yes. To be a model Guard member . . . not so much." Zach grinned briefly. "But with this. Yes. I honestly can't make much sense of what all I'm seeing, but there are moments of clarity, and this is one of them. Take her with you."

"I can't. I can't put her in that kind of danger."

"She knows the risks as well as anyone can. She's choosing to go. Respect her ability to know her own mind."

"She's not my Shadow, but if I let her come with me—"

Zach put up his hands. "That's your own problem. I don't let people in. I'd be a hypocrite to tell you to."

Brian laughed, understanding Zach better than he had before.

Zach finished his bagel, humor lurking in his eyes.

"Thank you," Brian said again. "I really mean it. For coming all this way. For everything."

Zach shrugged. "I've haven't done much yet."

"Yes, you have. See you on the other side?"

Zach nodded and they did a handshake bro hug. "See you on the other side."

"Our Uber is here," Alexis said, joining them. She gave Zach a hug too.

"So, you're coming?" Brian didn't bother asking how long ago she'd requested a ride. He would ask how much it cost later and get her money. There was the emergency cash he'd gotten from the Airbnb, but he needed that for expenses until he got his family back. He dismissed the thought that he might not live long enough to pay Alexis back.

"Yes," she said.

There were a million reasons to argue with her. He could use the help, desperately wanted her company, and yet he had nothing but danger to offer her. He certainly couldn't offer her any kind of romantic relationship at the moment. Though maybe it was egotistical of him to worry about that. She'd not in any way referred to his kiss last night. Maybe she understood that it had been an impulsive goodbye kiss, not anything more. Or maybe her magic showed her that he wasn't a long-term relationship person. Trying to work it all out was enough to make his head spin.

There was the danger of Nick, his guns for hire, and magic, but Zach was right. She understood those risks. He'd been upfront about that. He offered her his hand. "Let's go, then."

She laced her fingers with his and smiled. "On to Baltimore."

Thirteen

Alexis was swept up in a rush of enthusiasm as she stepped into the Uber. Normally, when she was offered a big responsibility, she'd consider it carefully and decide somebody else would do the job better. However, when plans A through F had been scrapped, it was a different story. It didn't matter if it happened when a camper had an allergic reaction at the far edge of camp or when a hung-over counselor couldn't do her job, anything that required Alexis to unexpectedly step up changed everything. Adrenaline and excitement overcame her reservations as she listened to Terra explain Plan G or W, and Alexis felt as if she could do anything, because there was no other option.

She'd been humming with the same energy boost since she'd realized that Brian was going to Baltimore without the Guard. Alexis was far too sensible to think his goodbye kiss was in any way responsible for her mood. Sure, there was a warm, tender melting in her chest whenever she thought about it, but she doubted it had meant nearly so much to him. Maybe, when the adrenaline wore off . . . Well, maybe they could build a relationship together. But there were too many variables, too many possible futures. Alexis took a deep breath and pushed those thoughts out of her mind.

Outwardly calm, she pulled her laptop out of her bag as Brian said hello to the driver.

"You two seem a bit old to be running away from home," the driver said in a strong French-African accent. "Why such a long ride?"

"We're on an adventure," Alexis said; it was true enough after all.

"Where are you from?" Brian asked, clearly trying to change the subject.

"Senegal," the driver said cheerfully.

Alexis tried to tune out the conversation as the driver chatted happily about Senegal, the US, his recent trip to Baltimore with his kids, and about his day job. Alexis concentrated on following more leads on who Nick might be.

Disappointment tugged at her when she finally was able to track down an article about P. Steele and his two sons. It was one of those fluff pieces about a wealthy family's tradition of donating to local charities. The eldest son, leaning against his father's desk in the picture, was only twenty-two, way too young, and his name was Nicholas. She doubted the guy who'd kidnapped Brian's family had used his real name. That ruled out the Steeles on two counts, but something about them had caught her attention at the meeting. And he had blond hair. Shrugging, she saved the article just in case.

The next lead was more promising. Jason was a fan of the Searcha website and was a frequent commenter on the message boards. Finally, she found his social media page and it showed him to be a charismatic blond guy, aged twenty-four. Still not quite old enough, but closer.

She showed the screen to Brian.

"No." Brian shook his head sadly.

Alexis sighed with disappointment.

"This has got to be an expensive Uber ride. I'll definitely pay you back," Brian said.

"Thanks. I've got really good credit, but . . . Yeah, thanks." She realized the conversation with the driver had fizzled out. "So, what's your plan when we get there?"

"Um." He glanced at the driver, but seemed to accept that they had to talk at least a little about where they were going next. "I figure we'll need to get a decoy Compass and then wait for the call. Nick shouldn't know what it looks like, so a fake one ought to give me enough time to get all of us out of there."

Alexis waited for more.

"What?" Brian asked.

"That's it?!"

He shrugged. "We'll figure it out as we go."

She looked at him incredulously. She knew he was a by-the-seat-of-his-pants kind of guy, *but seriously?* "How can you not have a plan?"

"I have a plan. Use a fake compass."

"Where are you getting a compass that will pass muster?"

"Surely there's lots of touristy shops along the Inner Harbor."

Alexis didn't even bother pointing out the problems there. "What if he realizes it's fake?"

Brian shrugged again. "I'll come up with something."

Alexis rubbed the sudden ache in the middle of her forehead.

"Oh, come on, when's a plan ever useful? They always fall apart as soon as the slightest thing changes, and things are always changing," Brian protested.

"Okay, forget today for a minute. In general, you don't plan anything?"

"Ugh, no! You miss all the fun stuff along the way."

"But you're in college. How'd you get there without a plan?"

"Everyone else was going to college, and my parents expected it of me. So, why not? I filled out the paperwork, did the steps as they came up, and voila. It's been fun so far."

Alexis stared at him for a long moment; she would have missed a step if she hadn't had a plan, but maybe he was lucky. "But how'd you choose a major?"

"I'm on my second major. The first one sounded cool, Parks and Recreation, what wouldn't there be to love? I learned some interesting stuff about trees, but hated the main teacher in the department and loved one of my elective teachers. Who would have thought Child Development would be interesting? I took another class with her. One of the most challenging classes I ever took, but it was awesome, so I found time to do the work. Got a B+ and switched majors to early childhood education."

He made it sound easy, but Alexis was all too aware of the time and money he'd lost by not figuring it out the first time. She'd worked hard to finish a semester early, even after she realized working in marketing wasn't such a good fit for her after all. Yet here he was, apparently unbothered by an extra one. "What are you going to do when you get out?"

"I have some vague ideas about looking for a job at one of the international schools overseas, like the ones I attended growing up, but I'll see where life takes me. I could always teach English somewhere interesting until something more long term comes along. There's always cool things to do if you're not afraid to fail and keep your eyes open."

"Maybe for someone like you."

Brian sat up straight. "What's that supposed to mean?"

Alexis found the view of passing suburbia fascinating. Her cheeks were flaming, but she tried to find words anyway. "You're smart and confident." She wimped out on saying *good looking*, but he was. Of course, people who were all those things didn't have to try as hard as the rest of the world.

"I'm not that smart. My sister, Vicky, now she's brilliant. And Em is fearless. I'm terrible at standardized tests and always had a problem with theoretical information. Learning through doing I can manage, but abstract thinking? You might as well be speaking Greek. Which do you think you spend most of your time in college learning? And, if you haven't noticed yet, I tend not to look before I leap. What I will admit to is having decent social intelligence and a strong faith that what I need will show up when I need it. I use those things to gloss over my shortcomings. Knowing your strengths and not letting your weaknesses get in your way is a skill worth having."

"Okay," Alexis said, trying to wrap her head around that. "That's all well and good, but without a plan, I'll take photos I'll never do anything with, watch too much TV, let Mia drag me on adventures, and not get anywhere in life. Having a plan keeps me moving forward, even when things get hard, because I know it'll be worth it and I'm prepared as often as possible for when things go sideways."

Brian shrugged. "If it gets too difficult or goes too sideways, there's always another path I can take. Life's too short not to enjoy the journey."

"You both sound right to me," the driver said.

Alexis started, having forgotten there was a third person in the car.

Brian laughed, sounding just as surprised. "What's your advice?"

"Plans are meant for changing, but they're important. I make plans when other people are involved, especially my wife. If it's just me, I more, you know, wing it."

"You've got a point," Brian said with a sigh, before turning back to Alexis. "Okay. So other people are definitely involved. You're the Shadow and like plans, what should we do?"

Alexis stared at him incredulously. It was his family. *Isn't it his job to come up with the plan?*

"What?" Brian asked.

"I can't just think up something off the top of my head."

"Exactly. We'll just wing it."

She scowled. "I didn't say that. Let me do more research."

"Okay." He shrugged.

Alexis started to get mad, but then she saw his shadow, crisp and in focus. He was covering up his fears and concerns for his family with indifference. "We're going to figure this out," she said, hoping like hell she was right.

"Thank you." He met her gaze for a long moment and then leaned against the side of the car and closed his eyes. "With or without a plan, your abilities should be enough to show us how to get through this mess. I'm glad you're here."

The weight of his words, the responsibility in them, landed on her shoulders. She took a deep breath and tried to push the perfectly logical voice saying, *I am in no way qualified for such a responsibility* out of her mind. She hadn't felt qualified to deal with kids bullying each other or to keep campers safe forty feet off the ground or a million other things she'd managed to do well enough at camp. *But this is the real world.*

"I still wish we could talk to the FBI," she muttered, low enough so the driver wouldn't hear.

"They're not equipped to deal with magic," Brian muttered back.

Alexis wanted to point out all the ways she and Brian weren't equipped to deal with kidnapping, but she concentrated on something she could do something about.

It was easier for Alexis to think on paper, so she pulled out a notebook and started making a list of A: the things she did know, and B: all the questions that might be relevant. Column B was a lot longer than column A, but at least it gave her a place to start.

"What we need is more information," she said while she subcategorized her list. "Where's that book Sadie was looking for?"

"I think he's asleep," the driver said.

Alexis looked up from her notes and saw he was right. "Well, that's one way to get out of planning," she said as lightly as she could while grinding her teeth.

The driver laughed.

Alexis took the opportunity to try and study Brian's shadow. It was like staring at a person—more comfortable to do when they weren't looking. Maybe his shadow would hold some clues to how they were supposed to proceed. It had gone out of focus, though, and was an unhelpful, blurry image. She tried his reflection in the car window. Nothing. Her brow wrinkled as her frustration grew. Just a plain, normal reflection. No movement, no distorted images, and nothing with the saturation turned down. *Is there no magic this far north?* But if magic had made it all the way to Richmond . . . *One thing at a time.*

She wasn't going to wake Brian—he needed the sleep—so she turned back to the driver. "If you were looking for a really old fancy book, where would you go?"

"There are some antique stores and the universities," he said thoughtfully. "Or the Peabody Library? It's nicknamed the Cathedral of Books. My wife dragged our kids there last time we visited the city."

Something flickered briefly in the shadows, so Alexis did a quick search on her phone and found the Peabody Library. A hunt through their catalog found the book Sadie had been talking about in the kitchen yesterday. *The Travels of Sir Walter to Exotic Lands* was available to read in the library when it opened at 9 a.m. Though the book couldn't leave the library, it was in English rather than Old French.

"Do you want to go to the Peabody?" the driver asked.

Alexis glanced at Brian, sound asleep. "He's going to be hungry." She did a search for breakfast places nearby, checked their reviews, and then gave the driver an address.

"Can do."

"Thanks!" Alexis returned to her list. Next, she figured out where to buy a nice quality, old-fashioned compass. One look at prices and she steered away from the expensive antique stores. Her credit might be good, but it wasn't that good. She settled for finding midlevel stores that would hopefully have a good mix of nice and crap.

After she filled in the most glaring omissions from Brian's "plan," it was time to return to her hunt for Nick. Every time she got stuck, she'd try to adjust her perspective or filters, but it was a relief when the driver said they were almost to the restaurant; she'd run out of ideas half an hour ago.

Looking out the window, she could remember how the world had looked in her dream when Storm showed her the city, but Alexis couldn't tell if she could see it for herself or if she was just imagining the images of past that seemed to float like a mist amongst the predominantly brick city. The character of the buildings made her itch to get out her camera and see what she could do with composition, but that would be a distraction.

There were no signs of the hospital from her dream, but a different structure caught her attention. "Is that a clock tower?" Alexis asked the driver, uncertain if the red brick tower that looked like something belonging to a medieval castle was actually there or was something she was seeing in a shadow.

"That's the Arts Tower," the driver said. "Pretty cool, right?"

Should have known, it's in color. "Yes, cool." Alexis tried to keep the disappointment out of her voice. Seeing magic would be more helpful, but it was nice to have clear evidence this was the same city Storm had shown her.

Alexis reached for her camera again, but set it aside. Keeping her mind on figuring out how to rescue Brian's family was more important than trying to take photos out the window of a moving car.

Brian woke reluctantly, but brightened noticeably at the word *breakfast.* Alexis wanted to rehash their plans over chicken and waffles, but Brian would be more helpful after he'd eaten, and a crowded restaurant wasn't the right place for a magic/kidnapping conversation. She did her best to ignore the taunts of her mental list.

Instead, she asked questions about the places he'd lived and tried to listen to the answers. Her headache eased as she ate. Maybe it was the food or maybe it was the fact that she and Brian were bonding over how they both felt like they'd lived in foreign cultures growing up.

Alexis had been born just outside Boston and been raised in several states, but mostly Alabama. Her dad had finished his doctoral thesis about the time she was born and had taken several postdoctoral research positions before settling into a tenure track. Her mom did computer tech and could work anywhere, usually from home.

Brian lived in way more exotic places, but as they compared and contrasted, Alexis and Brian agreed there were some interesting similarities between expat communities and college towns. They laughed for a while over accents. Alexis was a better mimic than Brian, but he'd had more exposure. Brian enjoyed the bits of a British accent that slipped into his everyday speech, while Alexis had worked hard to keep the southern accent out of hers.

It was intriguing to get a peek past his easy self-confidence to the loneliness and lack of belonging that had clearly existed at different times in his life. Alexis felt privileged to be allowed past the happy stories he'd entertained her with when they'd first met. She glanced down during breakfast and realized she didn't know how long they'd been holding hands. A smile in her eyes, she looked up to answer his last questions.

She didn't let go until he needed his hands to pay the bill. She offered to split it, but he pointed out that he already owed her for frozen pizza and a ride.

"So," Brian said, a little too casually, as they left the restaurant and started walking toward the Peabody. "Any chance the shadows here have given you an amazing answer for how we're going to save my family?"

Alexis winced. "Sorry. No. I'm getting flickers, but they won't settle down long enough for me to see much. Do you think the magic here is weaker? Too far north, maybe?"

He looked around, his eyes focusing on things she couldn't see. "It looks fine to me. The sparkly things aren't as big, maybe, but the webbing seems as thick."

Alexis rubbed her forehead. "Then I don't understand why I can't see it!"

Brian looked around. "Maybe it's the time of day or something. I'm sure you'll be able to see them clearer soon."

Alexis didn't think it was that simple, but she didn't bother saying so aloud. He didn't need her getting all upset and panicky right now. Taking a deep breath, she checked the map on her phone. "This way."

Brian reached for her free hand and she laced her fingers with his. The tension eased from Alexis's shoulders, and the shadows around her shifted just a little. Black-and-white shadows of people from the past walked by, shrouded in darkness, as if they were in underexposed images. They didn't draw her attention, but something else did. As she focused harder, she saw it. There was a burnt-red tint to everything, as if a sepia tone had been added to the grayscale. Or had there always been a bit of red to the shadows, and she just hadn't noticed before? *Maybe it's because it's morning?* Alexis shrugged off the nagging feeling that she was missing something and looked for a clue among the phantom people living in the shadows of the old buildings, but they faded away the harder she looked.

The library was a serious marble building in an historic Baltimore neighborhood. The wooden doors were big and intimidating, but Brian didn't seem to pay them any mind as he pushed them open. The guard at the worn wooden desk pointed them to the left, and they walked through a museum-like room that celebrated old books in glass cases.

"This isn't going to be much help," Brian muttered, before spotting the next doorway. "Oh, here we go."

Alexis stopped at the entrance and looked up in awe. It did rather look like a cathedral, with a dramatic open space. Around the four sides were marble columns stacked on top of each other to make five more floors of balconies, with intricate cast-iron railings, all the way up to the vaulted glass ceiling. Each arched section between columns was lit with globe light fixtures that gave off a warm glow, highlighting the gold leaf. The floor contrasted with black-and-white tiles that were both grand and showed that this library was well loved and well used. In the middle were antique-looking wooden tables and chairs. A few people were scattered about, apparently deep in research.

"It's smaller than I expected," Brian said.

"It's gorgeous," Alexis breathed.

"Sure, but more church sized than cathedral sized."

"But—"

"It's nice, I'm just saying it's not as big as, say, the National Cathedral. But I guess books don't really take up that much space."

"There are three hundred thousand books here," Alexis protested.

"My point exactly. It's a great size for that many books. Sorry. Can we just find the book we're looking for?"

She gave him another disbelieving look before looking around again. She itched to try to capture the dramatic power of the room in a photograph, but it would take a while to find a vantage point that could truly capture the glory of the space, and Brian was right—they were here for a reason.

"I think we're going to need a librarian," Alexis said.

"Alright," Brian led the way to the back. Not bothered by the big glass doors, he stuck his head in and asked for help with a cheerfulness that contrasted sharply with the tension in the hand Alexis was holding.

The Travels of Sir Walter was ancient and smelled ever so lightly of mildew, with a heavy cover and unevenly cut pages. The print was blocky, slightly skewed on the paper, but thankfully not as small as Alexis had expected. The shadows around it seemed to be steeped in history, not just times and places, but also people. Alexis carried it reverently to an alcove and settled in at the table. Brian took the seat beside her and started leafing through the pages.

Fourteen

Brian
Saturday, 9:18 a.m.
The Peabody Library
Baltimore, MD

Brian flipped through the pages, rather hoping to land on the right one by chance. The bold letters stared back at him coldly. The few images were gloomy and absurd. The forward explained how it was an 1858 reprinting of a copy of a fifteenth-century translation of a—

Brian gave an impatient sigh and turned back a few pages. After a quick perusal of the lines, he pushed the book toward Alexis. "This table of contents isn't much help."

He leaned back in the wooden chair and looked around at the few people in the library. Most looked like graduate students, with deep passion for whatever they were studying. Two people were clearly tourists; they took a look around, snapped a few photos, and left to get to the next place on their list. No one looked like Gandalf or

Dumbledore or any sort of old wise man who could point Alexis and him in the right direction.

"Why don't you look through the new stuff in my Nick search, while I see if I can make sense of this book?" Alexis offered.

"Cool." He poked through the tabs on her laptop, but he kept glancing sideways at Alexis. *This is going to take forever. We're crazy to think we can wrestle an answer out of that book before tonight.*

Alexis had a notebook at her right hand and her cell phone close by, which she was using to look up words to help her better understand what she was reading.

"So, is it a spell book?" he asked.

"At first glance it looked like just what it says it is." She didn't look up from the text. "Some guy's travels through a bunch of lands that have either completely changed names or he was incredibly geographically challenged. I'm hoping there's another way to see his writing."

"Do you think it's in code?"

"I hope not!" Alexis said, looking concerned. "I don't know if that could have survived multiple translations. No, I don't think it's that complicated."

Brian tried to gauge how sure she was, but he couldn't tell. He let out a long breath and forced himself to turn back to the information she'd collected. Her organization system didn't make any sense, and very little of what she'd collected seemed relevant to finding Nick. As much as he appreciated all her work, he really hoped she was having more luck with the magic. Her information about where they might grab a bite to eat or find a compass made a little more sense, and he skimmed that set of Word files, maps, and links.

"Seriously," she muttered after maybe ten minutes, "did people actually speak like this? It would have taken forever to get anything done or discuss an idea."

"At least it's not in Old French," he grumbled.

"True that!" Alexis grinned at him. "I needed a silver lining. Poor Sadie."

Her smile was infectious and he returned it. "Any luck with it?"

"Some. How about you?"

He shook his head. "Sorry."

"No, I'm sorry I haven't found anything useful yet on the Nick front."

"Not your fault. You're doing a great job." At least he was pretty sure she must have been, because she'd definitely spent a lot of time on it. "The antique places you've found where we might get a passable compass look really helpful. Wait,"—he looked over at her, noticing her word choice—"what about the magic front?"

"Well . . . I'm starting to think several things."

"Besides the clunkiness of old-fashioned word choices?" he couldn't help but ask.

Alexis smiled before putting up her pointer finger. "Yes. First, this guy never left home. There's no way he could have been to these places and made such absurd observations—people with faces in their chests and ants the size of bears, it's impossible. And second, I think I figured out the right lens to see this through. If I'm right, the spells are mixed into the history of each culture and creature he encounters. Of course, it's been translated and copied multiple times since the original, but I'm starting to see the picture through the noise."

"Anything to teleport people home?" Brian asked, trying to make it sound like a joke.

Alexis rubbed her forehead. "Not yet, the only 'spell' I'm pretty sure I've found is for making light, but with electricity I can't see that being helpful. We might want to try it out anyway though. I bet we can learn something from it."

Brian tried not to groan aloud. *We don't have time to waste.* "Let's try a little longer before we resort to that."

"Okay. Do you want to see if we can look at the book at the same time?"

Brian shrugged, out of his depth, but he looked at the book when Alexis placed it between them and listened carefully as she explained her approach. It quickly became clear that he was better at reading the old-fashioned language than she was. His time with the Guard did have its advantages. He might not be able to understand Greek, but he had grown up reading crap like this. Alexis took over the Googling and note taking while he filtered through the pages for useful pieces.

It was painstaking work, and there was no guarantee it would help. Time was running by with each convoluted paragraph he summarized aloud. He hated that it was their best shot.

A fake compass was sounding more and more like a Hail Mary play now that Alexis had started to plan how it would work and he could see its shortcomings.

He pushed his hair out of his face, fighting to stay seated. Wading through the run-on sentences and roundabout wording, he kept waiting for her to exclaim, "I've got it!" That she'd figured out whatever was hidden in the pages and lost to time and translation, but it didn't come.

"It feels like we've been at this forever!" Brian groaned, leaning back in his seat and stretching his hands over his head.

"Almost two hours." Alexis looked away from her notes and caught her breath. "You okay? You're starting to glow a bit."

Brian looked down at his hands. "Shit!"

Alexis glanced around at the handful of people in the library. "You're okay. No one's noticed."

Yet. Brian closed his eyes and took a deep breath. He let it out really slowly. The glowing faded; the heat dissipated with it, leaving him clammy. Now, aware of the magic in him again, it bubbled just below the surface. Clawing like hundreds of digging ants, but trying to get out instead of in.

"Maybe we could take a break and stretch our legs. Maybe go look for a compass?" Alexis offered.

He opened his eyes and checked his hands before looking over at her. They weren't going to stop trying to figure out the book just because he couldn't handle a little frustration. "We're close. I can feel it."

"But you need to stretch your legs, how about you grab us an early lunch and I'll stay and keep at this?"

Brian rolled his shoulders. "I got this. We're faster together."

"True, but I could use the time to consolidate my notes. It'll make it easier to figure out where the important parts are. We can get back to the book when you return."

"Alexis!"

"What?"

Brian took another deep breath, fighting to keep his magic buried. "Nick might call while I'm gone."

"You could take my cell," Alexis said. "Mia might text or my mom might call, but you can just ignore them if they do."

Brian considered that. She wasn't going to drop it if his skin was on the verge of glowing like a neon sign, but they would get this done faster if he could just focus. Pushing his hair out of his face didn't help. He leaned his head toward his right shoulder and then the left, cracking his neck both ways.

"If there's an emergency, you're the person I'd call, and if you don't have a phone . . ." He let out a long breath. What he needed were solutions, not problems. "Maybe we should stop at a store to get a burner phone. Who even sells those?"

"Communication!" Alexis tossed her palms face up. "Remember that tribe of earless people that lived in the mountains?" She waved a hand at the book.

"You really think they used some kind of spell to communicate?"

"Yes! Where is it?"

Brian flipped back to the right page. "Okay," he said and then read through the section.

Alexis looked up from some hasty scribbles. "What if we use the magic clay stuff you found yesterday and this morning? You know, the magic marble? And the connecting magic strands that you can see? I think it might work!"

"Still kind of sounds like a waste of time with modern technology."

"Nothing else I've come across has made sense. There were some complicated ones that could have been useful, but I'm pretty sure those are for spell casters and not meant for the kind of magic we have."

"Wouldn't it be faster just to buy a phone?"

"If we can figure it out, maybe we can communicate with your family. If we could just figure out where they are, maybe we could get them out before the exchange!"

Brian brightened. "Okay, let's see what we can do."

The bubbling itching of his magic settled down as he painstakingly translated the story of the earless people into regular words, organized into reasonable sentences. Alexis asked close to a million and one clarifications as she tried to figure out the magic theory hidden below the boring encounter between the author and the implausible group of people.

It was slow work. They spent a lot of time saying things like, "Maybe the ones that come out at night are Shadows," and "Invisible ropes could be the strands of magic," and "The magic marble could be the fruit of the water weeds. No, that's not right," but eventually Brian leaned back in his seat.

"I think we figured it out," he said in a long breath.

"Are you sure we're not missing something?" Alexis frowned as she checked her notes.

"Only one way to find out," Brian said, fighting his excitement. The possibility of being able to talk to his family made him realize how much he wanted to, no, *needed* to hear their voices and know they were okay. He wanted it so badly it hurt.

"Okay." Alexis took a deep breath. "Let's start with the lump of magic, then."

Brian pulled the rock-like lump out of his pocket. "Hopefully this is enough, I haven't seen one nearly this big in Baltimore."

Alexis frowned as she took it.

"What?" he asked.

"Is it more translucent than it was yesterday?"

Brian's brow furrowed. "Huh? I can't tell a difference."

Her frown deepened as she molded the clay. "Does it feel more brittle to you? To me it feels like half-dry clay with little granules in it, very different from yesterday."

Brian took the lump of magic. "You're right, it's more like aging concrete than rock. What does that mean?"

"I don't know."

He handed it back, wishing they had more information. If Merlin hadn't decided that all magic had to go, then the Guard could be stronger. Members would have proof, and it would have been easier to pass information onto the next generation, but instead they were working in the dark. Of course, if there had been free magic, human civilization probably never would have gotten out of the Dark Ages.

He looked over at Alexis. She was staring at the magic in her right hand and rubbing her forehead with her left.

"You're going to wear out your forehead, rubbing it like that. What's wrong?"

Fifteen

Alexis
Saturday, 11:53 a.m.
The Peabody Library
Baltimore, MD

Alexis looked up from the dry, crumbly magic in her right hand to Brian and all his enthusiasm; his hope weighed on her as if she were carrying every one of the three hundred thousand books in the library on her shoulders. "I'm sure it'll be fine."

This shouldn't be any worse than when we left DC, she tried to reason. Forcing down her panic like it was just another day on the climbing tower, she tried to work the clay without thinking, without really breathing. *If I don't breathe, I can't think, right?* It seemed like sound logic.

The clay broke into two pieces. *It's all right,* she told herself before she could start hyperventilating. She would need two pieces anyway. A hint of bright citrus clung to them, but more sunbaked than the fresh, clear scent they'd had yesterday. With painstaking focus, she pushed each lump into the shape of a headphone earbud. They were lopsided, gritty, and clear enough that she could see the fine lines on her palm through them, but she was afraid to mold them any more. Two pieces were all they needed.

"Okay," she said, forcing herself to breathe more normally.

Brian's brow smoothed, as if he was trying to hide a frown. "A bit lopsided, but they look like they'll do the job."

"Your turn." Alexis leaned back in her seat to watch.

He reached for an invisible strand she could barely sense. She knew he was taking several of the magical strands that ran between them and wrapping them around each lump of clay.

She glanced around to make sure they weren't attracting attention. Then she shifted in her seat to watch the shadows around Brian. There had to be something helpful in them, but they were dark and opaque, as if she were using the wrong light sensitivity on her camera. Only slivers of light were visible around the edges, and nothing shone through that was helpful.

"Okay," Brian said. "Try this."

She took the magic he offered her and put it in her ear. It was like sandpaper, but she ignored the discomfort.

"How do you think it works? Do we just talk?" Brian asked.

"Your guess is as good as mine," Alexis said.

"Well, I don't think I hear you through the magic earbuds."

"Maybe we're missing something," Alexis said, but she was distracted by the words *magic earbuds.*

"So dumb. Wish Sadie were here."

"Excuse me!" Alexis exclaimed, her outrage turning to hurt faster than it had come.

Brian glanced around. "Not so loud. Excuse you, what? I don't know what we're missing."

"But Sadie would know?" Alexis asked, forcing herself to use the soft volume they'd been using. It was a good thing no one was sitting close by.

"Sadie? Why would she know?"

"But you just said you wished she was here."

Brian stared at her, clearly confused. Then something seemed to dawn on him. "*Magic earbuds.*"

"What about them," Alexis asked, her hurt turning to frustration.

"You can hear me."

"Of course, I can. I'm sitting right here."

"*No, I mean you can hear me,*" he repeated.

And then it hit her. He wasn't moving his mouth. "*You're not speaking out loud.*"

"*But you can hear me, just like I heard that.*"

Alexis caught the difference that time, it was subtle, but it was clearly coming through the magic earbud, and his voice had a faded quality to it. She would have noticed it sooner if she hadn't been upset.

"That's a bit . . . weird," she said uneasily.

"Just a bit." He looked as uncomfortable as she felt. "I thought of Sadie because she's better at coming up with cool names for things. Magic earbuds sounds a bit dumb, or at least a bit on the nose."

The knot in Alexis's stomach eased. She quickly tried to think of something else before he read her next thoughts. The gold leaf in the building really did add a nice warm hue to the whole library.

"*Okay, now I'm not getting anything, how does this work?*" Brian thought and then started to repeat himself out loud.

"Maybe we need eye contact?" Alexis pulled her eyes away from the balconies overhead.

"That's not very useful most of the time."

"Maybe I missed something." Alexis rubbed her forehead. *"Maybe I didn't make the earbuds right."*

"I think you did just fine. Maybe they just take practice. How about we try with numbers? Basic and simple. That way we can test if we're sending and receiving information clearly."

Alexis took a deep breath and nodded. "Okay."

Brian's idea turned out to be a great one. It helped them figure out how to send a specific piece of information instead of random thoughts. They could mentally send a number, and then the other could use counting fingers to verify that they got it, allowing them to practice across the length of the library. The trick, it seemed, was to clearly think of a word or sentence and sort of project it.

They got a few sideways glances, but the researchers were busy with their books, and tourists were busy gawking at the building and moving on. When Alexis started to worry that they were drawing attention, Brian pointed out that if you were confident enough, most people didn't ask questions.

As they got better at communicating, Alexis was relieved to find it was very similar to the difference between saying something out loud versus inside one's head. There was definitely less concentration needed the more she practiced. Brian must have felt the same way, because she stopped hearing his stray thoughts as well. Visual contact became unnecessary, and the connection got only a little staticky when Brian stepped outside to check.

"Saves us from getting a prepaid phone," Brian said when they were both back at the table with the spell book. "But unless I can get a magic earbud to someone in my family, I don't understand how it's going to help me communicate with them."

Alexis didn't like that he was probably right. "We can keep look-ing. Maybe we can do it without the earbuds, just the strands. We're still going to need to know the range. Should be easy enough to test. Do you want to go get the compass now? I'll pick us up some lunch and print what I've got on Nick. What do you think?"

"I'm all for testing the range, and I am hungry."

Alexis didn't bother adding that he had a green tinge to his skin. It was subtle, but it was definitely time to regroup. Plus, she wanted to get out of the library herself. Maybe outside the light would be better and it would be easier to figure out why the shadows looked so dark.

It took only a few minutes to plan their individual excursions and when they'd be back. Brian headed off while she returned the book and spent an extra few minutes checking, or stalling, perhaps, in the hall with the display cases just outside the main part of the library.

Brian's check-ins were like an alarm set on a five-minute snooze. Each time Alexis sent a mental confirmation that she could hear him. Finally, she couldn't avoid going outside any longer.

Alexis let out her breath when she stepped into the sun and saw the shadows around her shift. They were still dark and underdevel-oped, with a clear tint of red to them, but she could at least make out bits of the images. People passing by, who were long gone or not yet arrived, didn't hold anything she could see as helpful. A silhouette of herself walking to the office-supply store where she wanted to do her printing was a call to get moving.

Brian's thoughts came in crackly, like a badly tuned radio, but she could still make him out. *"I'm at the store. There's more touristy stuff than antiques here. Do you think a compass with a Game of Thrones' dragon is too recognizable?"*

"Yes," she thought back as clearly as she could.

Alexis walked into the office-supply store and headed for the printing area.

"So no to all movie and TV show merchandise?"

"Safer that way."

She flipped through tabs on her computer, trying to figure out how many trees she wanted to kill in her quest for Nick. The shadows flickered when she came to the article on the Steele's donation, so she added it to the files she was printing, wishing she could see more than a flicker in the shadow.

"How about steampunk?" Brian thought.

"No!"

She stared hard at the shadows while waiting for her stack of files to print. Shifting side to side, low or high did nothing to help the clarity.

"I'm out of ideas." Brian's frustration came through with his thoughts.

Alexis stepped outside into the sunlight, thinking hard. A chalice flickered across the pavement, like a washed-out still from a movie, as she started to walk.

"How about shiny and looking like it's made of gold?" he asked.

"Indiana Jones!"

"What?" His thought was almost lost in the static.

"Indiana Jones and the Last Crusade. The Holy Grail—" she started to say, but her earpiece dissolved into sand mid sentence.

Fighting panic, Alexis tilted her head to the side and shook out the broken magic. It floated down like glitter before dissolving into nothing.

Alexis stared at the sidewalk. The magic was gone. And the shadows looked like unremarkable shade cast by the sun. Not a hint of magic or color flickered in their matted depths.

Sixteen

"Shit!" Brian exclaimed aloud, shaking magical sand out of his ear. The grains glowed as they fell like snowflakes, evaporating into a quickly dissipating mist. He was about to use more colorful language when he noticed the antique store clerk frowning at him.

"Can I help you?" the man asked.

"I'm sorry. I got something in my ear." Brian gave his head one last good shake.

"Um-hmm?" The clerk said, but got distracted when a family with four small children bounced into the store.

Upside—Brian no longer had a rocky piece of magic in his ear. Downside—the earbud was broken. He tried to reach out magically. The strands connecting him to Alexis were still there, but the message wouldn't go through. *If the spell was this shitty, why the hell did we waste our time on it?* If the spell fell apart as soon as the earbuds broke, then there was no way this was going to help get his family out before the exchange. *We've wasted the whole morning!*

His skin started to itch. *Shit!* He took a deep breath and looked around. He was here for a decoy compass, not just to test the range of the earbuds. All he needed was for it to buy him enough time to get his family into a crowd of witnesses. *Nick wouldn't hurt them after that, right?*

Brian pushed his hair out of his face. *What'd Alexis say? Indians? No, Indiana Jones. What? Hadn't she just said, "Nothing from a movie?"* He looked down at the shiny-looking pocket compass in his hand with a fake ruby in the stem. *Oh, the Holy Grail.*

He walked over to the store clerk, who was watching the family with a pained expression. "Quick question. Any chance you have a more boring, yet old-fashioned-looking compass somewhere? Something that could have been in people's pockets for hundreds of years and been overlooked by thieves and villains?"

The store clerk tilted his head a bit to the right, perhaps trying to gauge Brian's sanity. "Um, what about those over there?"

Brian investigated the box of random baubles. There were three compasses, all a bit worn. One was plastic, but the other two were in metal cases. He'd been hoping for something with Celtic knot work on the case, but the more he thought about it, the more he liked the plain, pewter-colored case with the dent in the lid. The compass inside was modern, but he thought he could pry it apart and pull out the paper plate. To be safe, he also purchased one of the over-the-top pocket watches he'd studied earlier. He hoped that with Alexis's help they'd be able to cobble the two together and make it passable. All that mattered was that Nick believed it long enough to get Brian's family out of there.

Stepping outside, Brian took in a deep breath of fall air and hope. One setback with the communication spell was hardly anything compared to how far they'd come. A bit of magic, the size of a raindrop, glittered in the sunlight. Maybe new magic was what the earbuds needed. If he could collect enough, Alexis would probably have better luck molding it. At the very least, it would feel a lot better in his ear. Clearly, the magic had dried out after it was picked from the strands. He took the compass and watch out of the paper bag he'd gotten at the antique store, stuck them in his pocket, and used the bag to hold the magic.

The magic nodules were smaller than they had been in DC, but there were a dozen or so scattered around in a way that reminded him of an Easter egg hunt. Em would love this; she'd make it into a game and try to collect more than he did. And Vicky would figure out where the highest concentration of magic was and come out even without having to break a sweat.

Thinking of his sisters made Brian both smile and hurt at the same time. He checked his collection of magical nuggets. *Should be enough*. Picking up his pace, he jogged the rest of the way back to the library.

Alexis was waiting by the statue of Lafayette on horseback, near the entrance to the library, looking concerned.

"Any idea what happened with the earbuds?" she asked.

"I think you were right about the magic being too old. The magic clay dries out after it's been picked, like playdough left out of the container. So, I got more." Brian opened the paper bag so she could see the glowing contents.

"Magic?" she asked.

"Of course. We can try making new ones."

"Oh."

Brian could see her swallow hard. "What's wrong?"

"I can't see that either."

"Either?"

"I can't see anything in the shadows. I'm sorry! I keep trying, but I think I've lost my magic. I know I promised I'd help . . . but I don't know what's wrong with me." She spoke softly, with her eyes on the grass.

Brian shoved his hair out of his face. "How can you just lose your magic?" His chest was tight.

"I don't know."

He needed a solution. "Maybe you're thinking too much about it. Mine works better if I let it be."

"I can't just not think about it!" Alexis flashed him an angry look, but there were tears just below the surface. Then her expression changed to concern. "You're starting to glow again."

Taking a deep breath, Brian fought for control, partially over his magic, but mostly over himself. None of this was Alexis's fault, and getting frustrated at her wasn't only unfair but it wasn't helping anything. *I need to cut my hair*, he realized, pushing it back out of his face again. *Mom would have seen to it.* He closed his eyes and pulled in a deep breath.

When the itching faded, he opened his eyes and tested his voice. "I think we're both hungry."

She nodded; her concern for him had clearly overruled her other emotions at the moment. Picking a grassy spot under a tree, she unpacked two sandwiches, chips, and apples.

Brian shifted uneasily. "Hey, magic or no magic, you've been a huge help already. Without you I'd have ended up with a compass that had a dragon on it, and it would have been useless, or one with a big fake ruby."

"You understood my Indiana Jones reference? I wasn't sure how much got through before my earbud crumbled," Alexis asked quietly.

"Check it out." Brian handed her the compass and accepted the sandwich she handed him. It had turkey, Swiss cheese, and a generous helping of roasted vegetables. He eyed it closely—that was what he got for saying he'd eat anything. His first bite was careful, but he smiled as he chewed the juicy, slightly spicy sandwich. The roasted vegetables were actually a good addition. "If I got a compass you don't think will work, we can try again later, there are still a bunch of places left on your list to check, but I feel like this one will work. Thanks for getting food."

"This is perfect." She flipped it open. "Well, almost perfect anyway."

"That's why I picked this up too. Thought maybe we could use some of the pieces to make the compass look weirder on the inside. It's supposed to point toward magic, so it's no problem if we break the compass needle."

"How does the real Compass work?"

Brian hesitated. Everything in his family's training said he wasn't supposed to share that information, but this was Alexis. He was trusting her to help him get his family back; he could trust her with this. Besides, maybe if she didn't think about her own magic for a bit, it would help.

He set down his sandwich and unsnapped the leather cuff from his wrist. The cuff was dark brown, an inch wide, and lightly imprinted with a Celtic knot design. It'd held up well under the wear and tear of being on his wrist since it had been passed to him five years ago. Of course, he usually took it off when he went swimming, because even after listening to Elliot preach about the Searcha, it was hard to imagine someone actually stealing it. Well, at least not after the first week or two of wearing it. Mostly he was just impressed that he'd only misplaced it once. He would have approached the whole thing differently if he'd realized there were actually people like Nick out there.

"How is that a compass?" Alexis asked.

Brian grinned at her. "That's the trick of it. I was really into this at seventeen, which was when I swore my long-ass oath to protect the Compass. Every protector of a magical artifact picks a different way to carry it. And technically, no one is supposed to know how, but we all knew Mom carried the First Knot on a chain, as if it was an amulet. My dad carried the Compass in the wooden medallion on his key ring. I joked with the Guard that I'd carry it in my cell phone case, but I never told them where I really kept it." He grinned at Alexis before turning the cuff over. The groove pocket on the underside was custom crafted. A gift from his parents, who had known what he wanted it for.

"My roommate, freshman year, had a guitar, and the first time he restrung it I thought I was crazy. Because it turns out the Compass looks very similar to a low E string from an acoustic guitar." He tugged the Compass free, showing her the five-inch-long wire, apparently wrapped in a fine bronze thread.

"Okay, first—very cool," Alexis said, clearly intrigued. "Second—how is that a compass?"

"Without magic, it's just a weird wire. I've no idea how they crafted it in medieval times, but with magic in the world . . ." He placed it flat in the palm of his hand, like he'd done dozens of times when he'd first become responsible for it. But this time was different. This time it started to glow orange at one end, blue at the other, and float about an inch above his palm. It spun like the needle of a compass and settled into a direction not quite parallel to the street beside them. "Well, the orange end is supposed to point the way toward the closest Knot." His brow wrinkled.

"What's wrong?"

"If what I was taught is right, we're fairly close to a Knot. It's supposed to be a short-range locator and not work at any distance more than five kilometers or so. The colors shift as the Compass gets closer to a Knot. If all the measurements were accurate . . ." Brian tried to do the math in his head, but it would take a lot of time, and it was hard to imagine the directions had survived accurately all these centuries. He shrugged. "Umm . . . Maybe a few miles? That's weird, right?"

"Yeah, very weird."

"Maybe it's a coincidence. It is an old city."

"If only I could see the shadows."

"Seriously, food will help." He nodded to her sandwich. When he picked up the Compass, the wire stopped glowing. He slid it back into the leather pocket, not wanting to think about what it was telling him. Habit made him wince in pain; his left wrist still had some healing to do. He shifted the cuff to his right. The click of the snap closing eased the lines on his forehead.

Alexis picked up her own sandwich. Her lunch looked more green than his, pesto maybe, but she seemed just as happy with it as he was with his. After several bites, her shoulders relaxed from where they'd been up near her ears. Brian was able to breathe a little easier.

Not paying attention to his sandwich, he was a bit surprised to look down and realize he'd eaten it. Frowning, he licked the oil and cheese goo off his fingers and reached for an apple. There were a variety, so he picked what looked like a Gala or Fuji and avoided the green one. Polishing it on his sleeve, he tried to organize his thoughts.

"I couldn't see magic yesterday," he said, before biting into the crisp fruit. Maybe now that she no longer looked like she was trying to hide in plain sight, she'd be able to figure out what was wrong with her magic.

Alexis shrugged, her eyes on her sandwich, as if finding the right angle to take another bite.

"And that wasn't just because I was overthinking. It was because I was stressed and frustrated. Those things make me glow, but they also make it hard for me to see the strands. When I went for a run, I could see them again. Maybe exercise will help?"

"I tried some while I was getting lunch, but I'm not much of a jogger."

Brian took another bite of apple and thought that over. The apple was sweet and tangy, a good complement to the sunshine. His family wouldn't be enjoying the sunshine, but his feeling guilty about that wouldn't help anyone. "Everyone is probably different. Maybe something else will work for you."

Alexis shrugged and chose a chip from the open bag. "But if I was just better at this—"

"Hey, none of that," he said, searching for a way to loosen her shoulders away from her ears again. "You're not perfect. If you were, that would be both boring and terrifying."

She looked surprised and then her face lighted. "That doesn't make sense, terrifying can't be boring."

He laughed. "Oh, it so can be."

"Fine," she said, not quite managing to hide her smile. "But seriously, where does that leave us?"

"When the magic was invisible for me, I could still feel the magic marble. I bet you could make the earbuds even if you can't see them," he said while he set his apple core on top of the bag of trash and then reached for another one. "I think they'll be helpful. Every tool we can have over Nick the better. But magic or no magic, I'm still really glad you're here."

"What about your family?"

"They'll be glad you're here too," he said, mostly just to see if he could make her smile.

It didn't quite work. Instead, she crumpled up her empty sandwich wrapper. "Okay, let me see what I can do with the magic."

"I didn't mean because of your magic."

"Sure, but let's see if I can work with the magic. Even if I can't see it."

Brian handed over the paper bag.

"Oh." She molded two nodules together. "You're right. The magic feels smooth and easy to mold. Like it did the first time. And the citrus smells fresher. What makes it invisible to me and what makes it hard to mold are probably different things. I think you're right about it drying out."

"At this rate we'll have magic figured out in no time."

She grinned briefly before becoming absorbed in her work. Carefully pulling out one magic lump at a time, she started to mold them into balls of magic clay. It was slow work, especially since she still couldn't see what she was doing.

After nearly finishing off the bag of chips without realizing what he was doing, Brian looked around for anything besides eating to do. He'd already had two apples, and there was only a Granny Smith left. *What else is there to do?*

"You could take a look through my notes. See if they make more sense now that they're not on the computer," Alexis said, not looking up from her hands.

"You sure I'm not still wearing an earbud?" Brian asked.

"You're fidgeting."

"Right."

"In my bag."

Brian found the stack of freshly printed papers and leafed through them. The same stuff as before. He tried reading through some of the chat-room threads, but the wack jobs and their pro-magic opinions made his skin itch. He had no idea how Alexis expected to find Nick in any of this or how knowing his identity would actually help. But glancing over at Alexis, working with magic she couldn't see to help his family, he knew the least he could do was keep working his way through the stack. Alexis and his family all deserved better from him.

"Bloody hell!" Brian pulled the piece of paper free from the stack to get a better look. There was no mistaking the man leaning against the desk in the picture.

Seventeen

Alexis
Saturday, 1:14 p.m.
Baltimore, MD

"What's wrong?" Alexis asked, nearly dropping the magic clay. It had just started to take on a slight green tinge, but when she looked down it was invisible again.

"You've found him!" he exclaimed.

"Who?"

"Nick. Right here!"

She looked at the paper he held. It was the article about the Steele family's charity work. "But that guy is only twenty-two. I thought—"

"Seriously? I thought he had to be closer to thirty, but that's definitely him. What's the article about?" His voice trailed off as he started to read the puff piece.

Alexis put the magic clay on top of the bag, where she'd be able to find it again, and picked up her laptop. There wasn't a lot beyond the article to go on. The elder Steele had some kind of business with a boring, though expensive-looking website that didn't actually explain what the company did. Nothing on social-media sites showed up for either of them.

"I don't care how much money his family gives to local charities or some fancy research hospital, anyone who kidnaps people is a monster," Brian said.

His tone made Alexis glad his anger wasn't directed at her. "I'm not getting anything on my searches. I've looked into the hospital—it's in Baltimore and might be the one I keep seeing relating to Nick, but they take their privacy laws seriously. Still, knowledge is a form of power. Should we call the FBI now that we know who Nick is?"

"They can't deal with magic, and if knowledge is power, then money is too. How am I going to convince the FBI some rich guy's son kidnapped my family?"

Alexis conceded the point by returning to her computer screen. Still, nothing useful was coming up. "What about the Guard? Will they know something helpful about these people?"

Brian seemed to consider that before shaking his head. "No. Sounded like the Guard asks for money once a year and doesn't hear back. I can't imagine they'd know much."

Frowning, Alexis tapped her keyboard as she thought through their options. *Surely there is something that will work, we're so much closer!* And yet still so far from anything actually useful. "How about my friend Mia? She's really good at this kind of thing."

"Negotiating with kidnappers?" Brian asked in that way of his that didn't quite sound like a joke.

"Internet-stalking people."

Brian seemed to digest that for a moment. "What are you going to tell her about the why?"

"I'll keep it vague." Alexis really hoped she could talk him into it. Not only was Mia their best chance at finding more information about Nick, but Alexis also really wanted an excuse to call her. "She's my best friend, it's not like I'm going to be able to keep all this a secret from her anyway. It was one thing when you were just a guy with a unicorn, but now . . ." She shrugged.

"Will she think you're crazy?" Brian asked.

"Nah, she's more New Agey than I am. She'll be cool," Alexis said with more confidence than she felt. "But I'll save the magic stuff for the in-person conversation."

Brian shrugged. "Okay, then. Thank you."

Alexis checked that the volume on her phone was turned down to a regular level and called Mia. By the second ring Alexis was contemplating how awkward it would be if she had to leave a message.

"Alexis!" Mia said, her voice full of enthusiasm. "You're calling! Everything okay? How's camp? You'll never guess where Eric took me last night for dinner."

Alexis leaned back against the trunk of the tree, tension easing from her shoulders as she listened to Mia cheerfully bounce from one topic to another. The earth was solid under Alexis. The scent of citrusy magic and cut grass drifted around her. She yawned once, not because she was tired, but because her body was breathing deeper. She asked a few questions, but mostly just listened. It really was a rather nice day, with the sky such a bright shade of blue.

"Sorry," Mia said, with another of her sudden topic changes. "You know you should stop me when I'm rambling on and on about me. How are you? Have you found your photo yet?"

Alexis sat up a bit, not quite ready for the conversation's turn. She glanced over at Brian and realized how antsy he was. "Not yet. I kind of got sidetracked."

"Are you trying too hard again? You know, perfectionism—"

"Is the enemy of done," Alexis finished. "Yes. I know."

"But do you walk the walk? Are you being a perfectionist?"

Alexis frowned at approximately where the lump of magic clay was. "Maybe a bit, but it's not my photography that got me side-tracked. Would you mind doing a search for me?"

"Oh, it's your tall, dark, and handsome? Now that's my kind of distraction."

Alexis glanced at Brian, then hastily returned to the computer screen. "Not exactly. It's a long story. Better told in person."

"He's standing right there, isn't he?"

"Yep."

Mia chortled before giving a dramatic sigh. "Okay. I can be patient if I need to be. It's not easy, but I'm strong. What am I looking for?"

"Nicholas Steele," Alexis said, then read through the rest of the information she had on him.

"Humm, a brooding blond with money. Square jawed and bor-ingly symmetrical. Why would you want to waste our time learning about him?"

"Sorry? I'm trying to figure out what ties he has to Baltimore. Maybe somewhere he might keep . . ." Alexis tried to think of a rea-sonable end to her sentence, but had to give up. "Oh, say, hostages."

Brian dropped the Granny Smith he was eating. A pity, she'd wanted an apple.

Alexis waved a hand for him not to worry and continued talking to Mia. "I'm hitting dead ends on all the usual sites. He might also go by Nick."

"Alexis?" Mia said, her voice suddenly serious. "Did you get into a mess without me?"

Fighting an unexpected surge of emotions, Alexis blinked back tears. "I'm okay. Really. The guy I was telling you about, Brian, I'm kind of trying to help him with a mess."

"Alexis! You're supposed to be finding the photo you want, not helping some lost puppy. Yes. This Brian has officially gone from tall, dark, and intriguing to a puppy."

Alexis couldn't help it—she laughed. "I still have time to find a photo. So, you'll help?"

"For you, of course. But seriously, are you okay?"

Taking a deep breath, Alexis made sure she could mean it when she spoke. "Yes. I'm not sure what I'm doing, but this is where I need to be right now."

"Well, I'm sure you'll figure it out. You're a rock star at doing things you didn't think you could, at least as soon as you get out of your own way, if that makes sense. Like the climbing tower. Remember that first summer?"

Alexis did. She'd been so afraid of heights she'd not been able to get five feet off the ground. She insisted that there was no way it was possible for her to make it a single step higher. She simply wasn't physically capable of it, and there was no way she was going to make it to the zipline at the top. But she'd proven herself wrong. By the end of that summer, Terra had recruited Alexis for the climbing team for the following year. Alexis still hated heights, but she loved to work at the top of the zip platform, helping kids handle their own fears.

"Thanks. I needed that reminder."

"You're welcome. Now go win that competition."

"I'll keep my eyes open for the right photo, but at this point . . ."

"Don't give me that crap."

"I'll do my best. Let me know when you have something." Alexis could almost hear Mia rolling her eyes, but her friend let her go without more advice.

Shaking her head and smiling, Alexis picked up the still-invisible magic clay. Mia was right, she was being a perfectionist about it. A few tweaks, and she offered Brian the new earbuds.

He was staring at her.

"What? I think it's right. I made a little hook there to tie the magic string to. I have clay left over so I can make backup sets."

"Your friend sounds like a handful."

"She's the best."

He seemed to be about to say something but shook his head.

"Seriously, will the new earbuds work? I still can't see them, so you need to tell me," Alexis said.

"They look perfect." He pocketed them. "But for now, we've got something more important to do."

Eighteen

Watching Alexis on the phone with her friend had been a sharp reminder that Alexis was a human being with a life, goals, and a whole world that didn't include him or his problems. He'd gotten pieces of it from talking with her, but she had so willingly jumped in to help him, he hadn't quite realized how disruptive it had been to her life. Just because she'd agreed to help didn't give him the right to forget who she was.

"Where are we going?" Alexis asked as she helped him clean up their picnic.

"When's the last time you took a photo?"

"Um . . ." She seemed to think hard and then shrugged. "Yesterday, when I was trying to get a picture of Storm."

"That doesn't count, you were doing that to help me."

Alexis shrugged. "It was interesting."

"Let's go find something you can take pictures of because you just want to."

"I'm not going to find anything for my competition here, and there's still a lot we need to do for your family."

She had a point, but then again . . . "We've got a decoy compass, we've got handy-dandy communicators, I just need to tie them into the magical web stuff. We've learned all we can from that spell book, and your friend is looking up information on Nick. We need to take care of ourselves for a bit if we're going to have enough mental energy to handle tonight. Time we have some fun."

Alexis didn't look convinced.

"You do take pictures for fun, not just to win competitions, right?"

"Well, yes, of course, at least I used to, but now's not the time."

"It's the perfect time. Let's get to the Inner Harbor, so we'll be where we need to be when Nick calls. That gives us a destination. Come on, do it for me, my brain is going to melt if we have one more serious minute for at least the next two hours."

Her lip twitched toward a smile. "We can get a bus from over there."

"How about we walk? It's not that far, right?"

She shrugged. "Okay."

"In the meantime, how about those statues? Where's your camera?" Brian put his hands on his hips with mock seriousness.

She rolled her eyes, but humored him. After a few clearly thoughtless pictures, however, she started to get absorbed in what she was doing. When she would surface and remember where they were supposed to be going, he'd find some way to slow her down again. One time he stopped and pretended to admire a skyscraper, but he was actually counting as many windows as he could before boredom threatened his life. Spotting a coffee shop, he decided they needed pastries and spent forever choosing the perfect one. Seeing a music store, he stopped in for a guitar string, because the Compass did seriously look like one, and there was a slim chance Nick might know that. Mostly he used people watching as an excuse to slow down. The city was full of diverse and fascinating people going about apparently interesting lives.

His favorite person to watch, though, was Alexis, when she became lost in her photography. Her posture shifted as she started to unwind. Her shoulders relaxed down, she stood comfortably straight, and her walk became more fluid. Her patience amazed him. When she became fully focused on something, she could stand for minutes on end waiting, sometimes shifting from one vantage point to another, and sometimes just watching for something he couldn't see.

If she had a photo she was excited about, she'd show it to him on her camera screen. When he asked about it, she'd explain what she was trying to do with it. Then he would be able to see a composition or a color or how the light played across a surface in a way he hadn't noticed. She'd always insist it would be better after she'd played with the photo digitally, but he could usually see what she was trying to accomplish.

He was grateful for all the museums his parents had taken him to as a kid. Every city they visited or lived near seemed to have a collection of art and statues. His favorite had always been the medieval weaponry exhibits, but he'd absorbed enough information about art and photography to ask questions and understand Alexis's answers.

When nothing caught her interest to photograph, she'd walk beside him, her hand in his, people watching with him. There were even times he momentarily forgot why they were in Baltimore, but as they reached the Inner Harbor, Brian became more and more aware of the time crawling by like a spider on the back of his neck. Luckily, there were walls and steps to climb and space to move about. He tried to do a handstand, but his arm still hurt from when he was trying to get away from Nick. Pushing the thought away, he noticed there were more flakes of magic he could collect. Glad to have a mission, he left Alexis to her photography, so that he could use up some of his restless energy. His family needed him at his best tonight.

Nineteen

Alexis
Saturday, 1:48 p.m.
Baltimore, MD

Alexis snapped a few boring photos. There was plenty to see, but at first nothing seemed to click. Slowly though, she settled into the world. Settled into the composition, color, and light that called out to be captured in a photo.

The pressure of saving Brian's family and the future of the world fell away. Even time lost its meaning. The mystery of deep shadows in an alleyway, the expression of confidence in the stride of a passing police officer, and the loneliness in a crowd, each absorbed in their own cell phone, were all moments that begged to be captured. Seeing the first few, the rest came more easily. Playing with the light, vantage point, and composition, patience seeped into her bones. She let herself become absorbed in trying to show the strength of a rope anchoring a historic ship in the harbor. When she felt she'd gotten it right, she moved onto the next thing that caught her interest.

She wasn't even aware when the shadows started to speak to her again. It was a subtle shift, but visible as the emotions she was trying to capture in each photo. They interacted with the world, a part of it, no less than she was.

Not wanting to push the shadows away, Alexis let them be, seeing what they showed her and not searching for answers. Brian had been right, they needed time to take care of themselves.

Thinking back over their conversation, she realized he'd been right about her photography too. She would want to continue taking photos whether or not she ever made it a step further in her goal to be a professional photographer. She'd been putting so much pressure on herself to win the competition, to build a career as a photographer, as if that would validate who she was as a person. Being a photographer was part of who she was, like being best friends with Mia, or having brown eyes. She didn't need to justify it by getting paid or prove that she was good enough at it by having strangers appreciate it. Photography was a passion, a talent, a skill, but most importantly it was a way she enjoyed seeing the world. A lens, just like her ropes-course training or her place in her own family. It was a lens she wanted to share with people beyond her family and friends, but if no one else ever saw her photos, she shouldn't stop. She wouldn't be whole if she did. She just had to make the time, no matter her day job.

There was a peace in that. It filled her with a warmth and a well-being that permeated from her chest to her fingertips.

Checking a shot on her camera, she smiled. It captured exactly how the drummer with the llama mask made her feel entertained and curious. That was what all those technically perfect photos she'd been taking lately lacked. An emotional component.

A shadow flickered and got her attention. The drummer with the llama mask played here often and loved bringing joy to people but was shy and was trying to work up the nerve to ask the hippie who sold jewelry down the street on a date. She'd been there every day this week trying to find her chance. She'd work up the nerve tomorrow, and the hippie would say yes. Alexis laughed. That was what was missing from her magic too. She needed to feel what was behind the images.

All around her the shadows came into focus and the exposure sharpened. She used the way she thought about light, shadows, and cameras to exert some control over what she was seeing. Mentally shifting through the shadows of the people on the street, none of their stories came in as clearly as the drummer's, but the understanding and control remained. The power of her magic became something she could do instead of something that was being done to her. Without her photography training, years of practice, and hard work, she'd never have figured it out.

Today might be daunting and difficult, but it was the path for her. Brian couldn't save his family without her. That was as clear as the sunlight across his dark hair as he kicked a soccer ball with some teens.

Her phone rang. The light changed. Brian's shadow turned dark, and ice crystallized across its surface.

Alexis waved Brian over and handed him the phone. The light breeze turned cold, and goosebumps marred her arms.

"Nick," he said, looking at the caller ID.

Alexis nodded. Brian answered the phone with one hand and took her hand in his other. His fingers laced with hers, solid in a world of turbulent shadows.

"This is Brian." He leaned close so she could hear both sides of the conversation over the laughter of a family nearby.

"Good. Just checking to make sure you and the Compass are on your way," Alexis could hear Nick say.

In the shadows around Brian, Nick flickered in black-and-white across the pavement, easier to make out now that she knew what he looked like.

"Yes. Is my family still okay?" Brian asked.

"They are. We've discussed what it will take to keep them that way."

"I'm doing everything you've asked. I want to talk to them."

"Fine. Here's your littlest sister."

"Brian?" a girl's voice asked. The shadows around them flickered, and Alexis could make out layers of closely knit family.

"I'm here, Em. You okay?" Brian asked.

"We're okay. Just really looking forward to getting out of here tonight. This place is *boring*."

Alexis caught a reflection of what looked like an office space with chessboard-patterned carpet and a cubical behind the girl. Mentally, Alexis shifted the angle, searching for clues. So much easier now that she knew what she was doing, but it could only take her so far when she didn't know what to look for.

"Are you playing cards to pass the time?" Brian asked.

"Nah. Even if we had cards, I'd just end up drawing the three of diamonds or five of spades again."

"Enough," Nick's voice said. "They'll continue to be fine as long as you do as I say. I assume since this number still works, the girl is still with you?"

"Yes. But she's not a problem. I needed a ride, though, so she's giving me a lift. She'll just drop me off."

Not holding her breath during the following silence was hard.

Finally, Nick said, "Fine. When will you be in Baltimore?"

"I'll be there in time."

"Go to the National Aquarium. I'll text you the details for how to get your ticket. There is an event being held there this evening. You'll have to go through security to get in, so don't try anything. I'll meet you at the top level of the rainforest exhibit."

Alexis nodded when he looked at her.

"I'll be there."

He hung up the phone and reached to give it to her, but Alexis couldn't take her eyes off his shadow. She could see Nick with the Compass and the consequences that saturated her vision.

Crimson liquid spilled across the stones. Pale tendrils fed on it and rose up in the shadows, ensnaring everything they touched. Around her black-and-white reflections of strangers and people she loved all screamed silently in terror. The angry tendrils snagged the reflections with teeth like thorns. They melded with each person before rotting them away, leaking an ocean of life's blood. The metallic scent filled her nose and mouth. Choking, Alexis fell to her knees.

Brian caught her and pulled her to him. Alexis buried her face against his chest. It was like her whole immune system was under attack. Everything around her shook. No. She was the one shaking.

The rest of the world was still. Nothing had changed. Not in the world everyone else could see. But in the other world, the world of magic futures, the blood lit on fire and consumed the buildings along the harbor.

Twenty

Brian

Saturday, 6:32 p.m.

Inner Harbor

Baltimore, MD

Brian held Alexis tightly. He wanted desperately to demand what was wrong. Had something terrible happened to his family? It couldn't have; Em had sounded okay. Brian shoved his own worries away. There was nothing he could do for his family at the moment, but there was something he could do for Alexis now.

Murmuring soft reassurances into her hair, he held her and waited. Slowly, her trembling stopped, and her breathing shifted from gasps to long inhalations and exhalations.

She looked up at him. Her brown eyes were dark with fear. "We can't give him the Compass. We can't." Two tears spilled down her cheeks.

"We aren't planning to, remember? What did you see?" he asked tightly, fighting panic. He began counting his own breathing.

She closed her eyes and took another deep breath, as if trying to sort out everything she'd seen. Brian had to restrain himself from shaking her; it felt like the only way to get an answer. She let out a long, slow breath, then opened her eyes. The pain in her face punched him in the gut.

"I saw what happens if he gets the Compass," she said, her voice barely above a whisper. "Magic will be released unchecked. It will spread and devour the world. All these people." She waved a vague hand at the children playing, couples strolling, and the two police officers walking by. "All these people will be destroyed. Devoured. It was like my nightmare, but this time I could taste it." She shuddered.

"I'm not handing over the Compass," Brian insisted.

"Even if it's the only way?"

"I'm not losing my family." The words might have come out as a growl.

She looked at him with tears still falling. "If he gets the Compass, there will be no world for them to live in."

"What the hell is that supposed to mean?"

"I don't know. Don't know how to explain, but I don't think you can go to the exchange tonight."

If she had stabbed him in the back, it couldn't have hurt more. He wanted to push her away, but he doubted her knees would hold her. "You don't understand!"

"I wish I didn't. I saw the people here, and Mia, I saw my own family. Everyone lost to darkness." Alexis buried her face into his chest. "If you give him the Compass, there'll be no world for anyone. Just rivers of blood."

"Does that mean our plan fails? The fake compass doesn't buy us enough time, and handing over the real one is the only way to save them?"

"I don't know."

Brian wanted to demand she tell him what she did know, but that wouldn't help. Instead, he wrapped her close; he was no longer sure which one of them was holding up the other. He could smell the cucumber scent of her shampoo and the bite of the water off the bay. Around them people talked and laughed, unaware that his world had just crashed down around him.

"How the hell could anyone want that? The death of all these people, I mean. Is Nick crazy?"

Alexis just held him tighter, evidently assuming it was a rhetorical question. Brian guessed in a way it was. It didn't really matter why this was happening. It was. They stood together, looking out over the water, but he was barely aware of her and didn't see the water at all. If he were to give it any thought at all, numb wouldn't seem like a strong-enough word to describe how he was feeling.

One thought started to filter through his haze. There had to be a way. Alexis had to be misunderstanding what she was seeing. One magical artifact, especially one as basic as a compass, couldn't end the world, no matter whose hands it was in.

"I wish like crazy that I'm wrong, but I'm not," Alexis said softly, wiping her tears away. "It's only been a few days, but I know what I'm doing now. Give him the Compass, and you lose your family and the rest of the world to the worst magic has to offer."

"What can we do?"

"We can take another look at our plan and see what we missed."

"We should have stayed with the Guard. That's what they wanted all along."

Alexis shook her head.

A cell phone ring jarred them.

He glanced down at her cell, still in his hand. "Zach."

She just watched him. He pulled her close with his left arm, not wanting to see the misery in her face, and answered the phone with his right hand. "Yes?"

"What did you do?" Zach asked.

"Nothing."

"Something's changed," Zach insisted.

"What do you mean?" All he was doing was standing in Baltimore with Alexis. The Compass was still safe. He hadn't done anything . . . yet.

"I can see the end of the world. An actual apocalypse, but I don't see a single zombie or demon anywhere. And since there's no news on the radio about an impending nuclear war, I assume it's something you've done."

Brian let out a long breath; his last shred of hope that Alexis was reading the shadow wrong slipped away. The stupid, scary stories he and his sisters had made fun of as they got older were actually true. Magic really was a destructive force that no longer had a place on Earth. Letting more loose really could end the world. But they couldn't be right. It couldn't be his family's life for the world. This couldn't be happening.

"Nick just called," he admitted at last. "He set a place for the meet."

He could almost hear Zach thinking.

The silence ate away at Brian. "I guess Elliot's stories are true then, not just some excuse to keep us from running up and down the halls when we were kids?"

Zach snorted with surprised laughter. "My mom told him he had to stop scaring us with those stories when I was seven." Then his voice turned serious. "Shit, I think you're right. But if those stories are even half true we're in deep shit."

Alexis looked up at Brian. "Can the Guard help?" she asked.

Zach must have heard her, because he answered. "No. I'm struggling to see almost anything, but Alexis is right, I don't think it's a good idea for you to return to the Guard just yet. There is something very wrong here. It's subtle, but it's there. Trouble is, at the moment Elliot's anger is blotting out everything around him. He was furious you were gone this morning, and then that we couldn't find the Compass in the marsh. It took both Seth and Terra to calm him down. Seth is still glued to his side. But if it turns out the Guard can help . . . well, we'll see you soon enough. We're on our way to Baltimore to try to intercept you."

"Are you in the car with other Guards right now?" Brian asked.

"No. Nearly got sick a few minutes ago. Felt like I got hit by a wave of blood and rotting flesh. I'm in a gas-station bathroom now, trying not to vomit my lunch. I don't know how to fix this mess, but you better do it soon."

Brian pulled Alexis more securely against his side.

"What the hell am I supposed to do?" he asked.

"Did you ask to speak to someone in your family? Did they pass you a message?"

"Yes, but nothing helpful."

"I'll be there soon enough. If I can help, you know how to reach me. Got to go. Elliot and Seth are coming to check on me." Zach hung up.

Brian stared at the phone for a long time. They couldn't seriously expect him to choose between his family and the world. Between them and the lives of all these people around him. He couldn't do it. His mind literally couldn't contemplate those kinds of stakes. Couldn't untangle all the consequences.

His knees started to give way. Blackness infiltrated the edges of his vision. He was going to lose everything. There was going to be nothing left.

"Brian!" Alexis said, as if she were repeating herself, trying desperately to get his attention.

He was leaning heavily on her now, but he couldn't find the strength not to. Couldn't find a reason not to.

Somehow, she got him to a bench. They sat down together, awkwardly, and he rested his head between his knees. He concentrated on one breath at a time. Slowly, his vision cleared. Eventually he was able to sit up again.

Numb, his fingers, toes, and even his face felt as if they belonged to someone else. Just a few moments ago he'd been talking to Em, and she'd sounded so alive.

"Stop it," Alexis snapped.

He looked blankly at her. He was never going to hug his parents again. Never going to hear Vicky give another long-winded explanation of a book she was reading.

"It's going to be okay."

"Ha." He knew a platitude when he heard one. "If I give Nick the Compass, the world is dead, if I don't my family is."

"We'll figure out what we've missed and fix it."

"Sure, how?" he said sarcastically, just for the sake of arguing. It was better than thinking, after all.

"Let's start with the message Em sent you."

He shrugged. "She said it was boring, so they're being held in a standard office building. Three of diamonds meant a brick building, third floor. Five of spades means there are, on average, five bad guys with guns. She didn't have a chance to pass more info, even if there was more to say. But none of that helps us, there have to be a million brick office buildings in the city alone."

"You have a secret code to pass information?"

"We used it more as a game. I never expected it would actually be something we needed. Not that it's helped."

"Every bit of information helps. *Office building* supports what I saw in the shadows when you talked to her. I don't know what we're going to do with it yet, but it helps."

Brian gave her a look to clearly express just how little faith he had in her words.

"We just haven't gotten the plan quite right yet," she countered. "I'll know it as soon as I see it. Remember? Know your strengths and weaknesses. My strength is that I'll be able to recognize it. I think seeing magic for us is like using peripheral vision. When we're stressed we get tunnel vision, but if we can find a calm space within and relax, we can see a panorama without moving our heads. You find that peace in movement. I can find it in photography. I've got this."

Brian fought the urge to point out that at lunch she'd not been able to read a single shadow, much less see a plan. The part about magic made sense, but inner peace didn't have an on/off switch.

"Since we can't give him the Compass, there's nothing we can do if things go sideways." Brian didn't realize he meant it until he'd said it. It was true though. It wasn't his family or the world. If there was no world, there would be no place for his family. They would be lost too. If it had just been Alexis saying it, maybe he could have dismissed it, but the fact that Zach saw it also . . . no. There was no way to get his family back.

"We don't need the Compass to go to the meeting. There will be a way to save your family. I'll see it." Alexis sounded like she believed what she was saying, but Brian couldn't. His positivity had stretched beyond its limits, snapping like a rubber band and smacking the shit out of him.

Alexis didn't seem discouraged by his silence. "We know Nick would rather not kill your family, that gives us an advantage."

Something terrible and violent stirred in Brian. He'd never believed in revenge. Always thought it was a dumb idea. Letting go and moving on always seemed a healthier life choice, but maybe it was time to reconsider.

"Crap!" Alexis said. "Careful, does that guy look familiar? The one who looks like a bear."

Trying to look casual, he checked over his shoulder. *Shit!* He ducked lower on the bench, trying to hide behind her. "It's one of Nick's hired guys."

"That's not good."

"Of course, it's not good!"

She gave him a look that made him want to shake her again.

"What is it?" he demanded.

Alexis tried to hide behind her hair. "He doesn't like that your family's seen his face. He's afraid Nick's plan will land him and his friend in prison. He's hoping to kill all of you instead. Let's move before he spots us."

He took her hand and followed.

Twenty-One

The restaurant was on a roof deck overlooking the bay. They'd chosen the spot for the view, not the expensive food. It appeared to be a good call, considering the way Alexis kept scanning the people below. Brian picked at his overly fancy hamburger; nothing about it was appealing, but he'd gotten it because of Alexis's pestering. And because she was right, he did need to keep up his strength. He ate one of the mushrooms that had slid out of the bun but couldn't make himself go back for a second one.

"Okay, we know Nick doesn't want to hurt your family. That makes his hired guns the real problem," Alexis said. "Well, and that shadow figure with the knife."

"He can destroy the world, but doesn't want to hurt a couple of hostages?" Brian countered.

She shrugged. "I don't understand the logic, but he doesn't want to hurt your family. That part, at least, is clear in the shadows."

"Just because he doesn't want to hurt them doesn't mean he won't."

She winced a little. "True, but I don't think he will intentionally kill them. That gives our Fake Compass Plan a good chance of working."

He shrugged. "So, what do we do about his hired guns? None of my magic blocks bullets. And we didn't find a spell in that book that could."

"Yeah, that's more of a police thing."

"I know, you'd rather call the FBI."

Alexis gave a one-shoulder shrug and looked away. "I get why we can't. Magic and all."

She looked so sad and drained, Brian pushed aside his own pain and searched for anything to lighten the mood a bit. "Too bad Storm isn't here. I bet she could handle guys with guns. She can go through walls and burn her hoofprints into wood, after all."

Alexis grinned briefly, but an idea seemed to spark behind it. "I wonder—"

Her phone rang. "Mia," Alexis said to him before answering it.

Brian wasn't sure exactly what it meant when Alexis started taking notes, but it had to be a good sign that she started to ask about brick office buildings. He leaned back in his chair, and his french fries looked interesting. He tried one. Not too shabby. The Old Bay seasoning was a nice touch. He reached for the ketchup.

"Thank you, Mia, this is super helpful! Do you have time to check into one more thing for me?" Alexis said, causing Brian to look up from his last fry. "An event at the aquarium tonight? Yes.

Thanks. Bye." Alexis leaned back in her chair and looked over at Brian. "Okay."

"A good okay?" He asked.

"A very good okay. Mia's a ninja master when it comes to social media. Nick's father has an office in Baltimore. It recently moved to the sixteenth floor of a high rise, but he still owns the building where his office used to be. It's an empty, three-story brick building. From the pictures Mia found on the rental site, it looks like it has the same black-and-white-patterned carpets I saw in the shadows." Alexis showed him the photos Mia had texted.

"Bloody hell!" Brian exclaimed.

Alexis grinned. "Exactly!"

"Why are we still sitting here? Let's go."

"I don't think we can risk it. The building is halfway across town, and by the time we Uber there . . . If we're wrong, it'll take too long to get back. There are too many variables. We'll need to be here, ready for the exchange."

Brian didn't like it. He checked the time. They could probably make it, but it was a big gamble. "If we're right, we can't just sit here."

"Do you think Zach would be willing to check it out?"

"Oh." Brian let out a long breath. "Of course."

Alexis handed him the phone.

Brian took a half second to weigh texting versus calling. Zach picked up on the second ring.

"Now's not a great time," Zach said. "I'm in the car."

"I think we know where my family is being held," Brian replied.

"Oh?"

Alexis waved to get his attention and said softly. "Zach's not the one calling the shots, we're going to have to convince someone on the Council."

Brian nodded and said to Zach, "Who's right next to you? Can I talk to them?"

"Elliot is, but Terra is riding shotgun up front. Let me give you her."

"Thanks."

"Hello," Terra said, sounding official.

"Hi, it's Brian." He thought about apologizing for running off, but he wasn't sorry, besides that wasn't what was important. "We figured out where Nick is holding my family. Alexis and I need to be here to stall for time if something goes wrong. Can you please go see if you can get to them before Nick moves them for the exchange?"

There was a long pause. "Where are you?"

"Alexis and I are safe," Brian said, intentionally misunderstanding. "So is the Compass. I'm doing the very best I can, I promise. I won't jeopardize the whole world for my family, but I'm willing to do whatever else it takes to get them back. Please, please, see if you can rescue them now."

Brian's skin started to itch while he waited for Terra to say something. Alexis reached across the table and put her hand on his arm; his skin was humming with a low glow. He took a deep breath. Her fingers were warm on his forearm. Glancing up, he was caught by her eyes.

They weren't a single color of brown, and for a moment he was utterly distracted by the shades in them and at the same time completely aware of the person they belonged to and the empathy radiating from her.

"It's not going to be an easy sell," Terra said. "We're at the Inner Harbor, and Seth just found a parking place. What if we get the Compass from you and then go look for your family?"

Brian didn't need to check with Alexis to know that wasn't a good idea. "There isn't time. Zach knows I'm right," he gambled.

Elliot could be heard in the background wanting to know who was on the phone. Then Terra must have put her hand over the phone, because everything on her end became muffled.

Finally, Terra came back. "We'll send someone to go with you to talk to Nick."

"No, Nick thinks I'm working alone, it needs to stay that way. Chances are good he'll recognize Guard members. Alexis"—he started to say she was a Shadow, but she shook her head hard—"she's got my back. Besides, I won't need to go to the meeting if you can get to my family first."

There was more muffled conversation, or loud debating, before Terra said, "Text the address. We'll go now."

"Thank you!"

Grinning, he ended the call and handed back the phone. "They're on it." He picked up his burger. Chewing thoughtfully, his mind was conjuring up images of pulling Alexis close when this was over and kissing her until they were both senseless. He would run his hands through her hair and then down her body. Slowly he'd undo the buttons of her flannel shirt. He looked into her face to see if her mind was on a similar path. He let out a long, steadying breath, trying to cool his racing blood, when he noticed she had the faraway look she got when reading shadows. And she was frowning.

He was forced to clear his throat before he could ask, "What is it?"

"I can't tell if that will work or not." Her frown deepened.

"Hey, that's why we have a backup plan. You and me. We got this."

Like he was hoping, she smiled.

Somehow or another, they'd get through this. Without hope, they didn't stand a chance, so he let himself believe. Even if it hurt more later.

"Right. Together." Alexis laced her fingers with his.

Unbidden, green tendrils of magic unwound from his center, dancing like sunlight and static electricity across his skin. They wove geometric designs down his arm and around her wrist. Slowly, they melted back into him, but marks were left on both their wrists, as if they'd gotten matching forest-green bracelet tattoos with a Celtic design.

"Can you see that?" he asked.

"Yes. What happened?"

"I don't know." But it was something important. As if their lives were now entwined in a way that extended beyond this moment. Beyond this crazy weekend. Beyond whatever would happen next. Beyond the possible end of the world.

She let go of his hand to examine the mark. "Mia is going to be so impressed that I got a tattoo."

The absurdity caught Brian off guard. He laughed. As she laughed with him, something terrible inside his chest eased.

Alexis grinned mischievously at him. "So, here's what I'm thinking."

Twenty-Two

Alexis changed quickly in the restaurant bathroom, while Brian went to find the drop point for the ticket Nick had texted about. She was glad she always packed a nice shirt just in case. This time it was emerald green, with a scoop neck, and a fitted shape that flattered her curves. Her jeans were black, but a far cry from black tie. To compensate, she had her student ID clipped to a belt loop and her camera around her neck. Perhaps not the most exciting cover, but sticking as close to the truth as possible seemed like the advice given to undercover characters on every TV show she'd ever seen. She didn't like that this was the most sane part of their plan.

Walking to the aquarium, she watched the play of shadows across the ground, trying to figure out her best approach. Everything was more precise after Brian's magic had connected them with the magic tattoos, as if she were using a high-end camera. It was a good thing, because otherwise she might have missed the flicker of light. Looking closer, she saw herself later grabbing her backpack from behind a rock. Grateful to have a place to put it, she slipped her pack behind the rock in the shadowed garden by the aquarium.

Straightening her shoulders, she headed forward again. Glancing at the green twine of magic, still visible on her wrist, a smile touched her lips. But now wasn't the time to start dreaming about a future with him. Now was the time to find a way into the exchange.

One of the shadows of the people around the aquarium was brighter and more inviting than the others. Alexis headed for the tall man casting it. He was one of four people standing near the smaller entrance; the clipboard and headset distinguished him and his colleagues from security.

"Hi." She forced herself to stand to her full height and smile. "I'm Alexis." She put out a hand.

Politeness overcame the fact that he clearly had no idea who she was. He shook her hand. "What can I do for you?" The words were friendly, but the tone was frosty.

What had she been thinking? *This isn't going to work.* Up close she could see just how much security the place had. *Head up.* "I'm a finalist in a national photojournalism competition. I'm on fall break and am trying to get the perfect shot. I just learned about this amazing fundraiser, and I was wondering if there was any way I could talk to some of the people involved?"

Within five minutes of chatting, she found out he was an alumnus of her school, and that he knew several of her teachers. His sister was a journalist for a radio show in Wisconsin, and his dad was an amateur photographer. The world could be a very small place if one could find the right vantage point to see it from. *Thank you, shadows!*

By the end of six minutes, he was happy to help. Without quite understanding how it had happened, Alexis had a press pass from a local paper that had bailed on covering the fundraiser. She promised to show the amazing things the hospital was doing with pediatric medicine. Her research had paid off, allowing her to sound like she knew what she was talking about. She had enough connections at the school paper that she was pretty sure she could keep her promise, but it still felt wrong.

Pushing away guilt, she went to find Brian.

Twenty-Three

The invitation was waiting for Brian exactly where Nick's text had said it would be, along with the neatly packed clothes. He quickly changed into the black-tie appropriate shirt and suit. The clothes should have given him confidence, but mostly they gave him a nau-seating sense of unease.

Alexis wolf whistled when he came out of the bathroom. "Nice."

He smiled briefly, but shifted his shoulders against the tightness of the suit jacket. "I wondered if James Bond was ever this uncom-fortable."

"He wears custom-fit jackets, not one stashed above bathroom ceiling tiles. Still, Nick did a decent job guessing your size."

"It seems like a lot of work for Nick to go through for a hostage exchange?"

"The clothes will keep you from standing out. It looks like Nick is serious about keeping everyone honest. This event is exclusive. Nick probably only has access to it because his family donates to the hospital. And there's a lot of security. No way you could bring the Guard to the exchange. But that works to our advantage, too, because I don't think he can bring his mercenaries either."

"I've heard of using charitable donations to get out of taxes, but for a hostage exchange? That really takes philanthropy to a new level. You'll be able to get in, though?" He took a moment to really look at her, and his mind started to slide away from where it needed to be. "You look nice." *And that's an understatement.* She was curvier than her flannel shirts let on, and he had to pull his eyes away from her hint of cleavage.

"Thanks. Yeah, I was able to get a press badge." But she was still frowning. "Any word from Zach?"

"Not yet."

"I don't want to do this if we don't have to."

"I get that." He pulled her phone out of his pocket and checked it again. "It's almost time, what's taking them so long?"

Alexis shrugged. "Maybe that's a good sign. Maybe they found them and are dealing with getting them out of there."

The phone rang. Brian almost dropped it. Hastily he answered. "Zach!"

"Sorry, we missed them. They were here. I can see that in the shadows, but we missed them. I'm so sorry," Zach said.

Brian covered the phone and cussed with all the fluency he had in several languages. Inhaling slowly, he tried to breathe around his tie before accepting Alexis's outstretched hand. Alexis laced her fingers with his.

Resigned, Brian lifted the phone back to his ear. "It's okay, it was a long shot. I'm glad to know we tried another way. In the meanwhile, we've got a backup plan."

"I really am sorry. Seth tried to help, he gave us directions for the fastest way, but there was construction and a detour. Anyway, Brian . . . Heads up—after Seth told us how to get across town, he got out of the car. He's in the Inner Harbor, trying to find you. He wants to help. It was the only way everyone would agree to go after your family—he had to stay and try to protect the Compass."

"Thanks for letting me know. This is a big place. We haven't seen any sign of him yet."

"Tell Zach we're at the aquarium," Alexis said.

Since Zach and the others wouldn't be able to make it back in time to help or hinder, Brian passed that along.

"I gotta go," Brian finished. "Time's up," he added to Alexis. *Or close enough.* He didn't want to be late.

She didn't acknowledge his comment, too busy frowning at his leather cuff.

"Doesn't really go with the suit," he joked. It also felt wrong on his right wrist. His left arm was healing, but it wasn't there yet.

"I could . . ." She hesitated, took a deep breath, and then tried again. "I could hold on to that for you. Just in case."

"In case I'm tempted to risk the world for my family's lives?" He didn't notice the anger in his own voice until she paled. Fighting with his tie, he tried again to take a deep breath. Finally, he was able to fill his lungs and control a long exhale. He had to get a grip; his emotions were shifting faster than he could handle.

"I get what's at stake," he said by way of an apology. "I won't hand it over to Nick no matter what." He prayed he wasn't lying. "But I've given an oath to protect it. I won't let it out of my sight."

She rubbed her forehead. "I get that. I've just got a bad feeling we're missing something." She must have seen something of his thought in his face because she hastily added. "We're almost there. We've got a good plan. Here's the decoy compass."

He took the makeshift device. It had the authoritative gravity of the metal case, with the impressive makeshift internal workings they'd thrown together at dinner.

"You've got your invitation?" Alexis asked.

"Check," Brian said.

"Magic earbuds?"

He offered a pair to her, while putting his own in.

"Check," he said mentally.

"Check," she said in the same way and grinned. The smile brightened her eyes and eased some of the tightness in his chest.

"I think you're set," she said out loud.

"Almost. *A kiss for good luck?*"

She leaned up to meet him halfway. For a moment Brian let himself forget everything but her lips and body against his. For a moment, all was right in their corner of the world.

Too soon, though, she leaned back. "Check."

He laughed. Not a bad way to start a rescue mission. "See you on the other side."

"This is our best shot," she said.

He wasn't sure which one of them she was trying to convince.

She headed for the aquarium without looking back.

Brian set his shoulders and walked, breathing the way he did when swimming laps. Each breath, each pause connected him to the present.

The strands of magic came into focus. There seemed to be more than there were before, or perhaps they were just becoming easier to see. He found the bundle that tied him to his family and traced a finger along it as far as he could reach. They were close.

He looked up at the aquarium. The side facing him looked like a cross between a skyscraper and a greenhouse. Modern glass panels reached perhaps five stories high. The rainforest behind it was illuminated softly, but enough to be visible through the condensation on the glass. There was something terrible about using such a magnificent, creative building for a hostage exchange.

Brian squared his shoulders and walked up to the front doors. Fifteen minutes and counting.

Twenty-Four

"*I'm in,*" Alexis thought as clearly as she could.

"*Good. No sign of Nick yet.*" Brian's thoughts came in crystal clear.

She worked her way around groups of women wearing shoes she'd only ever seen worn by actresses on TV and men who looked their equals. Laughter and conversation sparkled around her, but she tuned it all out to concentrate on the shadows across the floor and the reflections off aquatic tanks. The blue glow at the heart of an invisible thunderstorm was here somewhere.

She saw traces of him darkening the shadows of other people and flickers of polished steel, but where was Nick? She swallowed hard.

Cinnamon, she could taste it in the air. *Why am I tasting cinna-mon?* She cast a table of appetizers a nasty look before she shook the thought.

A flash of red and white caught her attention. A huge lionfish swimming in the middle of a circular tank, but there would be time to investigate another day. The storm cloud had to be her focus.

Arms of a dark rain cloud indicated the way. Just ahead, through another exhibit. There he was, a pinnacle of blond hair and dark suit amongst a hurricane of anger and fear. Nick was in a group of talking people, but he was cut adrift from all of them.

Alexis swallowed hard. She cringed away from him, from his pain. She was horrified at the realization. *What is wrong with me?* Usually, people in pain drew her to help, but his pain was twisted and warped into a toxic cloud of rage.

The crowd around him seemed to feel the same way, because they receded like a wave from the shore. Leaving him as physically alone as his shadow. Nick didn't seem to notice. He checked his watch and looked in the direction of the rainforest exhibit. Up close she could see he had dark circles under bloodshot eyes.

"*I see him,*" she thought to Brian.

"*Can you get a read?*"

Alexis frowned; she couldn't see anything useful through the churning layers of his shadow. "*On my way.*" She forced herself to step forward.

Nick would have brushed right by her, but Alexis stuck out her hand. "Hi, I'm Alexis."

He automatically shook her hand. Alexis was braced, but invisible lightning burned down her arm like acid. He jerked back; she didn't try to hold on. She shifted her feet, so they were better planted, and refused to let the darkness block out her other thoughts.

"Excuse me," he said and walked off. He glanced back once, as if to try and figure out who or what she was, but he checked his watch again and kept going.

Alexis leaned against an information panel about the water cycle and tried to catch her breath. Her heart was loud enough that she wouldn't have been surprised if Brian could hear it. There was a lot going on in Nick's shadow, but she tried to bring the answer to one question into focus. *Where is Brian's family?* The image floated up through the storm, like the answer in a Magic 8-Ball.

They were outside with Nick's hired hands. Brian wouldn't be anywhere near to help them.

Twenty-Five

Brian
Saturday, 9:04 p.m.
Inner Harbor
Baltimore, MD

"He's headed your way." Alexis's voice was clear in Brian's head. *"I got something. Call for help and stall."*

Just like they planned, he wrapped his hand around one of the strands connected to him and made a mental call for help. There hadn't been time to test it before, but Alexis sounded confident it would work. He took a deep breath, let go of the strand, and clenched the railing tightly in both hands. His eyes might be looking out over a man-made rainforest filled with plants and animals, but he didn't see any of it.

"Glad you're on time."

Brian spun to find Nick standing on the other side of the platform, looking far too calm and in control. No one else was nearby; most of the guests were inside, where the hors d'oeuvres, drinks, and aquatic animals were.

"Where's my family?"

Nick appeared to send a text message before waving at the big windows beyond the plants. "Right over there."

His family and two mercs walked into the glow of a light, making them visible, despite the reflection from inside. The mercenary with the scar said something. Em waved before they walked into the darkness.

"All safe and sound. Now where's the Compass?" Nick said.

"They're outside," Brian thought.

"I'm on it. Stall," Alexis thought back.

Brian wished that he was the one outside, risking his life for his family, while Alexis stood here and distracted Nick. But this is where he was, so he had better do his best. "Do you know what it'll mean if more magic gets out?"

"I'm not here to have a philosophical debate with you. I'm here because we both want something the other has."

"But this isn't some abstract thing. Magic will destroy the world."

Nick scoffed. "It's part of the world. That's like saying thermodynamics or gravity will destroy us. Get over yourself."

Brian wracked his brain for a way to explain. "DC used to be a swamp. Swamps are good and a natural part of the environment, that doesn't mean we can return DC to being a swamp overnight without destroying the city. What you're trying to do is way bigger than that."

"I don't care."

The chill of his words made the hairs on the back of Brian's neck prickle. "How many people will have to die so that you can get what you want?"

Nick's eyes narrowed. "Would you like me to start with your family?"

Alexis said she was sure he wouldn't hurt them, but standing there, face-to-face with Nick, Brian wasn't nearly as confident.

"Fine," Nick said. "I'll just text the mercs. Hope that wave was enough of a goodbye for you."

The blood drained from Brian's face. "Stop! Fine. I did the best I could." He offered up the metal compass.

"Brian, don't!" The words jarred Brian, and apparently Nick, too, because they both spun to look at the newcomer on the platform.

"Seth?" Brian tried to figure out how the Council member had gotten inside.

"You can't give him the Compass," Seth said.

Taking a deep breath, Brian made up his mind. Well, I'm supposed to stall. He channeled his improv skills and prayed Nick would buy it. He turned to Seth. "You'd trade my family's lives for some relic!"

"I'd trade their lives so that everyone else on the planet can survive. We couldn't survive another Dark Age," Seth pleaded.

"Shut up!" Nick said. "Stay out of this, Dr. Murphy. Brian, you have five seconds. I'll have them kill the youngest first."

Brian didn't let him reach three. If Nick was lying, he was very good, and that was a gamble he wasn't willing to take. He handed over the metal compass.

Nick snatched it. Triumph filled his face.

"No!" Seth said.

Brian held his breath.

Nick turned over the compass, then he flipped it open. He pulled the piece of guitar string out and turned it one way, then the other. Fury darkened his face.

"What the hell?" Nick growled. "You're playing games with your family's lives." He reached for his cell.

"*Alexis!*" Brian mentally shouted. "*Time's up!*"

Twenty-Six

Trying not to draw attention to herself, Alexis strode toward the stairs. Seven semesters of college and a rather ordinary life didn't qualify her to rescue anyone held at gunpoint, but they were running out of options.

Magic, which hadn't been there three days ago, reflected the price if she failed. She had to force herself not to shy away from the pooling blood—it wasn't really there, not yet at least. The fact that magic had spilled into the world couldn't be changed, but there was still a chance she could stop another disaster before it happened.

Alexis raced down the stairs, but stopped to fight the tight panic in her chest before stepping through the glass doors. She inhaled deeply, took the lens cap off her camera, exhaled, and then plunged forward. It was like jumping off a zipline platform, she didn't dare check how far she had to fall.

Brian's thoughts interrupted hers. He wouldn't be able to stall for long. Time was running out.

Holding her camera like a shield, she followed the shadows cast by streetlights to the two dangerous men flanking Brian's family.

She snapped a photo of the native-plant landscaping and a display about trash in the Bay. The light was terrible, but hopefully that wouldn't be the first thing on the mercenaries' minds. Turning on the flash, she shifted her camera and snapped a shot of the mercenaries.

"Hey, lady, what are you doing?" the mercenary with a scar on his square jaw demanded. *Pretty*, Alexis mentally named him.

"Sorry." But she took another picture. The flash reflected magic off the guns beneath their jackets. "I'm doing an article for my college's paper and need some general human-interest pieces about the Inner Harbor. Can I talk to you guys about it?"

"No," the bear-looking mercenary said.

"She's got a picture of us," Pretty muttered.

"Give me the camera," Bear said.

"Seriously? I can't post anything without your permission, it's not a problem. I can delete it if you'd prefer."

"Just give me the camera, lady."

"No, it's expensive." *Where*, Alexis thought, *is my backup? Did she not hear Brian's call?*

"You might want to do as he says," Brian's mom said softly.

Alexis only took a second to notice that she had Brian's hair, only hers was longer and braided back. Even as hostages, they looked like a nice family. And the shadows showed wide, woven strands of connection between them.

"Alexis!" Brian's thoughts sounded like a shout in her head.

Bear held out his hand for the camera.

"No." Alexis held it to her chest and edged toward the rock where she'd left her backpack. Preparing to scream if she had to. Someone would notice.

Pretty pulled his gun. "Just give it."

Alexis's breath caught in her throat.

Where the hell are the cops? They'd been everywhere an hour ago. *Now, Storm, please!*

The sound of hooves on stone echoed in her mind. The four beats of a gallop. The scent of rain wafted around her.

Alexis took a half breath.

"Time's up!" Brian's thoughts were frantic as they reached her.

Storm jumped out of the magical plane and landed five feet from the mercenaries. She reared and screamed like lightning.

Pretty fired the gun, already in his hand.

Storm shifted out of phase. The emptiness of the air hurt Alexis's eyes.

"I don't know what the hell is going on!" Pretty turned his gun on the rest of them. "But I've had it!"

Storm shifted into phase beside Alexis. Trusting her instincts, Alexis grabbed her backpack, jumped onto the rock, then onto Storm's back. The unicorn phased out again, taking Alexis with her.

Bear pulled his gun too. "The next person to move gets shot!"

"Hands in the air," a policeman said.

From the magical plane Alexis watched as the cops and aquarium security swarmed. A gunshot in the Inner Harbor had gotten even more attention than she'd hoped.

"You okay, Storm?" she asked, patting the unicorn's shoulder.

The unicorn snorted derisively. She was made of magic and a thunderstorm; bullets weren't a problem for her. But she was blowing hard and trembling from the exertion of shifting between planes.

Brian repeated his call for help.

"It's okay!" she thought back. *"They are safe. It worked! The cops are here."*

Alexis wanted to whoop for joy, but she wasn't sure how invisible she was. She settled for savoring the moment.

She was looking around for a place for Storm to let her off, when she noticed a substance like oil spilling across the shadow world. Storm reared and backed up like a spooked horse. Alexis tried to soothe her, while holding on tight. The oily blackness started to boil, then lit on fire.

Mouth dry and panic in her chest, Alexis thought, *"Brian! What's going on?"*

Twenty-Seven

Brian
Saturday, 9:12 p.m.
Inner Harbor
Baltimore, MD

It wasn't until the cops became visible in the glow of the lights outside that Nick seemed to understand why no one was answering his texts.

"They're safe." Relief made Brian lightheaded. "My family is safe. The police are arresting your mercenaries."

"Oh, well done! Alexis's doing, I gather?" Seth said. "Terra is convinced that she's a Shadow?"

Nick sank to the ground.

"Yes. I just needed to stall while she took care of things out there. Thanks for the help. Even if you didn't know the plan."

"You monster," Nick muttered.

"The Compass is safe?" Seth asked.

"Yep. Right here." Brian held up his wrist with the cuff on it.

"Well done. I'm really impressed. You saved everyone." Seth put out his hand to shake.

Seemed a little formal, but Brian shook Seth's hand warmly. He struggled to understand. *It actually worked!* He had to get to his family. It wouldn't feel real until he'd hugged all of them. *It's over.*

Seth unsnapped the cuff from Brian's wrist.

"What?" Brian asked, reaching to get it back.

Seth pulled a small handgun out of his suit pocket. "Try, and you'll be dead before anyone can stop me. I'd rather not go to prison, but it won't really matter if I have this. My friends will carry on the fight." He pocketed the cuff.

Alexis's panicked thoughts tore through Brian's mind.

"What are you doing?" Brian asked Seth. He didn't know what to tell Alexis.

"You're so blind, Brian. The whole Guard is. I wish I could make you see," Seth said apologetically. "Society is rotting away around us, but humanity isn't content to just destroy ourselves. We want to take Earth down with us. Magic will restore the balance. It will save us. But now's not the time for this conversation.

"Come on, Nick. Let's save your brother."

Nick took the offered hand and got to his feet.

Seth glanced at Brian sadly. "I'm sorry, but I'll have to shoot you if you follow. This is more important than any of us."

Brian stood there, his jaw literally hanging open, as Seth and Nick walked away from him with Merlin's Compass.

Alexis's thoughts screamed through his brain fog, trying to get his attention.

Twenty-Eight

Storm backed away from the spreading shadow fire.

"Easy, girl." Alexis held on tighter as the unicorn shied. "It's just shadows, there's not really any fire there." Suddenly she wasn't so sure. Maybe it could hurt Storm. *Brian!* she thought-yelled again.

"Seth . . . he took the Compass." His thoughts were soft, but crystal clear.

"Seth?!"

"He played me. He played all of us."

Storm did a swift sidestep, almost unseating Alexis. Taking a big handful of mane to stay on, Alexis thought back over Seth's shadow, looking for a clue she'd missed. *"I never got a good read of his shadow. He was always hiding it behind Elliot's fear of magic."*

"What are you doing?" Alexis asked Storm as the unicorn shied again.

Storm snorted and then spun. She must have used her magic, because Alexis didn't slide this time.

"We can't go this way." A sheer, three-foot drop to the channel was directly in front of them. "How about the bridge?" But the magical fire cut them off while she spoke.

"*Alexis?*" Brian asked.

Storm nickered and collected herself.

Alexis realized what was going to happen a moment before they were in the air. She bit back her scream and held on tight.

The water was dark. It splashed around them and came up to Alexis's waist. Icy water bit into Alexis's jeans, stinging like a thousand needles. She held her camera over her head with one hand and held on tight to Storm's mane with the other.

"What the hell did you do that for?" Alexis asked.

Storm tossed her head at the fire on the shore, before swimming under the bridge.

"*Alexis?*" Brian repeated.

"*I'm okay,*" Alexis answered, trying very hard not to think about what was in the water.

"*Seth and Nick are leaving. We can't let them get away with the Compass.*"

"*I'm under a bridge, invisible. I don't know what the hell I'm supposed to do about it at this precise moment. Sorry. I was supposed to be saying that just in my head, but . . .*"

"*I get it. But under a bridge?*"

"*You'd think trolls were the only thing that hid under bridges. I guess unicorns do too.*"

"*Huh?*"

"Don't ask. Why do I smell cinnamon?" It was clear and distinctive, despite the fishy scent of bay water. Alexis tilted her head, thinking. Then she heard them.

"Are you okay?" Seth asked.

"Just trying to understand."

Alexis recognized Nick's voice.

"You were playing both sides," Nick said. It sounded like a neutral statement; she wished it was an accusation.

"I wanted to tell you." Seth sounded apologetic.

"Seth smells like cinnamon, the way Storm smells like rain," Alexis realized.

"You see him?" Brian asked.

"Yes, well, no. I can hear him. Shhh."

"Why didn't you get the Compass yourself? Instead of telling me about it?" Nick said. "You made it sound like you wanted magic to help my brother, but couldn't find any."

"I was hoping not to lose my ties to the Guard. This is just the beginning of the magic revolution. I couldn't take the Compass from the Weavers without giving myself away. Had you scared the Weavers into putting the Compass and the First Knot into the Guard's vault, I could have risked sneaking them out. I'd complained enough about the bad security to make an outside theft believable. Let's stop here for a minute and try it."

Alexis breathed as quietly as possible. They had to be almost directly overhead.

"Oh," Nick said, his voice so soft Alexis had to strain to hear. "It's just like you described."

"I haven't seen it in years, but yes. The instruction manual was a little unclear." Seth trailed off, clearly working.

"You didn't think I'd be able to get the Compass and Knot myself?" Nick's voice was cold again.

"That would have worked, too. I was concerned when you only got the Knot. We need the Compass to find the rest of the magic. One or two Knots aren't enough. As you've already seen. And Brian found Alexis, making everything more difficult."

"The one you said is a Shadow?"

"Exactly. She wouldn't admit it, but my colleague was certain she was."

"That was fast."

"A unicorn and a dog from a line of King Arthur's Shadow hounds brought them together. I'm surprised magic hasn't brought you to someone similar. But the kidnapping was inspired. You couldn't have picked better leverage against Brian if you'd known him his whole life."

"Family is important," Nick said flatly.

"It almost worked. A shame I had to blow my cover in the end."

"You're getting the magic just to help my brother and the other people at the hospital?"

"Nick, this is so much bigger than your brother. This is about the world," Seth said, his voice swelling with enthusiasm.

"Did you mean what you said about magic bringing on the next Dark Ages?"

"That's probably an underestimation, actually, but it's the change we need. Look at the Compass! I told you there was a Knot around here somewhere. Come on."

They moved out of hearing range, but Alexis had to fight to breathe. That's what the shadows were so riled up about. A new Knot was about to be cut.

"How are we getting out of here?" Alexis looked around at the sheer sides of the canal.

"What?" Brian asked.

"Sorry, just thinking loudly. Again. Just give me a minute."

While she was still working on a plan, Storm swam over to the side, surveyed the edge and then jumped out of the water in a way that defied physics. There was a splash, but the water stayed behind.

"Never mind, Storm knew what she was doing." Alexis patted her jeans, grateful to find them dry, and then glanced hastily around. Out of phase with the physical plane sounded fancier than invisibility, but she assumed whatever it was, it had limitations. And Nick was a Shiner, after all. If anyone could see them, it would be another magic user. Luckily, he and Seth were just ducking into a door in an old brick power plant converted to retail space, and only Seth looked back.

The numbness she'd felt from Seth taking the Compass started to wear off. She tried to fight her anger at herself for not seeing what Seth was. The way he talked about Searcha should have been a clue. He'd made their views on magic make sense to her and made the reasons for them being nuts sound overly biased. Of course, he'd wanted her to look them up. Had he hoped to recruit her? Join him instead of telling the others he was a traitor if she saw his shadow clearly? In the sterile light of the lab, without Brian beside her, she'd not been able to read his shadows, and the bastard had known it. Seth had pushed to get her tested as a Shadow, so he knew what he was dealing with. He had wanted to know when Zach would arrive so he could be on guard against him. And *The Travels of Sir Walter*. It wasn't Guard contacts that had gotten Sadie a copy in a language she had to translate instead of letting her go to Baltimore for one in English. It was Seth's contacts.

Alexis shook her head hard. Wasting energy on anger at herself didn't fix anything, but that was so much easier thought than done. It didn't help that none of her other thoughts were helpful either. Things had been bad before, but now . . . She couldn't make herself give the shadows around her more than a passing glance. Nick had wanted magic for his own use, and if people were hurt, he'd find a way to live with that. Seth wanted it to destroy civilization, to knock humanity off the top of the food pyramid. This is what her nightmare had warned her about.

Images of monsters raged around her and Storm, ghosts from long-trapped magic knots, fighting for their place in a new world, mere whispers of what they could become. Storm shuddered.

"You don't want this either." Alexis patted the unicorn's dripping neck.

Storm nickered in agreement.

The world as it was now could use adjusting, but this war, this destruction, wasn't the answer.

"What are we going to do? Seth has a gun, and Nick has magic." She didn't add that Storm was starting to tremble, and not from the chill in the air. Fatigue radiated off the unicorn like heat waves off hot pavement.

Storm sighed sadly, then nickered.

It took Alexis only a second to see what had caught Storm's attention. Terra, Zach, Elliot, and Prince were coming around a corner. The shadows were boiling too much for Alexis to get a read on anything. *Well, anything beyond the rising tide at the end of the world, that is.*

"Want to go talk to them?" Alexis asked.

Storm gave a heartbroken-sounding nicker, as if she agreed, but didn't have any hope that it would help. Somehow her mood made everything way worse. Alexis fought the bitterness at the back of her throat and the tightening of her gut. The sound of a unicorn losing hope wasn't pretty.

"Brian," she thought, needing a second opinion. *"Seth and Nick are in a bookstore not far away, looking for another Knot. Terra, Elliot, and Zach are here. Thoughts?"*

For a long moment Alexis was afraid the riled-up magic had cut their connection. At last, though, his thoughts entered her mind.

"Do you trust them? Is there more than one traitor in the Guard?"

"We can't alienate all of the Guard just because one person betrayed us. I trust them." And she did. Elliot was afraid of magic, but seeing these shadows, she now understood why it was something to fear.

Brian's thoughts sounded relieved when they reached her. *"Okay, then. Go talk to them. I'm headed your way."*

She nudged Storm to a trot. When they were close, Prince looked up and yipped with joy. Storm touched noses with him, but wouldn't phase. They were too visible here, and Storm was close to collapse. Alexis wasn't sure she could handle another phase change.

"Okay if I get off?" People weren't paying them special attention. Nice to find a use for her Intro to Psychology class. Change Blindness should be enough to keep people from noticing if she appeared out of nowhere into a group of people, but a unicorn would probably be pushing things.

Storm snorted in agreement.

Alexis slid off. As soon as her feet hit the ground she started to phase back. Stepping away from the unicorn, she became fully solid. She doubled over, braced her hands on her knees, and fought down the bile that was rising up. It was like having heat stroke and dehydration sickness all at once. Fighting to breathe, she tried not to black out.

"Alexis!" Terra reached out to help her from toppling over. "What the shit is going on?!"

Alexis blinked. She'd never heard Terra use any language that wasn't camp appropriate. Her stomach settled into place. Storm nickered worriedly.

"Is that a unicorn?" Zach asked.

Twenty-Nine

Brian
Saturday, 9:26 p.m.
Inner Harbor
Baltimore, MD

Brian hesitated at the entrance of the aquarium. He couldn't express to himself how badly he wanted to go to his family, but they were eyeballs deep in law enforcement, and he still had a mission to finish. The mercenaries were in handcuffs; his family was safe for now. Brian ignored the thought that he might not make it back later.

Trying to walk as if he knew exactly where he was going and as if he was too important to be stopped, he skirted the crowd and headed for Alexis.

Luckily, Alexis had already gotten through a fast summary of events, and Terra was practical enough not to scold them, or let Elliot do so, until they had the Compass back.

"Do you see that?" Zach asked, his eyes on the ground.

"Yes. Seth called for backup. Searcha members are on their way," Alexis said.

"Do we have a plan?" Brian asked.

"Yes. You and I are going into that bookstore before Seth and Nick find the Knot that's apparently hidden there. Terra, Elliot, and Zach, can you figure out how to buy us some time when the Searcha gets here?"

Terra looked a little surprised at Alexis giving orders but not bothered by it. "We'll see if we can get the police involved."

"And check on the rest of the Weavers," Zach said.

Brian sent him a grateful look.

"You sure you don't want us to come with you?" Terra asked.

Alexis gave her a hug before returning to Brian's side. "No, Seth's got a gun. The fewer targets, the better. This is a fight best fought with magic, and you need Zach here to help with the Searcha."

Brian laced his fingers with hers. "Let's go."

"You coming?" Alexis asked Storm.

The unicorn was out of phase, more a mirage than a solid creature, or maybe it was that she was panting, lathered, and looked like she'd lost every inch of body fat on her.

The unicorn looked up at the brick building and shuddered. She looked sadly at Alexis and shook her head.

"It's okay, girl. You've done awesome. You need to rest. We got this." Alexis might have fooled the others, but Brian was too closely connected; he could sense her fear. It was contagious.

He set his shoulders; he didn't have a choice.

As they walked hand in hand to the brick steps leading up to the bookstore, he wondered again why she was there.

"It's not for you," Alexis said, evidently hearing his thoughts. "Or not just for you. We can't let them cut another Knot. And it's not like you can do this without me." She grinned.

He grinned back. "True. And you couldn't do it without me."

Her smile turned teasing. "Don't let it go to your head."

The old power plant was big and brick. Tall smokestacks rose high from the central roof peak. It had been converted into a multiuse building with retail on the bottom and offices above, but it still retained a historic and powerful presence. Alexis scanned the shadows around them, and Brian briefly wondered if she could see the history of the building in them as he checked the bookstore door.

"The lock is broken." He eased it open.

"I can see from the shadows that Nick disabled the alarm system somehow." Alexis slipped through the door behind him and switched to thought communication. *"At least the place is closed for the night."*

"Kind of creepy."

Alexis froze to watch a shadow shift.

"What's wrong?" he asked.

"Crap. They saw us coming from the second floor."

"Which way, then?"

She shook her head. *"I can't tell. The magic looks like it's boiling."*

"Look, there's a magic marble. Maybe that can help." Brian checked both ways and started for it.

Bang.

"Duck!" Alexis pushed Brian down. A bullet struck the bookcase just above them.

"Thanks." Brian led the way toward a seed of magic pulsing at the center of a row.

"They're up there," she whispered, pointing up at the second-floor loft above. "I think Seth has a silencer."

Coldly, Brian realized the bullet had missed them more because it was difficult to be accurate with a pistol at such a distance, and not because she'd seen it coming in time. He gently plucked the marble of magic out of a tangle of magic strands with numb fingers.

They reached the end of an aisle, and he peeked out around the edge.

"*Three,*" he thought, holding up his fingers.

Alexis nodded, letting him know she'd heard him, but didn't look up as she added the new marble of magic to the lump left over from the magic earbuds. She packed it on like a snowball, though it was only about the size of a lemon, and handed it to him.

"*Two.*" The way was almost clear. Seth was scanning to the right. Nick was casually leaning against the rail. Unafraid. Watching for them. *Bastard!*

"*One!*"

They moved swiftly, heading for the next row of bookcases. On the way, Brian slowed for a moment. The thought of his family held hostage made his blood pound in his ears, and he didn't think. He just threw the lump. It sailed through the air like a fastball, made it up a story to the loft railing, and clipped Nick on the shoulder in an explosion of green sparks.

Nick cried out and fell.

Brian whooped. *"It worked!"*

Alexis raced across the opening and leaned against a bookcase beside him, breathing hard. "But Seth's out of sight."

Brian poked his head around the corner and yanked it back in. The thud of a bullet hitting the carpet made him fight for breath. "Crap! I shouldn't have wasted that on Nick."

Alexis took his hand. "We got this."

"I'll make another one." Brian headed for the next seed, trying to make a solution. *If I'd thrown it at Seth first . . .* He needed more ammunition. There were more tendrils of magic here. They tangled around bookshelves like grape vines on arbors. Flecks of clay were nestled between the strands; the biggest were the size of a pea, but with enough of them, maybe he could make another throw.

Alexis followed. *"Can you pull the gun from Seth's hand?"*

"I have no connection to the gun, other than it being used to try and kill me." Brian tried anyway. "It's not strong enough for me to pull it."

Alexis dug around in her pack, her back pressed against a section of self-help books. "Here, try this."

Brian looked at the Frisbee. "I can't do any serious damage with this." *At least not at this distance.*

"The gun."

"Worth a try." Brian took it, trying to follow all the strands, using the one from the gun that had shot at him and the connection he had with the Frisbee. He looped the magic together and peeked around the edge of the shelf.

Seth had his head up, just above the railing, looking for them.

"I can't see the gun," Brian whispered.

"I'll move back a stack, that should draw him out," Alexis thought.

Brian flinched at the idea of her taking such a chance, but nodded. Seth didn't know which direction they were going next.

Alexis counted down and dove for the shelf. Seth lifted his gun. Brian threw the Frisbee.

The orange disk flew wide before sailing at Seth. Alexis rolled. Bullets tore into a bookshelf. The Frisbee slammed into the gun, and Seth dropped it. The weapon fell, but didn't go over the railing.

Seth ducked down.

"Nice!" Alexis mentally called.

Brian caught the Frisbee. *"Closer?"*

"You're attached to the Compass, can you get it from here?"

Brian tried again just to be sure. *"I'm too far away. The strand keeps stretching the more I pull."*

"The escalators are turned off, maybe the back one?"

"We'll be out in the open. What if we wait for him to run out of bullets?"

There was a smashing sound, and brick dust fell from the top story.

"I think they just found the Knot. We're out of time," Alexis thought.

Smash. More brick fragments rained down.

"Should we split up?" Brian replied.

"I won't be able to read anything around you if we do. I think we'd better stick together."

"I like it better that way, anyway."

They headed for the back escalator, using the bookshelves for cover and waiting for Alexis to check that no one was looking their way before crossing the openings that were visible from the upper level.

They made it three quarters of the way up the stairs. Staying low, Brian watched for an opening.

Seth must have sensed something, because he spun to face them. Gun back in his hand.

There was no way Brian could throw the Frisbee fast enough to save them now.

Thirty

Alexis
Saturday, 9:42 p.m.
Inner Harbor
Baltimore, MD

Alexis stared at Seth, her breath frozen in her chest. But she couldn't stop now. Behind him was a hole in the brick wall. In the hand not holding the gun was a tangled Knot even larger than the one in the Guard's vault. Angry, hair-raising magic radiated from it, stinging Alexis's skin worse than the cold water of the harbor had.

"Is magic really worth all the people that will die?" she asked softly. "I can see the chaos that comes from your plans, you know. I can see the rivers of blood. Is it really worth that?"

"I'm sorry, but this is more important than us. More important than your lives," Seth said, sounding truly apologetic.

"But is it worth the lives of millions? I can see it. I can taste it." Alexis tried to find the words to describe the images all around them. "What you're doing will lead the world to an apocalypse on the level of nuclear annihilation. Not just human life, but all life will be radically affected. How can that be good for anything?"

"I don't have to justify myself to you. Balance, when things are this out of whack, takes big action."

"Or slow, patient change."

"Shut up. Dead is dead, you won't feel better for having valiantly argued your side. People like you are destroying our society with your tolerance for evil. I truly am sorry, but people like you can't share in this new future." Seth raised his gun.

Alexis closed her eyes.

Brian slid his hand into hers. She held on tight.

She hadn't expected the end to sound so loud. Blood was racing through her ears.

Alexis peeked.

Crash.

Blue lightning flickered around Seth. He fell in a twitching heap. The gun fired wild, sending a display of toys into the air.

Nick stood up, blue magic etched across his skin. He'd hit Seth with a magic marble the size of a grapefruit.

Alexis took a steadying breath. "Nick?"

Pain flared around his shadow before settling into oily despair. "And I thought," he said more to himself than them, "I was crazy. Well, thanks, Doc." He gazed coldly down at the unconscious Seth. "I feel a lot saner when compared to you." Nick looked up at Alexis. His gaze flicked to Brian, but he couldn't look him in the eye. "The Compass is all yours."

Brian yanked on the thread; the Compass and his leather cuff flew off a table. He caught them neatly. The shadow world around Alexis shifted, as if she'd changed filters. The red saturation evaporated, leaving only grayscale, and the threat of apocalypse faded out, like an overlapping dissolve between scenes.

To be safe, Alexis let go of Brian's hand to snatch up the Knot from Seth's twitching fingers. It burnt like a hot frying pan, so she shoved it into her backpack. Holding the backpack at arm's length for a moment, she waited to see if it would burst into flames. When nothing happened, she gingerly slid the pack back on and looked around. The knot had a sinister presence, but at least it was safe for the moment.

Seth had just received the equivalent of a taser jolt, but she wasn't sure how long it would last. Brian seemed to agree because, using the sleeve of his jacket, he carefully picked up the gun and looked around blankly before turning to Nick. "We need Alexander the Great's Dagger."

"Going to keep it safer than Merlin's Knot or Compass?" Nick said, crossing his arms. "It's not like you're going to shoot me with that thing."

Brian's skin, already glowing green, flared up like a neon sign.

Alexis was glad Brian's finger wasn't on the trigger. She stepped hastily forward and took his free hand. Turning to Nick she said, "You don't plan on using the Dagger again?" The shadows wouldn't have settled down if he did. Letting him hold on to it for a few more minutes wouldn't end the world. She needed leverage to get it; the gun wasn't it.

Nick shrugged. "If I did, then that guy wouldn't be drooling on the floor."

"Thank you for that." She waved a vague hand at Seth.

Brian opened his mouth, but clearly changed his mind when Seth groaned. "What are we going to do with him?" Brian nudged the mostly unconscious man with the toe of his shoe.

"If we let him go, he'll try again. He's dangerous," Alexis said.

"How are we going to stop him? Guard HQ isn't set up to hold a prisoner," Brian said.

"What about the police?" Alexis had to ask, but she already knew the answer.

Brian snorted. "Have them arrest him for trying to destroy the world with magic? That'll go over well."

The shadows reflected Alexis's thoughts, and she was able to sort through a few possible futures, as if they were negatives that had only been partially exposed. Not particularly clear, but they helped her sort through the options. "What if," she said slowly, "we blame Seth for the kidnapping?"

"That could work," Nick said with a shrug. "Thirty years or so in prison should keep him out of your hair. He's the one who put me on the path to find magic, and he's the one who 'let it slip' where to find the Compass and First Knot. He deserves it." Nick dusted off his hands before turning as if to walk away.

"Wait," Brian said. "*Aren't we going to have Nick arrested too?*"

Something in the shadows came into focus. Alexis asked, "Nick, has magic helped your brother?"

Nick turned back and gave her a suspicious look. "How do you know about Peter?"

"I'm a Shadow."

"Right."

"So did it help?"

"No."

Alexis frowned. The pain and despair flaring like heat lightning in his shadows were clashing with the coldness of his voice. He was in so much pain. It practically gave her frostbite. "Why not? You did all of this, hired mercenaries, kidnapped good people, staged a hostage exchange, all for Peter, didn't you?"

"Shoot me, use magic on me, or let me leave," Nick snapped, emotions surfacing in his voice. He started to turn away again.

Alexis went with her gut and with what the shadows were telling her. "Can I see if we can help?" She didn't think there was anything she could do if he refused, besides let the authorities hunt him down and arrest him.

Brian stiffened beside her. "*What the hell are you doing?*"

"One Knot of magic isn't enough magic to save him," Nick said, his tone pure ice again. "And if half of what you say is true—"

"How do you know there isn't enough magic?" Alexis pressed.

"Dr. Murphy." Nick looked down at the drooling man.

Brian snorted. "He's a PhD, not an MD."

"He's an epigeneticist who's consulting at the research hospital. He was working on an experimental treatment."

"And it wasn't working." Alexis frowned at the shadows. "He told you magic was the only way to save your brother, right? That one Knot wasn't enough? If only he had more magic, he could save the people at the hospital? All the while he was trying to start an apocalypse. He had every reason to lie to you. He played all of us. Let us try," Alexis said.

"*Alexis!*" Brian shouted in her head

Alexis tried to figure out how to explain her thoughts to Brian. "*He just saved our lives.*"

Brian glared at her. "*He kidnapped my family!*"

"He did it to save his brother." But he had a point, so she turned back to Nick. "If we can help your brother, will you give us Alexander's Dagger? And agree to turn yourself into the police, explaining that you and Seth kidnapped Brian's family?" She wasn't comfortable asking him to lie to the authorities, but it seemed like the best of a bad set of options.

"He'll get off too easy by making a deal or something!" Brian protested.

Nick stared coldly at her, but behind that she could see he was thinking hard.

"Alexis!" Brian repeated.

"Without his help, how are we going to get the charges against Seth to stick? And Elliot will have a heart attack if Nick walks out of here with the Dagger."

"If you can actually help my brother, then fine, you have my word," Nick said.

"You seriously trust him?" Brian asked.

"About this? Yes. I'm not saying what he did was right. I'm saying his little brother is really sick," she insisted. *"I'm going to help a child in pain and put Nick in prison at the same time. His going willingly will be better for everyone. You don't have to come."*

Brian stared hard at her for a long time. Finally, he let out a slow breath. "Let's get this over with. What do I do with this gun?"

"Trash can?" Alexis guessed, with a helpless shrug. "We can tell the cops where to find it."

"Why not?" He tossed it in.

Thirty-One

Brian stood woodenly as Alexis called Terra. Around him were shattered bricks and scattered displays of toys and games. A gnarled hole gaped in the wall where Seth had dug the Knot free. Nick sat on the floor, his back casually leaned against the railing furthest from Seth's unconscious body.

Alexis held Brian's hand, a quiet comfort at his side, until Terra, Elliot, Zach, and Prince arrived. Stepping forward, Alexis explained what had happened. Brian sighed in relief; he wasn't needed yet. She answered questions and handed Elliot her backpack with the Knot. He accepted it with a jubilant relief and jumped into helping Alexis and Terra sort the situation. Zach stood with his hands in his pockets, speaking up only occasionally.

Elliot had seen something like the magic jolt Nick had given Seth during the Cold War. Though Elliot was cagey with the particulars, he was sure Seth would be out for at least an hour. Prince was given the job of making sure Seth stayed put until they figured out the details of getting the traitor into police custody.

Brian stared at the unconscious man as the others sorted through what needed to be done next. The numbing shock was slowly ebbing from his mind, more painful than a sleeping leg waking up. Seth had been a part of Brian's world for the last ten years. When Seth was in college, he'd discovered an old journal in his family's attic, and the journey to understand it had brought him to the Guard.

Even while he was studying for his PhD in epigenetics, he'd stayed an active member in the Guard, moving up to a seat on the Council. Doing his postdoctoral research in Baltimore had allowed him to stay close to Headquarters. Camila had often said how much she appreciated his help with Guard business. *But had it all been a lie? An excuse to sabotage us? When had he switched sides, or had he always been with the Searcha?*

"Even if you ask, he won't give you a straight answer," Alexis said softly from Brian's side. He hadn't noticed her join him, but he was grateful to link hands with her.

"Am I thinking that loudly?" he asked.

"A bit."

"You can't see answers in his shadows?"

"No. I can see what he wants for the future and him behind bars, but his past looks like an underexposed image, no matter what I try."

The silence stretched.

Brian shoved his hair out of his face. "He played Monopoly with us once. It was a Guard picnic when I was eleven, and the rain didn't feel like it would ever stop. He made it fun. I don't know why I keep remembering that."

Alexis leaned her head against Brian's shoulder.

Brian had to fight for a deep breath before he could speak again. "I don't know how I'm supposed to feel."

"You are allowed to feel however you feel. But consider not trying to figure it out tonight. I don't know about you," she added, her tone turning dry, "but for me it's been one crazy weekend."

Brian laughed.

Terra looked over at them. "Ready for step one?"

"You figured out everything already?" Brian had missed some big details, but he trusted Alexis and Terra to come up with the best plan for dealing with Seth and Nick.

Going to his family seemed like the next step to Brian, but they were still dealing with the cops. From what he'd gathered, they had been light with the details to the authorities, because magic was involved. Between Terra, Zach, and the spare magic earbuds he had reworked so they could talk to his family as soon as they got to them, they'd get things sorted so that Seth was implicated and charged. Elliot and Prince were responsible for making sure the still-unconscious Seth was found by the police.

Brian looked at Alexis and shrugged. "I guess it's time to help Peter."

Nick gave Brian and Alexis a ride in his white sports car to the hospital. It was a two-seater. *A bloody stupid thing.* Cramped for three people. Though when Brian relaxed a little, he had to admit to himself that having Alexis in his lap wasn't bad compensation for not letting her do this alone. Despite its flashiness, Nick drove the five-speed with patient focus, not challenging traffic laws or the abilities of his car.

Slowly it started to sink in that they had won. His family was safe, the Compass was securely back on his wrist, the newly found Knot was in Elliot's vigilant care, and Nick hadn't actually destroyed the world. Brian thought he should be relieved, jubilant even, but he was simply drained.

"How do the shadows look?" he thought to Alexis.

"Better. I don't think they'll ever be without possible dangers, but that's life with magic in it. We're safe for now." She rested her head on his shoulder.

An ache formed at the center of his forehead at that thought of magic in the world despite all they'd done. One day at a time. He rested his cheek on top of her head. *"We'll figure out how to get magic back into its Knot."*

Alexis started to agree, but she froze as the hospital came into view. *"This is where Storm brought me in that dream."* She shivered when she got out of the car. Brian pulled off his suit jacket and offered it to her. Absentmindedly she thanked him and pulled the jacket on, her eyes not leaving the brick complex.

The hospital was a big, brick labyrinth of a building, but the few staff they saw seemed to recognize Nick and were friendly to him as he led the way deep into the innards of the complex.

With her hand in Brian's, Alexis didn't seem to be walking in the physical world. Her whole attention was on what only she could see. She shuddered from time to time and would shift closer to him. He didn't want to ask what she was seeing, so he put an arm around her instead. It was a tad awkward walking, but it was all he could do to shield her. Alexis burrowed closer.

Visiting hours were long over, but Nick had no trouble sweet-talking their way past the nurse on duty. "I just want to poke my head in. I won't wake him if he's asleep."

Peter was blond like his brother, but looked half the size and age, except for his eyes, which held a quiet acceptance that was unnatural in such a young person. They lit up when they saw Nick.

"Hey," Nick said. "You solving all the world's problems?" He nodded to the notepad and tablet Peter had been working with.

The boy laughed, but it made Brian's gut flip queasily. *"He looks really sick."*

Alexis nodded slightly. *"Yes. His shadow isn't good."*

Unwanted empathy for Nick prickled in Brian. He couldn't or didn't want to imagine Em or Vicky in a similar situation. The ends didn't justify the means, but he could uneasily admit to himself that such a moral absolute would have been a whole lot easier four days ago. But then Brian remembered the hell Nick had put his family through, the danger he'd put the world in, and felt a little more justified in his anger.

"I brought some people by to meet you," Nick said to his brother.

"Hi," Peter said cheerfully, though his eyes were guarded.

Alexis offered her hand. "I'm Alexis."

Energy flared—Alexis was reading Peter. Brian couldn't see what she saw, but he did see several strands light up, bright white.

"Nice to meet you?" the boy said, clearly wondering when she was going to let go of his hand.

"Sorry, we're weird," Alexis said, not letting go. "Give me a sec. Brian, do you see this strand?" She pointed at a tangle about a yard from the bed.

"More like several dozen." Brian leaned closer. The fine strands kind of looked like Em's hair after a day of swimming and boating. Gently, he tried to tug them apart. Thankfully, they were stretchier than hair.

"What are you doing?" Nick demanded.

"Trying to help," she said calmly, but Brian could sense the huge amount of energy she was using to see her way through the mire. "Brian, how about here?" She pointed at a little cluster.

Reminded of a complicated cat's cradle, he attempted to spread the tangle more.

"How about now?" She pointed at a strand so fine he could barely make out the glow. She glanced up at Nick. "We're not going to hurt him."

Brian pinched the strand between his pointer and thumb. "Okay, yes. If you hold it, I'll see if I can untangle it,"

"I can't see it. Just how the light bends, going through it. I don't think I can hold it."

Brian shook his head to clear it. "Right." The strands were so obvious now, it was hard to remember that only Shiners could see them. He glanced at Nick, but shrugged the thought away. Frowning, he tried twisting strands around his fingers to hold the ones he didn't need out of the way.

"Just give me a few more minutes," Alexis told Peter, still holding his hand. "Yes! That's what we need."

"Nick deserves to be punished, not rewarded," Brian thought to Alexis. Part of him really wanted Nick to be hurt, not just willingly imprisoned, for everything he'd done. All he had to do was break this strand. It was so fragile in his fingers, he was sure he could snap it in two.

"I'm not asking you to forgive Nick. I'm not saying he'll go un-punished. What I am asking is that you help me help Peter," Alexis thought back.

Brian frowned at her. Then looked at the blond child. Slowly, he exhaled and let the worst of his anger go with the air. Peter didn't look like Em, even the blond hair was the wrong shade, but somehow . . . well, he refused to let his anger against Nick keep him from helping an innocent child. He liked to think he was a better human than that, and he would be.

Looking back at the strand he'd almost broken, he realized how close he'd been to losing this boy's chance at life. Self-anger boiled up. But he hadn't. The strand still pulled between his fingers. He looked over at Alexis with tremendous gratitude surging through his heart. Because of her he was strong enough not to let one man's evil actions smash his own moral compass. The magical band on his wrist glowed brighter, and her band echoed the glow back. Alexis smiled, as if understanding.

He pushed away all thoughts and channeled his attention into the tangle. With effort, he fought to connect with the strand. He fought to be open to Peter's pain and where this strand might lead. The magic took on a green glow. "There!" It was clearly visible, going out the door, free from the tangle in his hands.

"I see the shift in the shadows. Can you get it?" Alexis said.

Brian let go of the overzealous cat's cradle and picked up the strand, just where it bent around the door.

Alexis winked at Peter and let go of his hand. "See ya around! You coming, Nick?"

Brian followed the strand; Alexis and Nick followed him. It led to a middle-aged doctor, who was rather plain looking. She wasn't young and hot or old and distinguished, she was a bit short and a bit overweight. There was a sense of dishevelment about her that didn't make her the least bit endearing, but rather made one concerned that she didn't care about details.

"That's who we're looking for?" Brian thought to Alexis.

"Exactly!" Alexis grinned. She tilted her head slightly to read the woman's ID card. "Hi, Dr. Chiron. I'm Alexis," she said, putting out her hand to the doctor, who shook it and looked around, as if trying to find another clue to who Alexis was and why she was being talked to.

"Hi?" she said.

"You know a lot about pediatric cancer treatments?" Alexis asked.

"Yes?" The doctor sounded uncertain; Brian hoped she didn't feel that way about medicine.

"I'd be really grateful if you'd take a look at Nick's brother. I think you'll find he's a really interesting case."

"Where are your parents?" the doctor asked.

"My father's business interests tend to keep him overseas. I'm my brother's legal guardian." After a questioning glance at Alexis, Nick began explaining his brother's diagnosis.

A tendril of sympathy grew in Brian's chest. He couldn't imagine having parents so out of the picture that he was the legal guardian of his sisters.

Brian followed strands over the next few hours and watched as Alexis brought people together. Before long, the disheveled Dr. Chiron had checked charts, run a blood test, and the new people Alexis recruited got involved.

In the meantime, Terra arrived at the hospital with Alexis's bag, minus the Knot, and an update. Things had gone well at the harbor.

Terra had been able to put herself in the middle of the police situation with her concern for the Weavers. Following her lead, and with the help of the magic earbuds, Brian's family had shifted their story. Seth and Nick shared a similar build and height. Seth had brown, not blond hair, but that was a detail that could be fudged. Their testimony and Nick's would land both Nick and Seth in prison for a long time.

Zach had stayed in the shadows with the Knot sealed into a box and spotted some Searcha members slinking around. He'd relayed the info to Elliot, who'd gone with Prince to scare them off. Once things had calmed down, Brian's family had been settled in a hotel for the night. They were all tired but were as well as could be expected.

Brian thought about having someone put his family on the phone, but he wanted to see them in person, and according to Terra his sisters had fallen asleep hours ago.

He, Alexis, and Terra napped in a waiting room, passing the time until the people they needed to talk with got to work. Nick stayed a little apart from them, leaning against a wall or walking circuits large enough it didn't quite look like he was pacing. When Alexis and Brian were awake, they talked about their future. One where they'd be in each other's lives. Alexis laughed when he said they'd live happily ever after, as if he'd been joking, but she did admit his shadow showed them spending Christmas together with his family and New Year's with hers. Brian thought that was rather specific, but he didn't mind if some of her planning was mixed into her prediction. It would be weird getting to know each other outside the adrenaline rush of the past few days, but it was a journey he was very much looking forward to.

During breakfast at the cafeteria, Alexis found the last strand she wanted to follow and brought a shy Korean medical researcher onto the team.

Not long after that, the disheveled Dr. Chiron stopped by at the end of her shift. "We can't cure Peter overnight," she explained to Nick, while handing him more paperwork to complete. "But there's real hope that we can help him. I'm glad you found me. The researcher who was consulting on this, his diagnosis was way off."

Nick looked up from the paperwork. "What do you mean?"

Righteous anger flashed in Dr. Chiron's eyes. "In layman's terms, he called a horse a zebra. I've crossed paths with Dr. Murphy. He's smart. It's hard to believe he misdiagnosed this badly. I hope like hell he somehow missed not one but three separate tests that showed he was wrong. Because otherwise . . ." She shook her head. "His career is over. But we will get it sorted. I assure you. And the people you've introduced me to are amazing. I think helping your brother is just the beginning of what we're going to be able to accomplish."

"Thank you, Doctor." Nick shook her hand.

She yawned and left. Nick stared after her, clearly deep in thought, before looking down at the paperwork.

"She means it, you know." Alexis said. "She thinks Seth purposefully misdiagnosed Peter to funnel money into his research. And she's got the clout to destroy him. Not that it really matters, since he'll be going to prison for kidnapping, but it makes me happy."

Nick's frown deepened, but he didn't look up from the paperwork.

Brian turned to Terra, looking for a distraction from his mixed emotions. "Think this will scare off the Searcha for a while? Since they no longer have a double agent in the Guard?"

"We can hope. Russel's survey indicates that magic hasn't spread much past the Shenandoah Mountains west of here. It's a big area, but not huge. Elliot thinks that the Searcha didn't strike directly at us because they don't have the manpower to do so, not because they were trying something more complicated," Terra said. "What do you think?"

Alexis watched the reflections of sunlight off the water fountain and let her gaze move past it. "We have a bit of breathing room while they regroup, but they'll be back. They're going to be desperate to let more magic loose before we figure out how to lock away the stuff that's already out. And recruiting will be way easier for Searcha, now that they can prove that magic exists."

"Together we'll be ready for them," Brian said.

Alexis squeezed his hand and rested her head against his shoulder. "Yes, we will."

Nick handed over the clipboard to a nurse and turned to them. "Thank you both. I . . . I can't express . . . Thank you."

"Are you ready to hold up your end of the bargain?" Brian said, with a little more force than necessary.

Nick pulled the Dagger and sheath out of a holder under his jacket. "Take good care of it."

"We will." Terra tucked into her purse. "Would you like to call the police or should I?"

Nick stood straighter and his chest stilled, as if he'd stopped breathing. "Now that my brother has a chance of recovery, I would say I don't care what happens to me, that I deserve prison, but he still needs me. And . . . and I think"—Nick took a deep breath and started to speak faster—"if this is just the beginning, you're going to need all the help you can get. Use me as a double agent. Murphy betrayed me. Worse, his fake diagnosis could have killed Peter. He found me and Peter in our hospital in Virginia and convinced me this research hospital was our only chance. I pulled dozens of strings to make it happen, and my family donated a lot of money."

Alexis frowned at the ground. "Seth was in charge of reaching out to your family, among others, for donations to the Guard. That's how he found out Peter was sick."

Nick shrugged. "When Peter got worse, not better, Murphy 'let it slip' that magic might be our only chance and laid down enough bread crumbs for me to follow. I thought I was so smart. When I saw him yesterday, he made such a show of trying to help Peter with magic, finally giving up and saying it wasn't enough. More knots had to be cut. There was nothing he could do. It was all an act!" His anger turned into a rage so icy Brian shivered. "I'm going to tear that bastard apart. I'll start by putting him in prison. I'll tell the police that when I overheard Murphy planning to kidnap the Weavers, he threatened Pete's life and forced me help. My family lawyers make wolves look like puppies in comparison. They're going to enjoy this. Dr. Chiron can destroy his career. I'll destroy his life. Then I'll help you bring down Searcha."

In the silence that met those words, a whole list of objections rose to Brian's lips. He looked at Alexis for help, but Terra spoke first.

"How do we know you won't be playing both sides?"

"I let magic loose on the world to try to save my brother. I'm not a believer in the cause Murphy was spouting. And in the end . . . well, everything I did with Alexis and Brian, getting a second opinion, finding people who could help, I could have done without magic. I should have. I want a future for my brother, and some magic end of days isn't what I want for him. I can be more help to you out here than I can be in jail."

"How can you play double agent if you turn on Seth to get him arrested? Putting him in prison is nonnegotiable," Terra said firmly.

Brian tried not to grin.

Nick took a deep breath and stilled, but Brian had no doubt his brain was working double time. "I'll say he placed my brother's life in danger when he could have just asked for my help. That he deserves it. He'd burnt his cover with you, and his career. He is a liability not an asset to the cause now. That turning on him keeps me out of prison and is my best chance to help Searcha. Magic will save my brother, and I will do whatever it takes to protect it." He sounded utterly convincing at the end.

"But you don't believe that?" The disbelief in Terra's voice echoed Brian's thoughts.

"No," Nick said, his voice like flat ice.

There was a long silence. Finally, Alexis put out her hand. "Shake on it."

Nick swallowed hard, but offered his hand. His vulnerability made Brian uncomfortable. With Alexis, it felt like a two-way street, but not here. She wasn't giving anything of herself, instead she was guarding herself against Nick's pain. Brian kept his hand in her left, trying to give strength.

After thirty seconds, Alexis let go of Nick's hand and turned to Terra. "I'd take him up on it. He means it, and he'll be able to help." She turned to Brian. "Sorry," she said. "*But,*" she mentally added, swallowing hard. "*From what I can see in the shadows, this will be a lot worse on him than going to prison.*"

Brian could tell that made her feel a little sick. He pushed aside all of his warring emotions and put an arm around her. His family was safe, Alexis was safe, and the Guard stood strong to protect the world from magic. "I'm good."

Alexis smiled at him, and all was right.

Terra gave Alexis a long look and then nodded. She fished a business card out of her bag and handed it to Nick. "Stay in touch. We have a lot to talk about."

"I will," Nick said, not looking at any of them.

"I'm ready," Alexis said.

Terra led the way out of the hospital. Brian had no interest in ever setting foot in that particular building ever again.

Thirty-Two

"Brian!" a blond girl shrieked and threw herself across the room. Alexis grinned and stepped back as Brian caught the girl and swung her around with a big whoop.

Prince greeted Terra with almost equal enthusiasm.

Alexis itched to dig her camera out of her bag, but took a deep breath and let go of the urge. She savored the joy around her, not trying to capture it. Brian was now enveloped in his loving family. She didn't need magic to see the strands connecting them. Smiling, she leaned against the wall. His joy was overwhelming, and it spilled over to her. Distracted, she hadn't braced herself, and she stumbled back as Prince launched himself onto her.

Laughing, she ruffled his ears. "Miss me, boy?"

He gave her a slobbery kiss on the cheek.

Brian heard her laugh and brought his family to her.

"I want you all to meet Alexis. I couldn't have done any of this without her."

Alexis put out her right hand as Brian started to make introductions, but his mom hugged Alexis instead. The rest of the family joined in. After a hug from everyone, Em wanted to talk unicorns with her, and Vicky wanted to discuss the history of the Guard and how that might shape Searcha's next move. Alexis loved them all immediately, but she was starting to wish she was back against the wall. An ache was forming in her right temple as she tried to keep up.

"Alexis," Brian said, interrupting Vicky midsentence. "Sorry, sis. Alexis, do you think Prince needs a walk?"

If Alexis hadn't been in love with Brian already, she undoubtedly would have fallen for him in that moment. Prince was bouncing off the walls of the small hotel room like a jackrabbit, but everyone seemed too busy to notice.

"Mind?" Alexis asked Terra.

Terra looked up from her cell phone, clearly coordinating Guard business. "Please."

"Where's your leash?" Alexis asked. Prince tore off to find it by the shoes at the front of the hotel room.

"Who's going?" Brian's mom asked.

"I got this, stay and catch up," Alexis said quickly. "It's raining."

His mom looked like she might protest, but Brian hugged her again and started asking questions about what he'd missed.

Alexis smiled again at the joy radiating in the air before following Prince out of the room. The dog still quivered with excitement, but he settled enough to walk respectably at her heels. She took the stairs and led the way out of the lobby entrance. Tugging a windbreaker out of her bag, she put it on before stepping into the fall drizzle.

It was one of those bleak fall days where rain knocked leaves off the trees, sunk cold to the bone, and reminded the world that winter was just around the corner. Alexis pulled the hood up, and tension melted off her as water pattered on the nylon. Gray light cast soft, surface shadows, which didn't reflect any lurking darkness.

Alexis let herself absorb the cold. Soon enough she'd be warm; for now she let the chill soothe her raw emotions. With each deep breath in she brought in new peace and each long exhale she let go of the stress, fear, and concerns of the last few days. She focused on how each step felt, the sounds of cars on wet streets, and the contented presence of the dog by her side.

When the rain slowed to a soft drizzle, Alexis realized a warm smile had been plastered across her face for a while. Slowly, she brought more details to her awareness. The brick buildings were full of history, and the sidewalk had seen better days. The distinct scent of wet dog brought back bright memories of camp. The splash of passing cars was a reassuring illustration that the world was still there.

A large spider web pulled at her attention, woven between the orange leaves of a maple tree and a rusting wrought-iron gate. Water clung to the strands, making it visible at a distance. She walked around it, pulling out her camera. There was something there she wanted to capture.

There were some photos Alexis had to wait hours or days to capture. There were others that simply fell into place. Moments she might have missed if she'd not looked just the right way at the right moment.

A shiny red car was parked on the street, and the old buildings behind captured the blending of eras that was all around her. The spider web connected the vibrant natural tree with the loving craftsmanship of the neglected gate. The palette of reds was warm and friendly, so different from the blood and fire that had been haunting the shadows, and yet it echoed them somehow. Walking around the web, she found an angle that showed the way the web brought together everything around it. She knew exactly which settings she wanted, but the light wasn't right.

As if by magic the sun peeked through the clouds. Alexis caught her breath.

Without double-checking, she knew it would be perfect. There was more than one kind of magic in the world, and she was a photographer.

To be safe, she snapped a few more shots, shifting the settings to give herself more options to play with in editing. She was going to fade out the background to really draw the eye into the photo and not let anything distract from the sense of connection she was trying to capture.

Prince tugged on the leash, ready to be moving again, and Alexis let the moment go. She kept her camera out and looked for other images that might catch her attention. The sun retreated behind the clouds. She pulled her jacket closer against the chill.

Her phone buzzed. Alexis fished it out, thinking it was probably time to turn around anyway. Mia had written: *On our way back! Such an amazing time! Did you get the Perfect Photo?*

Alexis laughed out loud. She texted back: *Just found it! A spider web.*

Mia sent back a string of happy emojis with jazz hands.

Still smiling, Alexis put her phone away. She'd talk to Terra about where to meet Mia and how to tell her everything. School seemed like a million years ago, but there was still half a semester to finish and normal life to deal with. There were more unknowns than before, but Alexis was curious and not afraid to see where they might lead. She glanced back at the band of magic on her wrist, and her smile brightened even more.

The shadows weren't giving her the details, but she could clearly see where her path, and Brian's, could take them together. That image was wonderful and happy and so much more. It was an image that could help her get through any of the challenges that lay ahead.

"Ready to head back?" she asked Prince.

He looked at her, but didn't seem to have an opinion one way or the other.

"*Brian?*" Alexis thought as she started to walk back.

"*Yes,*" he thought back immediately.

"*I found the photo for my competition.*"

"*Congratulations!*"

"*Thanks.*" Warmth spread from her chest to her fingertips, despite the bite in the air.

"*How's the peace and quiet? Up for some company? Em and Vicky are ready for a walk. Parents are talking paperwork and boring stuff with Terra.*"

Alexis checked in with herself. "*I would love the company,*" she thought, truthfully.

"*Brace yourself then. We're on our way.*" Alexis could almost hear Brian's laughter.

Grinning, Alexis ruffled Prince's wet ears. "Don't forget," she told the dog with mock seriousness. "Always bring home a unicorn."

ACKNOWLEDGMENTS

Family and friends are vitality important to Alexis and Brian, and my family and friends were just as important in making Tangled Shadows a story I am so proud to share. From a million supportive phone calls and conversations, to helping me hash out characters and plot, to beta reading a wide range of drafts I was always sure were closer to finished than they actually were, and to all the other millions of ways that they helped me get here. I'd be here forever if I tried to name every one of them, but I am so grateful to each of them. Special thanks to my mom, who is the first person I want to share a new draft with.

I also have the Chain Bridge Writers to thank, not only for helping me with my manuscripts, but also for teaching me so much about how to give and take a good critique.

My substance editor, Trish Wooldridge, did an incredible job and she really got the story which made it a million times easier to accept her feedback and fix what needed work.

My copyeditor Christopher Hoffmann went above and beyond.

Will came to my rescue with the formatting.

Barbara and Thea both beta read earlier darts and yet were happy to proofread the polished draft too.

Jenny inspired me to write my first book and has been my critique partner from the beginning.

Meg gave Tangled Shadows its first glowing review, inspiring me to keep going.

I've circled back to friends and family, so it's probably time I stop, because it's been well over twenty years of support, encouragement, and feedback for seven manuscripts that have made this book possible. I am so grateful to them all.

Last, but not least, thank you for reading!

About Author

Christina Crothers has been writing stories almost as long as she's been reading them. Besides fiction, she enjoys exploring forests, practicing yoga, and spending time with family and friends. She lives in Virginia with her cat, who is a daily reminder she's not ready for a dog.

Zach's story comes next in Tide of Shadows. For more information and updates check out ChristinaCrothers.com